INK BLEED

A *Divine Villains* Novel

TRINITY LYNN

First Edition: June 2026

Edited by K.S. Elliott

Professionally typeset on Atticus

Cover design by Trinity Lynn

Originally self-published in 2026 by Trinity Lynn.

ISBN-13: 979-8-9959380-0-2 (Paperback)

ISBN-13: 979-8-9959380-1-9 (Hardcover)

For those who have learned darkness does not make you unworthy; it makes you whole.

PLAYLIST

Somebody's Watching Me—Young Medicine

Dethrone—Bad Omens

The Shower Scene—Ice Nine Kills

Code Mistake—CORPSE, Bring Me The Horizon

Never The One—Ocean Sleeper

FWYTYK—I Prevail

Flowers—Rain Paris

Straitjackets & Roses—Diggy Graves

Sweat—Mirakill

RAGDOLL—Vana

Build A Bitch—Rain Paris

ANGEL SONG (feat. David Draiman) - JD Remix—Nothing More, David Draiman, Justin Deblieck

CONTORTIONIST—Arankai

Blackmarketmonkeymagic—Archers

THE DRAIN—Bad Omens, HEALTH, SWARM

Emergence—Sleep Token

The Offering—Sleep Token

Vigilante Shit—Taylor Swift

Lovely (feat. Charlotte Buchholz)—Time, The Valuator, Charlotte Buchholz

DARKSIDE—Neoni

INK BLEED

Beg For Me—Braeker

Lethal Woman—Dove Cameron

Nightmare—Halsey

Villain—Rain Paris

Haunting—Braeker

Content Warnings

As much of my work contains dark and mature themes, it's important to include a comprehensive list of potentially triggering content for those readers who want to know what to expect. If you are sensitive to any of the following subjects, please either do not read or proceed with caution.

This book includes: explicit on-page sexual scenes and situations (consensual); profanity / offensive language; violence, fighting, killing, murder, torture, blood, gore, injuries; death; animal injury (not death); use of weapons, including guns; use of drugs and alcohol; smoking; cult-related activities; mentions of child grooming (past); mentally unwell characters; misuse of corpses by a medical professional; brief instances of anxiety, depression, and PTSD; blood play; knife play; gun play; questionable use of a cigar (consensual).

"Do not be afraid; our fate
Cannot be taken from us; it is a gift."
— Dante Alighieri, *Inferno*

PROLOGUE

POPPY

"Karma is a cold-hearted bitch, Doc," I say as I flick the rainbow butterfly knife inches from Sebastian's nose. "Isn't she?"

His curses can't quite make it past the wad of black lace panties stuffed in his throat. But I can imagine their flavor—the curses, not the panties—to be dark, bitter. I'm betting he's a café noir kind of man.

My lip curls in disgust. Never, *ever* trust someone who takes their coffee black.

"Oh, hush." I slide the spray-painted blade down his blood-stained shirt, hooking it into the *G* of his Gucci belt. "There's no need to shout, Doc. I hear you, loud and clear. But *no* means *yes* in your book, right? Well, here's a taste of your own *diction*."

My wrist flicks, slicing both the belt and the crotch of his tweed trousers. Out springs his flimsy cock, uncut and half-hard.

Gag.

The free-balling bastard manages to spit out the panties, barking, "Fuck you!"

"Oh, I kindly thank you for the offer." The tip of my blade flirts with Sebastian's navel. He stills as if he's looking straight into Medusa's stony gaze. "Sadly, you're not my type. Stalkers are romanticized and all. But, in reality, it's actually a sign of psychosis."

A flash of rainbow slices through skin and sinew. Scarlet spurts from Sebastian's femoral artery in his left thigh. Splashes across my gleeful smile. Paints my leather pants and biker jacket with death's favorite color.

He blinks.

And then he screams.

A bit delayed, but understandable. He *was* expecting me to cut off his dick.

I have something much more appetizing planned.

I always follow in Papa's carefully placed footsteps: maim my prey, let them suffer long enough to feel the grim reaper's breath on their necks. To feel the same fear of inevitability their own victims felt. People like Sebastian don't deserve swift ends. Neither do they deserve the solace of a crawling stop.

"Kill them too quickly, Poppyseed, they'll have no time to fear death," Papa warned me when I was old enough to wield a knife, using my childhood nickname while teaching his nine-year-old daughter a lesson on torture. *"Kill them too slowly, they'll beg for death's embrace. Kill them somewhere in between, dearest daughter. Give them a reason to shit themselves in terror before their undignified ends."*

Sebastian is nearly there. He just needs a little...nudge.

"Go fuck yourself, you psychotic bitch!"

"I kind of already did that today, *sooo* joke's on you."

I open up his other thigh from hip to kneecap in a crimson arc.

"So pretty," I croon over his deafening howls. "Red is *definitely* your color, Doc."

Sebastian's screams reach a fever pitch. No one can hear him but me. The fool chose to build his house in the forest outside the city, far away from civilization. Probably so no one would hear his victims scream for help that never came.

Such kismet, isn't it? Poor bastard probably didn't ever stop to think about if *he'd* be the one screaming.

Idly adjusting the skull mask over my face, I twirl a strand of pastel-pink hair around my forefinger. The tread of my combat boots sticks to the bloody planks as I pace back and forth across the floor of his living room. It's a habit I've had since I was little, to keep my mind grounded during chaos. It stems from the days Papa would come home soaked in death, murder's adrenaline gleaming in his arctic blue eyes. Mama would lock me in my room with my books. At the time, I didn't know why. It took me years and miles of wearing down the floorboards to understand what he does for a living, why he's always caked in blood after particularly long days at work.

My father is the king of Salem's underworld, a Nosferatu of corruption.

And I'm the apple sulking in the shade of his dark and twisted tree.

"Go to hell, you fucking cunt!"

Slowly, I turn toward Sebastian's lightless glare. "You first."

His attention slips over my shoulder. He immediately pisses himself.

"Doc"—I grin as an enormous black panther materializes from the shadows, prowling to my side—"I'd like you to meet Jezebel. Jezebel, meet Dr. Sebastian Bonaparte, a board certified piece of shit that does vile, unspeakable things to his students and keeps getting away with it. Well, until now."

I offer my bloody fingers to the big black cat. She licks them clean and I giggle, patting her pumpkin-sized head.

"Jezebel is a retired circus rescue. They were going to euthanize her when she refused to jump through flaming hoops after a bad stunt nearly burned her alive." I shake my head, throat scorching with a sudden, simmering wrath. "Since when is trauma punishable by death?"

Undying love radiates from her azure eyes to mine. Already, I feel my fury fading, leaving behind a cold, calculating calm.

"For years, she's been my emotional support animal. But for *you?*" I jab my knife at Sebastian and wink. "This sweet girl will be your personal guide to Lucifer's suite."

My fingers snap and Jezebel slinks forward.

Sebastian shrieks, scraping my senses. I shove the panties back into his throat to stifle them. He kicks his legs as if flailing like a fish out of water will save him.

It won't.

"I'd say strap in, but I think we already took care of that part," I muse as he screams and *sobs* in the face of death. "So, I guess all that's left is to just"—I grin, rubbing two sticky-red fingers together—"enjoy the ride."

The viridian veins in his neck and cock bulge in tandem, threatening to burst like a piñata. I'm tempted to see if he'll spontaneously combust into a confetti cloud, but it's late and I'm still tired from the last kill. Not to mention, I have a café to open in—I check my phone—two very short hours.

Snap!

Jezebel pounces with all one-hundred-and-fifty-one pounds of feline grace. Her fangs tear into Sebastian's favorite bits, staining her black muzzle red.

I wipe a tear from the corner of my lashes. I taught her that trick myself.

Of course, with those major arteries sliced, Sebastian will bleed out to a lifeless husk before he can watch Jezebel chew on his ballsack. What a shame.

"Have a safe trip south!" I wave with jubilance, flicking the butterfly wings shut around the blade and tasting iron on my lips. "Give the big man downstairs a kiss for me, would you? I'm a *huge* fan of bad boys with bat wings."

His delightfully fear-stricken gaze rips from the panther tearing out his manhood. He has the audacity to look at me like *I'm* the villain.

The funny thing is: he's not wrong.

Sebastian's eyes widen as I lift my fingers and *snap!*

Jezebel lunges for his jugular, wrenching his esophagus free. He dies instantly, and so does my smile.

Satisfaction should be coursing through my veins. Except, it's not. No matter how many of these predators die, there will *always* be more prowling in the dark.

"Unfortunately, Doc"—I sigh as I toe his piss-ridden blood into my personal trademark on the floor—"I'm no exception."

SAINT

BRONTË

"The dead make better company than the living, *mon ami*," I remark, snapping on a pair of blue nitrile gloves and grimacing down at the lifeless man gaping up at me with a missing throat. "Apologies for giving you the short end of the stick."

Feet shuffle behind me, grating my senses.

"Did he just talk to a corpse?"

"I think so?"

"Is that normal?"

"Maybe for someone in a straightjacket."

"Actually, it *is* normal." I drop my backpack and sling a scowl over my shoulder at the four police officers clustered in the lavish living room. Their uniforms are spotless, their badges pristine. Rookies. "It's no different than telling yourself affirmations in the mirror every day because your life is so pitiful you need a pep talk to be a functioning human." A young buck snickers, and a slow smile stretches my mouth a touch too wide to be friendly. "It's when they start talking back that you should consider bathing with a toaster, *mes amis.*"

He greens in the face and bolts for the door.

I stifle a snort into my thermos. "Fucking cherry."

"Lower the hackles, Bourbon," says Detective Shane Scull as he lingers behind the deceased. He's a Type-A brute in peak physical and mental shape for a man in his sixties, with a salt-and-pepper buzz cut, alpha complex, and amber eyes like a lion. I roll my eyes and he exhales another curt breath. "Do yourself a favor, and ignore them."

I try, but then someone grumbles, "Must've skipped his own pep talk this morning."

"He's positively feral," another sneers.

"Think he missed his annual rabies shot?"

The rookies snigger like hyenas, and my scowl deepens. If only disrespect incurred a death sentence. I'd wrap their hides around every copy of *Crime and Punishment* sitting in my Etsy queue just to spite the insolent pricks.

Sadly, I'm no murderer.

I *am*, however, a petty motherfucker.

Taking a long pull of my bold black brew, I draw the white sheet down the cadaver's pelvis to reveal the shredded meat that was once the sorry sap's cock and balls.

There goes another runner, dry heaving out the room.

I flip the sheet past the man's thighs. They each sport the same variety of slits as those made by a lame on a fresh loaf of baked bread.

Just like that, Scull and I are the only living souls left inside the house.

Thank every angel above.

"Every time, Bourbon," he grouses as I hide my satisfied smirk with another drag of coffee. "You run them out every *single* time."

"They're irritating," I snap, rummaging through my pack for a medical mask to staunch the stench of rotting meat, "and judgmental."

"They're *rookies.* They're meant to be irritating and judgmental. *You,* on the other hand, ought to be their patient and pleasant mentor, teaching them how they will be working with coroners once the training wheels are off. Not chasing them away every chance you get."

"Not my fault they can't handle a little gore."

"It's not the gore." *It's you,* he doesn't say. *You're the problem.*

It definitely *is* me.

Can I really be blamed? The living are such shit company.

Swallowing my pride, I click my penlight on and flash it over the body. The man was murdered in his living room. He's restrained by a pair of pink feather handcuffs. Lacy black panties hang from his mouth. A pentagram circles him, drawn in his own blood.

There is no other evidence. As always, the killer was efficient in cleaning up and leaving only their calling card behind.

Over the years, I've had my theories. They've ranged from a lone serial killer to a fully organized cult. Both are prevalent in Salem. Especially given the city's dark and bloody history.

"Care to introduce us, *mon ami?*"

Crossing his thick arms over his broad chest, Scull supplies, "This is Dr. Sebastian Bonaparte. Age thirty-seven. Professor of occult studies at St. Aurelius's Liberal Arts. The academy alerted local authorities when he didn't show up for work three days in a row. City cameras were scrubbed, along with those on the property. Unsurprisingly, there were no witnesses. There have been at least a dozen stalking claims and sexual assault charges filed over the past year, all dropped shortly after the reports came in. Since Sebastian's disappearance, the dean found historical email evidence of him blackmailing his targeted students to keep them quiet."

"Why wasn't there ever a formal investigation?"

He shrugs. "Between the streak of withdrawn complaints and lack of sufficient evidence to pursue any case, the higher ups chalked the accusations to girls crying wolf."

"Their mothers should've swallowed their batches," I snicker, pointing my penlight at the sick fuck that definitely didn't die slow enough. "Haven't they heard the wolf is real in the end?"

"For Christ's sake, Bourbon," Scull hisses, rubbing his temple. "It's Monday, it reeks in here, and we're awake before the fucking birds. Could you just keep your opinions to yourself for once and fill in the blanks for me?"

A bit of a pissy response, but I let it slide. Aside from me, he's the only person who actually gives a damn about finding the killer hiding in the shadows.

Swallowing the rest of my bitter remarks, I report the same details we've seen on these murder victims over the last decade: lacerations made with astonishing surgical precision, mutilated body parts, creative gags personalized to the deceased.

In this case, a rapist died with panties in his mouth. Justice served on a gilded platter, if you ask me.

Every single victim has been a criminal, typically the bottomfeeders of Salem no higher on the underworld food chain than rats. Whoever is killing them knows the cops aren't doing shit to find them. The most police have done is kept the news of these murders under wraps, blinding the public to our very own vigilante doing their job better than them.

Not that the cops care. Even after the DNA samples collected from each kill have consistently pointed toward an exotic cat used to deliver the deathblow, they've turned their cheeks. Why wouldn't they? The killer is taking a sizable load off their backs.

Or, such as in Sebastian's case, shouldering the entire damn precinct.

When I'm finished with my assessment I already know will go no further than a filing cabinet, Scull takes his leave to debrief his recruits.

Alone with the body, I scan the mangled cadaver. Searching for any imperfection discernible as remarkably *his:* tattoos, scars, blemishes, birthmarks. If he's doomed to a fiery grave like the rest, it's a necessary precaution before his hide becomes my next premium leather project.

My rebound books cannot be linked back to criminals meant for the incinerator. A single DNA test would spell my downfall, but I market the skin as animal hide to avoid any mishaps. False advertisement has saved me from a padded cell so far.

Thankfully, Sebastian's canvas is a clean slate.

"*Fantastique,*" I utter beneath my breath. "I think I'll wrap you around *Jane Eyre.* A tale *about* a woman, written *by* a woman. Seems fitting for your debut, no?"

He doesn't confirm or deny, which I take as a promising sign. The moment these dead bastards wake and talk back, *I'll* be the one bathing with a toaster.

As I head for the door, a flash of color snags my attention. Edging a pool of dim light on the floor beneath a nearby scene lamp, something pink winks at me. Grabbing a clear evidence bag and pliers from my pack, I kneel and pinch between the prongs a strand of someone's hair. It's long, sleek, and straight. Not synthetic, fully human.

A wicked smile stretches my lips taut. This may as well be a piece of priceless treasure. Even if the strand is from a wig or some type of extension made with human hair, it's as traceable as a fingerprint.

I should call Scull back in here. But if I do, his superiors will take this glittering gem and let it dull in an evidence locker until the case inevitably grows frost. And the mysterious vigilante will continue their killing spree. Their victims may be criminals, but there's no knowing when the city's guardian angel will turn on the innocent.

Heroes so often fall from grace. How long until this one trades their halo for horns?

The chambers of my heart stutter as a very insane, very *illegal* idea forms.

"I probably *shouldn't* test this to find out who they are so I can hunt them myself." I leer at the corpse of a predator searching endlessly for the paradise he'll never see. "Guess that would make me no better than you, wouldn't it?"

Yet there's a grinding gnaw at the back of my skull. It's the same feeling I had twenty years ago, when home was a deadbeat's house in Texas and every day was a game of survival. Listening to intuition saved both me and my brother then. I'll be damned if I ignore it now.

I seal the pink strand in the evidence bag and slip it into my pack.

"Don't judge me," I toss back to the dead prick, his gaze mercifully unmoving. "I'm no saint, but I'm *nothing* like you."

⸺⬦⸺

I deliver the felonious evidence to the local medical examiner's office, calling in a long overdue favor Quinn Wildes still owes me for her most recent rebind of *Dracula*.

After my brief explanation of the case and the gold I've just handed her, she stealthily slips the evidence bag into a pocket of her lab coat and pantomimes slitting her own throat to indicate her consent to keep quiet. I let loose an easy chuckle. Quinn is the only person aside from my brother who has the power to make me laugh on a bad day.

From outside the thin plexiglass window separating us, I ask, "How long, *ma chérie?*"

Quinn scrunches her freckled nose and glances over her shoulder at the lab bustling with staff carrying armfuls of specimens and reports. "At least a few months."

I blink. "Sorry, did you say 'months?'"

Her sharp sigh ruffles her wild cinnamon curls. "This is a forensics lab in Salem, Brontë. We're a *bit* backlogged."

"How can I jump the line?"

She starts to laugh then stops when I don't join in. "Oh, you're serious."

"What gave you the impression I wasn't?"

Rolling her deep sapphire doe eyes, she inches closer and murmurs, "Look, you know I'm good for my word. But if you want this to stay off the radar, there is no jumping the line. You're just going to have to wait your turn."

Leaning my arms on the counter, I tap a knuckle against the base of the window and rub my thumb and forefinger together in a covert motion asking, *Price?*

For a moment, her stare is all stone. I wait for her to tell me to piss off.

But she doesn't.

Instead, she casually reaches under the counter and withdraws a worn copy of *Carmilla* that hasn't seen a good day in at least ten years.

I know the feeling.

"Weeks is the best I can promise without raising any flags," she says quietly, sliding the book to me like it's secretly stuffed with cocaine.

My smile grows fiendish.

I know the perfect criminal to wrap it in.

TORN

POPPY

The bittersweet scent of coffee and parchment caresses my senses as I light the last candle and drift through the café I've called home since I was old enough to move out of Morgenstern Manor.

Beelzebub's is a revamped greenhouse overlooking the bay, brimming with dark florals and bright candles. Mama's Japanese roots are in the samurai artwork and kanji poems on the windowpane walls. Papa's prodigal influence resonates from the baroque style of it all: the tall ceiling and deep-set floors, the grand Gothic chandelier, the tinted windows dimming the setting June sun.

Separated into individual sights, it's a cobbled hodgepodge of light and lightless, foreign and familiar, traditional and modern.

But together, it's my home and haven.

I lower into my hammock at the rear corner tucked beside the coffee bar, cradling my pink skull mug to my chest and idly skimming my bare feet over Jezebel's soft midnight fur as she slumbers beneath me. The balmy bay breeze wafting through the cracked windows tangles my sharp fringe, playing with my hair like a lover's hands. Kahula Alohi, the baker in the back kitchen, sings along to Neoni's *Darkside* playing over the speakers, and I feel a smile warming my lips as serenity washes over—

"Judas fucking Priest," Remiel huffs, effectively popping my bubble of peace. She plops into the hammock beside mine with a dragon mug towering with whipped cream in one hand, her wriggling bobcat runt rescue, Hades, in the other, groaning, "Three *agonizing* years of this war with LuciImHome, and you'd think our friends would put money down on *me* for once."

"*I* put money down on you," I remind her with an indignant glower. In all honesty, I never gave three-eighths of one-fifth of fuck-all about her online rivalry with a masked gamer she's been secretly stalking since the night they became public enemies. But that doesn't mean I won't support her no matter how often she loses to him. "Literally every match, Emi. Not once have my Benjamins strayed from the magnificent and awe-inspiring Halestorm."

"You don't count." She tugs the hood of her gray sweats up and flops her wrist dismissively. "You're like my sister, Poppy. Your loyalty is a given."

I squint. "*Given?* I think you meant 'gift.'"

Emi's peach lips purse as she tilts her head toward me, catching the final rays of dusk kissing the sunset to sleep. The tired sun lathes her layered raven waves long as a mermaid's with deep golds, licking her dark skin and infusing her aquamarine eyes with a hint of heavenly honey.

But her loaded lour is downright *minacious.*

"What?" I squawk.

"You're missing the point, Pops. Our friends are ganging up on me and I need you to help me do *something*"—a pointed look at the pocket of my leather pants, where I keep my butterfly knife—"about it."

As my only tenant and a hacker-for-hire when she's not battling her arch nemesis online, Emi naturally knows every dark facet of my immoral life. Though sitting behind a computer and orchestrating a crime hive are two very different shades of black, we've bonded over our sins. Among them, the passion for bloodshed and violence against those who deserve it.

But she's just kidding about the knife.

...I think.

"Calm your tits, dove," drawls Fiona Walsh in her rhotic Irish lilt, taking the netted seat beside Emi and aiming a vulpine grin at her murderous scowl. She's every bit the embodiment of a Celtic princess: body built for soft seduction, summery gaze brimming with smelted golds and flecks of grassy greens, fiery copper curls mussed with artful care. She's a renowned heartbreaker. No one would guess, though, that she's a ruthless loan shark under that white button-down, plaid skirt, and round-rimmed glasses. "When you're tired of bending over and taking it in the ass, we'll consider switching sides."

"Judas," Emi utters into her mug, stabbing the air between them when Fiona glances at her phone.

...Not kidding about the knife, then.

"Easy, Hale. She *did* say 'when.'" Castor Ricchioni appears with a steaming coffee cake halfway to his mouth, completing our circle as he takes his seat between me and Fiona. As the owner of a local chop shop, the Italian is of course a walking Yamaha ad: biker boots, black jeans, a short-sleeve tee a size too small for his muscle-dense torso under his leather jacket. His onyx waves are windswept from his harsh yet captivating features. His obsidian eyes made for luring lost souls into their depths are transfixed, as always, on Emi. "Which is a far cry from 'if.' Counts for something, right?"

"She also said 'consider,'" I parry, elbowing him and snorting when he misses his next bite, "which is an even further cry from swearing fealty. Drops that *something* down to *nothing* in my book."

Cas sweeps crumbs from his lap, chuckling. "Pops has a point there, Gingerbread."

Fiona claps a hand over her heart. "*Et tu, Brute?* Whose side are you on?"

"No sides." Cas raises his palms in surrender. "I'll defend your honor, but that's it. You started this battle, you finish it."

Fiona gapes at the three of us, landing on a smug Emi. "What do you want from me, a feckin' blood oath?"

Emi *hmms* pensively. "You know, I think I like the sound of that."

Fiona scoffs. "What about Cas? He bet against you, too."

I suppress my wince. The mood shifts like rippling water as Emi and Cas share an uncomfortable, weighted glance. It's been three years since they split. At best, their friendship is as durable as a ripped page. We all see the tear where the ink doesn't align quite right anymore. Although it's had all this time to settle into its new shape, it can so easily be torn again.

Fiona, who wasn't part of our inner circle until *after* the Great Castastrophe, realizes her mistake a moment too late. "Ah, shite. I'm sorry, dove. I didn't mean to—"

"It's fine," Emi murmurs, casting her weary gaze out the window and to the sea beyond. "I think it's safe to say Castor did his time."

Fiona looks at Cas like she's drowning and desperate for a rope. But there's none for the latter to offer as he rubs his brow and avoids looking at any of us.

Unacceptable. Our lives are bleak enough when we're not together. Pulling up my text thread with Emi, I type:

> Forget the knife. Let's melt some Ex-Lax into their mocha tomorrow morning and watch them race each other to the bathroom. Bet Cas shits himself first.

Coffee suddenly rockets from Emi's nostrils, chasing Hades from her lap to Fiona's. She yelps as the bobcat's claws sink into her crotch, and she flails like a fish, tangling herself in the netting. Cas chokes on his cake, I cackle like a jackal, Emi sneezes hazelnut bubbles, and just like that, the tension shatters as we descend into a fit of laughter I'd gladly drown in if I could.

Almost. I *almost* forget that this is only half my reality.

As Cas hands Emi a stack of napkins, patching over the new rip in their page with a mending smile she returns, my phone buzzes with an incoming call.

From my father and the king of this city: Alexander Morgenstern.

Dread burns in the pit of my stomach like I drank too much dark roast as I make my way through the kitchen, step out the back door, and accept the call.

"*Hai,* Papa?"

"Poppyseed," he greets me, his tone grave. "Are you safe, baby girl?"

Not a comforting start. If he's asking about my safety like he's expecting someone that buys and sells people for a living to be answering my phone, whatever this is about isn't good.

I clear my throat, unable to unclog the knot. "I'm fine, Papa. At Beelzebub's with the crew."

"Thank the stars." His relief settles in my bones like the warmth of a fire on a cold night. Then he snuffs it out with a brisk, "I need you to do something for me."

My answer is immediate. "Anything."

Fire crackles in the background. I imagine he's in Morgenstern Manor's library. Mama is likely seated at the blazing hearth, eavesdropping while pretending to be buzzed on wine.

I lean against the glass panes, tilting my gaze up to the stars as I await my orders. As I have my entire life. My childhood didn't consist of classrooms and peers. My teachers were my papa and grandpapa. My lessons were on navigating the criminal underworld. I studied how to delegate sins to the appropriate sinners, how to cock the Glock when discord and disobedience inevitably arise.

No, my childhood wasn't normal at all.

Whether I like it or not, I am the second-in-command of my father's decrepit empire until the day he passes his crown to me. Along with his throne, I'll be inheriting every jailbird, crook, and vagabond in his grip working off their debts to the man who bailed them out of whatever tough bind they'd been in before selling their soul to serve the king of Salem himself.

My future as queen of the Morgenstern dynasty was written in the stars. I have no siblings, and though there are plenty of cousins who are just as capable of taking over the business as me, I am Alexander Morgenstern's only child. As his sole heir, I am the line of succession.

I never asked for it, but that's the crux of inevitability: it's unavoidable, inescapable. Which is why I spend my free time exterminating the vermin from the streets; to attempt penance, however small and undeserved.

If I'd had a choice, I wouldn't have lived this wretched life. My family has been the monarchy of Salem's underworld for centuries, but this—ruling as crime lords—was never in the original plan.

Grandpapa Lucian taught me our history before he passed away, unknowingly engraving on my psyche how far we've strayed from our origins. The Morgensterns had built a reputation in the city's black market during the days of the infamous witch trials. Our ancestors had been saviors of a sort, a resource for people to go to for herbal remedies to spiritual influence, protection against malevolent magic. Regardless of how ridiculous it all sounded growing up, it also sounded like something of a dream.

Now, the Morgensterns are known to be ruthless criminals not even the cops dare to fuck with.

"We have an unwelcome guest," Papa replies. "I need you to eradicate them before they can cause more damage than they already have."

Every vertebra in my spine locks. We haven't had a turf war in Salem since our battle with the Volkovs. I grew up during the bloody nightmare. Grandpapa Lucian was reigning at the time. So many lives had been lost between our families. Innocents were cannon fodder, friends were collateral, family was quarry.

The only reason we won the war was because the Volkovs turned on themselves. They shredded each other apart like rabid wolves. Leaving the remaining Volkovs working for us.

My jaw unlocks enough for me to rasp, "What has this unwelcome guest done?"

"So far, they've poached some of our best mercenaries and arms dealers, along with a few informants and chemists. Clientele are already closing their contracts with us. Whoever they are, they've tipped the hourglass, and we're very quickly running out of time. At this rate, we will be nothing but another dead legend in this city."

I detect something in his voice I've never heard before: fear.

Alexander Morgenstern may be many things, but frightened is never one of them. Fear is his sword. He's the master, not the slave.

"What aren't you telling me?" I ask carefully, kicking off from the panes and pacing to subdue my own rising anxiety. There's no reply for so long, I check the screen to make sure the call hasn't dropped. "Papa? Are you still there?"

"This is how the last war started." Even though his voice is clear, he sounds as distant as the moon. "Your grandpapa plucked the Volkovs' forces one at a time until their house of cards caved in. He didn't stop there. He targeted their entire bloodline, leaving alive only those who swore themselves and their lineages to the Morgenstern name. If this intruder is starting where my father did..."

Then our crooked empire will fall, and the entire Morgenstern dy-nasty passed down since the age of torches and pitchforks will crumble to ash and ruin.

All thoughts of light and laughter sink to the depths of the Atlantic as suspicion rises from the deep. "Could it be the Volkovs?"

"No." Papa's credence cuts through my theory. "What's left of that family remains loyal to us. This is someone else. Use whatever resources you need. Find out who it is, and bring me their head."

Some might question why he's ordering his own daughter to hunt down the enemy. But this is the man who raised me to rule on my feet rather than serve on my back.

I can still picture it, clear as the moon and the stars in the night sky above. Us, standing in an old chemical factory. Me, with a book cradled to my small chest. Him, replacing that book with a knife and pointing to a man on his knees and begging for his life.

While other little girls my age were dreaming about castles and fairytales, I'd been death's right hand.

I may be the daughter of a king, but I am no princess nor a damsel in need of protecting. I know how to protect myself.

I know how to kill.

"*Hai,* Papa," I vow, sharp as the blade I was forged to be. "Consider it done."

WITCH HUNT
BRONTË

Mozart flits across the studio speakers as I sew the ruby-dyed hide of a cannibal onto Quinn's copy of *Carmilla*.

My needle and glittering gold thread move in time with each rising note and melancholy chord. Dantë claims I'm a psychopath for listening to classic symphonies as I weave the dead together for sale on my Etsy shop. As if Taylor Swift would be more fitting.

In truth, no other music can soothe my senses so easily overwhelmed by the hum of the exhaust fans, the burn of toxic ammonia fumes, and the rancid sweetness of decay always slithering beneath. You'd think working in a morgue would acclimate me to death's stench. But befriending death is almost as concerning as having the dead talk back to you.

"Brontë?"

My hands stop moving. The stainless steel *C*-curved needle is stuck halfway through ringing the hide. I stare at the splayed book facing me cover-up from the worktable. Dim fluorescence filtering from the overhead recess lights casts dark shadows upon a cat's golden eye embedded beneath the title as a surprise for Quinn. It's staring back at me like it can *feel* what I'm doing to its skin. I swear it twitches in its glass casing, *blinking* at me.

"Brontë."

Fucking hell. How long should I wait to fill the tub, grab the toaster, and flip off the man upstairs to join the one down below?

"Brontë!"

I catch motion in my periphery and sigh in relief. It's just Dantë.

Pausing the music, I glare through the clear glass door leading out to the dark garage, where my twin leans against his chameleon McLaren and avoids looking inside. "What do you want, Ghostface?"

Dantë risks a glance of what he can see through the door—me, in black cargo pants and a simple shirt with the sleeves rolled to my elbows, sitting on my rolling stool with an entire mountain of packages to be shipped behind me—to toss a glare my way. A risk he likely takes because of the vexing nickname I gave him when he hit his big break as a masked gamer.

"Quinn is here," he drones, drawing his white hood over his equally white and slightly tousled hair with his hands inked in crimson tattoos. "Pissy as ever."

"Probably because I missed her calls." I grimace, clearing the notifications from my cell and slipping off my gloves. "I'll be out in a minute."

Dantë nods, his phone screen a neon glow against his squint as he hangs by his car like a haunting vision of the past. My brother always reminds me of our darker days when he lingers like this. It's a habit he never quite abandoned. When we were kids, standing within each other's periphery was in anticipation of our father raising a bottle or blade or, worst of all, his fists. We would be there for each other after the beatings were done and the wounds needed to be cleaned. We reminded one another that neither of us were alone.

It's why we live together now, all these years later. To feel less alone and remember that we both survived our own personal hells.

Dantë sticks to my side as we take the ascending stairs, murmuring from the corner of his mouth, "Are you fucking Quinn?"

I scowl. "Would it be a problem if I was?"

"Is that a no?"

"No."

"*Oui,* then?"

"Why are you asking?"

"She's hot."

I pause mid-step, eyes slitting. "You hate Quinn *on a molecular level.* Your words, in case you've forgotten."

"Doesn't negate the fact that she's hot. Besides, I wasn't asking for myself. I was asking for *you.*"

I scoff. "She's a colleague."

"Whom you've known for *years.*"

"So?"

"*So,* you should show her what she's been missing."

I scoff again. "Don't be ridiculous."

Dantë's wide mouth thins as he absentmindedly pinches his disheveled strands, the evidence of his afternoon tumble with his summer fling. Always a revolving door of women and men. Never anything serious. Not since his heart was crumpled up and burned by the only person he ever gave it to. "How long has it been, brother?"

"Since?"

His brow flattens over his red eyes. "Since you fucked someone other than yourself."

At least a year. Or three...?

Fuck's sake. Has it seriously been that long since the Swifty with the glitter obsession?

"You've made your point, *crétin,*" I grumble as I scale the last few steps and push through the door to the kitchen.

Overhead lights illuminate the sprawling driftwood and cerulean sea glass décor. A central island permeates the space smelling of summer heat and saltwater breezing through the tall bay windows. Beyond the strip of sand outside, the late July dusk shades the bare ocean with starry cobalts and moonlit maroons.

Twisting from the windows is an unamused and entirely peeved Quinn still in her scrubs, who shoves a black bakery box at me and snaps, "How hard is it to answer your damn phone, Brontë?"

Dantë wordlessly steers down the hall toward the den with a suggestive backward glance at Quinn's ass. My hostile glare chases him into the dark with a demonic cackle.

"Sorry, *ma chérie.*" I set the box on the island and peek inside. "Chocolate croissants?"

"They're your favorite," she huffs, irritated by my confusion, "aren't they?"

"Depends. Are we celebrating, or are you buttering me up for disappointment?"

These past weeks of waiting for this news have been a fever dream. Bodies haven't been piling up in the morgue at the rate they were last month. As if the mysterious vigilante just up and left for a summer vacation. Or they're plotting something big.

Either way, they won't be alive for much longer.

Quinn exhales through her nose, the anger in her dark blue eyes dulling with apprehension. "The results were inconclusive."

"Inconclusive?" Her cinnamon curls bounce with her nod as she pulls a report from her tote, the strand of pink hair in the clear evidence bag paperclipped to the front page, and plops it atop the box. I snatch it, unwilling to believe what I'm hearing, and scan the contents. Seeing hard proof of her claim doesn't make the truth any easier to digest. "How was a test on a strand of *human* hair *inconclusive?*"

"There was no match between the sample you provided and anyone registered in local, state, or federal databases. Which means—"

"I know what it means." Dropping the report, I lean heavily against the island. "Salem's latest Batman is a top-shelf criminal protected by an entire goddamn hive."

This mission has gone from insane to completely fucking impossible.

"Should I be worried?" Quinn asks warily. "You aren't going to do anything stupid like start a witch hunt for everyone in the city with pink hair, are you?"

Excellent start. "Of course not."

She taps her chunky white sneaker, obviously unconvinced. "You're a coroner, Brontë. Not a cop."

"Thank the angels for that." I grab a croissant and chomp into the dough. "I'd be suffocating on sand with the rest of them."

"Brontë—"

"Help me."

Her russet eyebrows knit. "What?"

"Help me." I step closer, carefully watching for any change in her expression and finding only hesitant curiosity. "It's been ten years, Quinn. The cops don't care. We can work as a team, hunt down this criminal together. You've already come this far. I know you want to see this through just as much as me."

I'm aware of how desperate I sound. But if I'm going to do this and get away with it, I can't have her perching on my shoulder and monitoring my every move.

"Oh?" She crosses her arms, taking a defensive stance. "An expert on what I want now, are you?"

"You willingly made yourself my accomplice, Quinn. You wouldn't have taken such a personal risk if you didn't have some sort of stake in this."

Quinn snickers, her jaw twitching.

It's not a denial.

"I'll brew a fresh pot," I offer innocently, gesturing to the coffee machine on the counter across from us. "We can strategize over caffeine and sugar."

She chews the inside of her cheek. Glances at the bakery box. Picks at the sleeve of her scrubs.

Still no denial.

A tiny nudge. That's all she needs.

Something within me stirs, like a beast being woken from a long, deep slumber. Perhaps there's a path I can walk that'll convince her to take the plunge.

I know Quinn like the back of my hand. She's a sucker for tattoos, and I'm covered in them. I'm built like my father, tall and framed by a healthy bulk, easily towering over her. My charcoal hair is styled in a faded undercut, the longer strands slicked. Rebellious tendrils straddle my brow deeply set in shadow, giving me a resting pissed face that oddly attracts others like moths to flame. Dantë claims he can see the fires of hell within my hazel eyes, though they've served me just as well as everything else.

She's hot. Show her what she's been missing.

I inch closer, crowding her body with mine just enough for my heat to bleed into hers. Her lilac perfume wafts to me, daring me to explore and discover exactly where she sprayed it. "I promise I don't bite quite as hard as those vampires you love to read about."

A subtle gasp of surprise escapes her lips.

My arrogant grin grows roots and sprouts. "Unless you ask me to, *ma chérie.*"

A warm flush of desire creeps up her neck, blooming in her cheeks. It fuels my bravado, and I reach for her curls.

Until she yips and *lurches* back.

"Shit, s-sorry," I stammer, palms up as I back off. "Are you all right? Forgive me, I—"

"For the love of God, Brontë, stop!" Quinn barks, a hand to her heaving chest. "I just—I'm sort of seeing someone at the moment."

"That's"—I try and fail to clear the discomfort lodging deep in my throat—"fair."

An awkward silence passes as she catches her breath. I eye the toaster, wondering how fast it can put me out of my misery.

"Look." Quinn moves closer, settling a palm over a tattoo of a weeping angel on my arm. "You have a heart of gold, but there's nothing more we can do. You need to let this go before you get yourself hurt—or worse. Let Scull do his job, okay?"

Not a chance in hell am I doing any of that, but I nod along anyway. She tips onto her toes to peck my cheek, patting my bicep with a sympathetic wince.

"Enjoy the croissants. See you at work."

I nod again, watching her take her leave out the front door.

"Well, *that* was a fucking disaster." Dantë materializes from the hallway, visibly cringing. "I don't know who's in more pain: her or me."

I sigh through my nose, thoroughly annoyed. "Shouldn't you be upstairs filming thirst traps?"

His mouth opens for what I assume is a snarky comeback. But then his attention snags on the croissants. "Where are those from?"

"The fuck does that matter?" I snipe, still scrubbing the image of Quinn leaping out of her skin from my brain.

Dantë closes the lid and taps the elegant *B* printed in pastel pink. "Thought so. It's Beelzebub's."

I realize a beat too late that he's waiting for a response. "Beelzebub, the demon?"

He skewers me with a glare sharper than a butcher's blade. "Margot's favorite café."

Margot. His runaway fiancée who disappeared with our mother's ring after he proposed last year, never to be seen again. The woman who ruined him for any other.

"Oh," I utter, casting a longing look at the toaster.

"*Oh,*" he parrots, grabbing a croissant and biting into it with an aggressive snap of his teeth. His clever gaze snags on the report still lying atop the island, the brightest rays of sunset glinting off the evidence bag and its damning contents. "So, this vigilante of yours has pink hair?"

I pinch the bridge of my nose, not bothering to hide what I've done. I wouldn't be surprised if he'd been eavesdropping during that entire catastrophic encounter with Quinn. "You weren't supposed to see that."

"You should be thanking the angels I did." He grabs his keys from the rack beside the fridge and heads for the door leading down to the garage. "Let's go."

"Where?"

"Beelzebub's."

"For what?"

"To stalk our first suspect, of course." At my questioning look, he grins like a wolf. "The owner, Poppy Morgenstern, has pink hair.

Which you'd know if you ever went anywhere aside from here and work."

I blink twice. "You could've led with that."

"And *you* could've told me about your obsession sooner. At least I didn't wait ten fucking years."

Fine. Even I can admit I deserve that.

As he strides past, I catch my brother's arm. "You're not helping me with this."

"I don't recall asking for your permission."

We're the same age, born fraternal twins within minutes of each other. Technically, his albino ass was the first of us to see the world, yet I've been stepping into the role of big brother our entire lives. A role I wouldn't have ever needed to take on if Mama hadn't died and deserted us and our older half-sister, Virgil, with a Purple Heart jarhead drowning in untreated trauma and deadly grief.

My job has always been to protect my brother. Even from myself. *Especially* from myself.

"Dantë." My grip tightens. "This is dangerous."

His smile melts like hot wax. "You fumbled your shot with Quinn. Who, in case you didn't notice, wasn't remotely interested in helping you to begin with. To make matters worse, she's familiar with Beelzebub's. She'd know of Poppy and should've given you at least that single lead instead of her 'there's nothing more we can do' bullshit. You work with dead people and are an antisocial hermit. So, the way I see it, I'm all you've got. I'm not letting you do this alone."

Before I can protest, he pulls away and treks downstairs, whistling an offbeat tune that sounds suspiciously like Rockwell's *Somebody's Watching Me*. I sigh and follow, lighting a cigar to burn what little remains of my guilty conscience to ash and smoke.

REUNION

POPPY

My motorcycle drifts across the threshold of the old tactile plant at the heart of the city, cutting the engine and rolling to a stop. Plopping my helmet onto my lap, I absorb the scent of burning chemicals and the sound of heavy guitar riffs blaring from the wall-mounted speakers.

I should be feeling some sense of comfort in this familiar place I chose to rendezvous with the assassins I'm assigning to my family's saboteur problem. Instead, the raving beat of death metal only urges my heart into a thundering stampede as trepidation dumps into my veins.

"Evening, Lollipop!" Baxilian Kemp waves enthusiastically, beaming at me with every ray of his sunshine as the tall, svelte street chemist and his sidekick, Jett Proctor, pour a bucket of colorful crystals into an unmarked cask.

"Evening." I point to a speaker above a shelf of rocking mason jars labeled: Boom-Boom Powder. "Bax, what is that?"

"Homemade fireworks." Bax pushes his safety goggles up from his ivy eyes, pinning back his boyish blond curls as a grin slashes a mischievous curve across his cherubic features. "Special order for some unlucky bastard in Boston. Requested by his *very* vindictive ex."

I cock an eyebrow. "Inspiring. Could you maybe turn Alex Terrible down a smidge before you blow us all straight to hell?"

"Relax, boss," he drawls, slapping the bucket until the last luminescent rock tumbles. "It won't blow without an ignition source."

I fling a hand toward the boiling liquids two *very* short feet beneath the rattling jars. "Seriously?"

Bax sighs, drawing his phone from his hoodie pocket and tapping the volume down to a tolerable rumble. "You're no fun."

"I *am* fun. Just not on days where I need to meet with the Volkovs."

Bax's easy smile slips at the same time Jett fumbles with the bucket, tin clanging a cacophony against the floor. Both are entirely reasonable reactions. After all, the three remaining Volkovs are our most infamous mercenaries. Not to mention, they hail from the family who lost everything to mine.

"How's the anti-anxiety juice?" Bax asks, recovering first. "Need a refill before they get here?"

I pat my jacket until I find my vape and pull the abysmally low cartridge out. "Got any more of your cotton candy blend?"

"Fairy Farts, coming right up. I'll even throw in a few extras if you promise to try Unicorn Cum. Tastes like a rainbow shot straight from a magical cock. Right, Jett?"

"Uhh..." Jett's sepia cheeks flush crimson as she averts her gaze, dragging her glossy black coffin nails through her acid-green pixie cut. "I plead the Fifth."

Bax jabs an accusing finger at her. "Those were *your* words."

Jett flips him off and pivots to the crystals, stirring them with a fire iron and dutifully ignoring his sniggering. "Anything else we can help you with, boss?"

As much as I adore her for asking, my family's impending ruination isn't exactly a topic I can discuss with her or anyone else that isn't a Morgenstern. Papa wants this settled quietly. Understandable, given that if our workers know how crippled our empire has become, they'll flee from our shadow to seek someone else's. Someone with more power.

Someone like the saboteur hellbent on bringing war to our streets.

"If you're ever unhappy here," I say instead, "come talk to me."

"This is our home, Lollipop," Bax replies with a bemused smile. "What is there to be unhappy about?"

"Yeah," Jett agrees. "The only one who's ever grouchy around here is Bax when something explodes in his face and burns off his eyebrows."

"That's literally never happened."

"Never, my shapely ass. You singe those fuckers off every time they grow back."

Bax rubs his blond eyebrows that are just shy of full. "At least I don't melt my nails with acid."

Jett scoffs. "That was one time."

"One time, my shapely ass," Bax mocks in a rasping mimicry of her high pitch. "You melt those fuckers off every time they grow back."

"You're a literal asshat."

"You can't talk to me like that. I'm your superior."

"You have a cock. That doesn't make you my superior."

"I can fire you, you know. Just ask Lollipop."

Bax throws a *back me up* glance my way, but I flash my palms. "Switzerland."

"Fire me?" Jett barrels on, planting her hands on her hips and scowling up at him. "How lost would you be without me here to make sure it's *just* your eyebrows that get burned, hm? Let's not forget how many times I've had to use a fire extinguisher on you so you didn't fucking roast yourself like a human marshmallow."

Bax whips her off, and she whips him off in return.

This, I think to myself longingly. This is the kind of atmosphere I wish my entire life consisted of. These are the kind of people I dream to have in my entire empire. Not the criminals who have no interest in redemption—but genuine, kind-hearted souls like Bax and Jett, who came to me from the streets and found a home here when they had nowhere else to go.

Stifling my chortles as the pair continue to bicker, I clear my throat and wiggle my vape. "About that refill..."

"Oh! Fuck, right." Bax plucks blue and purple vape cartridges from a wall dispenser that likely held condoms once, judging by the faded engraving of a Trojan helmet in the glass. He drops them all into a black velvet pouch and tosses it to me, his focus flicking over my shoulder. "Incoming."

Glancing backward, my mood sours right back to where it started.

Nikolai Volkov saunters through the door like he's nothing short of a god. As always, the assassin is wrapped in form-fitting black, his skin kissed by the sun to a deep olive, dark hair cropped close to his skull. A jagged line like a lightning strike streaks from behind his left ear, arcing up to his temple and down again, cutting his dark eyebrow in half. His gray eyes, cunning and knife-bright, instantly find mine. The same Cheshire smile I learned from him spreads his full lips wide over pearly whites that may as well be fangs.

Memories moan from where they lie buried in the graveyard of my mind. Rainbow blades, splashes of red. My own hoarse pleas. I shove them all down in the dirt, their distant cries reverberating in my bones.

Bax lays a steadying hand on my shoulder, anchoring me to the present. I toss him a grateful look then shoo him back to a solemn Jett.

Behind Nik, two silhouettes split from his shadow: Vladimir and Malakai, his cousins. Vlad and Kai, unlike Nik, are both built for speed rather than strength. They're not nearly as deceptively pretty on the outside, but they have the same bottomless stare.

"*Printsessa.*" Nik grins with a mocking bow of his neck. "How long has it been?"

Two years, forty six days, ten hours, seventeen minutes...and still counting every fucking second.

I twist a purple cartridge into my vape, inhaling the taste of a thousand vibrant colors and exhaling a lavender plume straight into his perfect face. "Not nearly long enough."

Nik's chuckle, echoed by his cousins, barbs every inch of my flesh. "You look"—he scans my usual leather pants and cropped tank and biker jacket then latches onto my hair that wasn't pink the last time we saw each other—"desperate."

Bait. Obvious bait to get me to snap at him and give him the satisfaction of knowing he can still get under my skin.

But he doesn't. Not anymore.

"This isn't a reunion." I place a casual hand on the mini Glock holstered at my hip. "This is business."

All three Volkovs straighten, their vicious grins sobering.

"Someone is fucking with us. I need your help in tracking them down. Start with gangs and clubs. Leave no stone unturned."

Vlad folds his arms and puffs his chest as if it'll push more muscle to his pancake pecs. "We're going to need more details than that to get started."

"Too bad. That's all I have."

"You can at least tell us what they've done, *printsessa*. Otherwise, we're going in blind."

"Are you doubting your own abilities?"

Vlad scoffs, but the burn to his ego works in deterring his dangerous questions. "What about our contracts?"

"They'll be taken off your plate and delegated elsewhere. This is your priority."

Kai cocks his head. "Compensation?"

"If you're successful, you'll each be paid a generous bonus worth more than any of your current contracts."

They share swift glances, and Kai asks, "What if we can't find them?"

"No bounty, no reward."

Vlad barks a laugh. "You want us to play bloodhound *blindfolded,* but you won't even cover the difference if we fail to complete a mission you're *forcing* us to do?"

"Would you rather we find out if a bullet can make your ugly mug any better?"

Vlad bares his teeth at me, and I bare mine back.

Nik claps his cousin's shoulder, digging his fingers into Vlad's shirt to hold him in place. Gray eyes glinting like an ocean predator in the deepest waters, he asks, "Dead or alive, *printsessa?*"

I'm almost surprised he has the foresight to ask. My habit of offing smaller fish isn't a secret. We once hunted the streets together. He taught me my best techniques. He knows in what condition I prefer my targets. He also knows this isn't my typical protocol.

Normally, I'd deploy our cyber team to dig into medical records, criminal histories, camera footage—anything and everything they can get their fingertips on. Then I'd do the rest myself. But this situation isn't normal. I don't even have a name or affiliation. I'm working with nothing but a swiftly draining reserve of resources at my disposal.

The Volkovs are my wolves flushing out my prey while I follow at their heels.

"Alive," I say, exhaling purple smog. "Bring them to Indigo, and call me immediately. The kill is mine."

Nik nods, muttering something Russian to his cousins as they turn to leave.

That's it. There's no handshake, no parting goodbye. Just a final, fleeting glance shared between me and the Volkov who is only breathing because I never told a soul what he did to me.

Not even Emi.

BIBLIOPHILE
BRONTË

"**W**e've been here for over an hour," I grumble, nursing my second cup of black and paging through the same book I've been pretending to read since grabbing it off a shelf labeled: Midnight Steam. All we've seen so far on this ridiculously amateur stakeout is too many living people, and none of them have been Poppy. "Are you sure this is the right place?"

"*Oui.*" Dantë nods from his seat across the table, his candlelit gaze lingering on the empty corner alcove nestled on the other side of the bustling coffee bar. "She's usually over there with her pack of misfits and her pet panther."

I pause mid-sip. "Pet *panther?*"

"Mhm. Big black beauty named Jezebel. Sweet as pie."

My lashes narrow on my twin. "Have you stalked Poppy before?"

"No." He snorts, lapping at the cream Kilimanjaro piled atop his caramel latte. "I stalked her best friend, Remiel Hale."

I rub a sudden ache in my temple. "Fuck's sake, Dantë."

"Listen, *she* stalked *me* first. Besides, I only did it a few times, and it was more like recon anyway. She's—"

"—Halestorm. Just as painfully obvious as you with Luci-ImHome."

He tilts his head back against his chair and sighs up at the wisteria weeping from the rafters. "You seriously need to get laid."

I roll my eyes, returning my attention to the book with a list of content warnings longer than a restaurant menu. Among them, a personal note from the author apologizing for ruining ice cream. *Impossible.*

Dantë kicks me under the table. "There she is."

My focus snaps up, panning through the bookcases and spying a group of dangerously beautiful people strolling through the café. Dantë leans close and rattles off details of each one in order of appearance: Castor, the chop shop operator; Fiona, the loan shark; Remiel, the freelancing hacker.

If I wasn't convinced of my brother's claim before, I certainly am now. They're *all* criminals.

Then I see *her.*

For a single moment, the planet stops spinning.

She's a blue-eyed samurai living in the age of leather and crop tops. Her combat boots boost her a few inches past five-foot-five. Her sleek, pastel pink locks frame knuckle-breaking cheekbones, a sophisticated nose, heart-shaped lips, and upswept baby blues winged at the corners. In another life, she'd be painted in the Palace of Versailles, alongside panoramic frescoes depicting winged angels flying through the gilded clouds of heaven.

Easily. She is easily the most stunning woman I've ever seen.

"Poppy Morgenstern, daughter of Alexander Morgenstern," Dantë murmurs with a hint of misplaced admiration. "Assassin and princess of Salem's underworld."

Murderer and monarch; a deadly combination.

My heart jolts as if struck by the kickback of a gun the moment I look into those knife-bright eyes edged by a fringe pointing straight down to hell.

No, she's *not* a woman. She's a devil.

Beside her is Miss Murder Mittens herself.

Jezebel spots Dantë and I as the group closes in on their corner. Long tail flicking, the big cat slinks over to us and peers up at me. Her irises are such a silvery azure, the sable slits are as depthless as oceanic trenches. Not once does she blink.

Dantë kicks me again. "Think she's imagining you with a giant apple in your mouth?"

"Piss off, Ghostface."

"With gravy drizzled all over your—" My glare shuts him up.

Then Jezebel pounces.

Gasps stream somewhere behind the wall of compact muscle and black fur tackling me. I'm convinced I'm a dead man. That is, until a barbed tongue tickles my face.

"Jezebel Lilith Morgenstern!" Poppy grabs the panther's scruff, hauling her off with impressive strength and passing her to a startled Remiel. As soon as I can breathe again, Poppy wrings her hands, looking utterly distraught. "I'm so sorry. Did she hurt you? Are you in any pain?"

What strange things for a murderer to ask.

I slip on an easy smile. "Not at all. She attacked with tongue, not teeth."

"Thank the stars." Angels above, her rasp is as heady as smoke. She waves off her comrades and rifles through her pockets, pulling out a wad of cash and sliding multiple big bills under my forgotten book. "This should cover everything you and your friend ordered tonight."

"How generous of you," Dantë drawls, drawing her attention to him, "but if I had a choice, I wouldn't be his friend."

Poppy blinks at my brother as if she's just now noticing his presence. "Dantë Bourbon? Is that you?"

Ignoring my perplexed stare, he grins. "In the flesh."

"*Kuso.*" She chortles, shrugging off her jacket and revealing a masterpiece Japanese dragon in black and pink ink coiling up her right arm. "How's Margot? I haven't seen her in a while."

"*Très bien,*" Dantë lies without losing his leisurely smile. "We've been busy living the dream."

"Good for you, *mon ami.*" Poppy flicks her gaze to me. This close, I can see every shade of blue in her eyes: sky and sea, cobalt and sapphire. Hints of silver thread through her irises like spools of unraveling starlight. "So, this is the recluse coroner who never climbs out of his shell? Brontë, right?"

I refrain from lancing Dantë with a *what the fuck* look as I manage a tight, "*Oui,* that's me."

A curious smile tugs at her lips. She scans me from boot to brow, latching onto the runes on my knuckles, then the army of angels and demons sprawling up from the *V* of my shirt to the edge of my jawline. "Nice ink."

"*Merci.*" I nod toward her own skin art. "Very *Girl with the Dragon Tattoo.*"

"You know, I didn't care for that book. Couldn't figure out what made Lisbeth so special aside from her tat."

"It's not about the ink. It's about how her persistence helped to solve the investigation of a serial killer."

I realize I'm about a thousand shades of stupid as Poppy cants her head, her small smile fading. "Is that so?"

Dantë clears his throat, lashing me with an admonishing glare. "Did I ever tell you about Brontë's Etsy shop, Bourbon Binds?" He pulls up my small business page on his phone.

Poppy's umber eyebrows hike the further he scrolls. "You take custom orders?"

Not from killers.

Dantë's *don't be suspicious* stare drills into my profile.

"*Oui.*" I nod. "The queue is long, but I can be persuaded to take on a new project for a fellow bibliophile."

A squeal unlike anything I've ever heard bursts out of her, and she commands me to stay put before darting into the kitchen.

Feeling eyes on me from the opposite corner full of criminals, I casually lean toward Dantë and, with a stiff grin on my face, growl, "Care to explain yourself, brother?"

"The Morgensterns own Salem, Brontë. You need to know what you're dealing with, and this is the only way to do it. If you want justice against the heiress of the most infamous family in this city, you need to play your cards right. So, stop acting shady and take this golden opportunity to learn thy enemy."

Poppy reappears, carrying an ancient, decrepit copy of *Inferno* that I'd personally burn just to put it to rest. "It's obviously on its deathbed, but it has sentimental value. Any chance you could work your magic and resurrect it for me?"

Such a hypocrite, this devil who takes lives asking for me to breathe life back into, of all things, a fucking book.

Learn thy enemy. What a joke. I've learned enough.

Perhaps justice will be her hide wrapped around the story of a man traveling to hell.

I offer my palm. "Let me have a look."

Poppy passes over the worn tome. Her bittersweet scent of coffee and cotton candy blankets me in an intoxicating cloud. I hold my breath as her slender fingers brush mine. I feel every scar flecking her digits. The wounds are old, unmistakably made by blades. There are as many embedded in her skin as there are marring this heap of coffee-stained parchment barely clinging to its broken spine.

Only killers have that many scars.

Checkmate, you little devil.

Gently dusting the cracked front cover, I grin in the face of the murderer I've spent the last decade of my life chasing. "If Frankenstein did it, so can I."

KARMA

POPPY

My footfalls are as silent as graves as I slink through the shadows of the luxurious beachfront villa. Even under night's heavy blanket, it's a Picasso of splendor. I'm shocked there aren't marble busts lining the walls and frescoes of cherubs flying up the ceilings. This Mediterranean dream belongs to the twin brothers that have been on my suspect list since they showed up at my café wearing fake smiles and lying through their fucking teeth.

Either—or both—could be my target.

Emi fished the dark web for anything on the Bourbon brothers. Although there wasn't much to be found, Dantë's dating life was a surprise. Last I knew, he was engaged to Margot Lovecraft, advisor of a local sorority. Apparently, the man has been going through bodies like a chainsmoker through cigarettes ever since Margot ghosted him last year. Brontë was spotted online twice: as the shopowner of Bourbon Binds, and as a coroner for a local medical examiner's office.

A coroner who's likely carted many of my victims to his morgue.

Emi hit a wall when mining for what Dantë does for a living, but it must be impressive if he can afford the custom-painted McLaren parked beside Brontë's vintage cobalt Corvette in the enclosed garage downstairs. He could be affiliated with the underworld. Or worse, the government.

I pass through an open-concept kitchen with a seaside view of the starlit Atlantic. Cross a hall into a homey den. Peer into an obnoxiously lavish study. Stalk up the main staircase. I crack the first door I see, to the right of the top landing. Honeysuckle and pine perfume the air as I poke my head in.

The room is brimming with anime paraphernalia. Quiet metalcore that Bax and Jett would enjoy is playing from the speakers. Top-tier gaming equipment encompasses the far wall. Swathed in sweats, Dantë is cuddling with an axolotl plushie and sleeping as soundly as the dead.

Who would have thought? Dantë Bourbon, playboy and nerd. I wonder just how many people he's fucked in that bed with his army of plushies watching.

I stifle a snort then close the door.

Across the hall is another room. I soundlessly peer in, breathing the spice of bourbon and cherry smoke. Built-in bookshelves wrap the room, stuffed with rebound books. An en suite bathroom stretches to the east, dominated by a priceless clawfoot tub. A bar cart is parked aside a leather wingback chair angled toward a small brick hearth.

I don't even need to see him to know whose room it is.

In a massive, circular bed piled with pelts and pillows, Brontë is asleep. A fur duvet is tangled around his long, muscled legs. He's in his boxers and nothing else, his warrior frame and throat-to-toe holy tattoos on full display in the slivers of moonlight trickling in from the far windows. He stirs, restless. Something tells me it's not a result of my presence.

Is he plagued by nightmares, too?

Focus, Poppy.

Before I do anything reckless like tuck him back in, I search the room and find nothing. Quietly shutting the door behind me, I creep back down to the garage. My assessment is as solid as the concrete beneath my feet.

The Bourbons are not my enemy.

My disappointment rises far above my relief. I'm nowhere closer to finding my target now than when I started.

My family is struggling to keep this systematic downfall a secret. Our ops are still being sabotaged from afar, our people leaving for greener grass. Slowly but surely, we are crumbling at the roots. We're in no better shape than the Volkovs were during their war with Grandpapa Lucian.

If this keeps going, our bones will be picked clean in a matter of months.

As I sneak toward the cracked window I slipped in through, I catch a glimpse of my own reflection in a glass door tucked beneath the stairs. Thick shadows bathe the room beyond, concealing its contents. Piled outside are boxes to be mailed, all labeled as Bourbon Binds.

Brontë's Etsy shop.

I inch forward, my imagination running rampant. Bodies strung up by the ankles like livestock, heads lining the walls like trophies, blood staining every surface like the aftermath of a horror movie.

Unrealistic. Yet entirely plausible.

Brontë may not be hellbent on crushing my family's empire. But he could still be a threat. He's seen the bodies I've been leaving in my wake. It's no coincidence he crawled out of his own hole to visit, of all places, *my* café. He looked just as uncomfortable as he did intrigued when we met. As if that wasn't suspicious enough, he'd been reading a serial killer rom-com while drinking a cup of black *and* made that odd remark about investigating unsolved murders.

The universe was practically *screaming* at me to read the signs.

Quietly, I push through the unlocked door.

A biting cold hits me first, shocking against the hot-as-Lucifer's-ballsack August heat still clinging to my skin. My exhale puffs white in the arctic chill. My inhale brings burning ammonia into my lungs, followed by the saccharine stench of death.

I flip on the dim lights and twist in a slow circle, taking it all in.

Cricuts crowd the shelves, pyramids of vinyl stacked beside them. There are mountains of border stencils and decorative paper. Rolls of ribbon and book cloth. Endless threads and needles. Every color of spray paint in existence, organized by type of finish on a shelf above glass jars brimming with syrupy dye. A slop sink is tucked into a corner, the deep basin artfully stained.

This is a bibliopegist's heaven.

Rather, it *would* be. If it wasn't defiled by death's odor.

My legs carry me toward the main workstation. Beside the medical gloves are several books in various stages of undress, including my untouched copy of *Inferno*. Nothing unorthodox.

Blowing out a defeated breath, I turn to leave.

But then I spy a hallway branching off from the main room, leading toward the unmistakable hum of exhaust fans.

"What are you hiding back there, *monsieur?*" I whisper, prowling into the dark.

The stench strengthens to a pungent punch before I round a sharp corner and push through a knobless door. Machines line the walls of another chamber. Above, the monstrous industrial fans whir, feeding the tainted air directly into the night. A heap of dry hide is stockpiled beside a suspiciously large chest freezer.

Brontë owns his own tannery.

Interesting.

I drift over to the leather. Some strips are dyed, others are natural pigments ranging from deep brown to pinkish white. I skim a palm over a slab.

Pause.

Ivory powder stains my fingertips. I rub them together, spreading the talc. Beneath it, the phantom texture of skin remains.

I've killed countless people. I know what human flesh feels like. Even treated beyond its original identity, it's unmistakable.

Swallowing dread, I crack open the freezer.

And gag at the sight of half a dozen frozen bodies.

Brontë Bourbon isn't innocent. He's a killer.

Fury floods my veins. I draw my knife, spearing for the exit. I'm moving so fast, I almost miss it—the logbook lying on a workbench by the doorway. It's open to a list of projects and names. Names of criminals, along with their transgressions. Many are familiar, as they are *my* victims. It spans the entirety of the last decade, since my early days of vigilantism.

My tongue clicks. "Stalker much?"

I flip forward, finding Sebastian Bonaparte fated for a rebind of *Jane Eyre*. Chuckling, I skip to the most recent log.

"Poppy Morgenstern." I grin so wide, my cheeks ache. Tracing a fingernail over the loops of ink forming my name beside *Inferno*, I muse, "Guess karma really is a cold-hearted bitch after all, Doc."

If I possess any sense of self-preservation, I'll go back upstairs and kill the man planning to kill me. It'd save me the headache later. Though I'd be forced to murder his brother, too. If there are no secrets between the twins, Dantë is aware of Brontë's agenda.

There's just one problem: I don't slaughter the innocent. Although Brontë's moral compass is as skewed as my own, we're on the same side.

And if we're on the same side...

I'm suddenly moving as fast as my thrashing heart. Grabbing the logbook pen, I scribble a note onto a blank page then tear it out. With bated breath, I plant it atop the book that had once been my escape from myself when I was a child learning how to be a monster.

HAUNTED

BRONTË

I've been wrong about women plenty of times in my life.

There was the college girlfriend who dumped me when I told her I wanted to work with corpses for a living. The Tinder find who didn't mind my career but had a furry kink I couldn't quite bring myself to feed when she insisted I fuck her in a James P. Sullivan onesie while she wore a Wookiee suit. Then there was the Swifty fling, and the brief yet scarring blip with Quinn.

Never have I been so wrong about a woman as Poppy Morgenstern.

I tap my laptop screen to replay the footage of the little devil stalking through my house. Questions swarm my mind like hornets kicked from a nest.

Why was she here? She was clearly looking for something she didn't find. Why didn't she kill me—*us?* She had every opportunity to slit our throats before *and* after sniffing out my secrets stashed in the studio. Instead, she left a note on the very book her hide was destined for and called it a night.

"What's our next move, brother?" Dantë sips his morning coffee, his focus lingering on the torn page lying atop the kitchen island.

Brontë, it reads, *I found your pretty skeletons. Sadly, I don't think the feds would admire your creativity nearly as much as me. I'll make this simple: If you don't want to worry about dropping the soap for the rest of your life, call me. I could use your help in serving poetic justice.*

P.S. Don't bother calling the cops. I think you know by now they're as useless as tits on a rock.

Poppy's number is scribbled in the bottom corner. I'm surprised it doesn't contain a triple 6.

"Not a clue," I admit, pausing the video on the little devil watching me sleep with a somber tilt to her head. She's not smiling nor sniggering like she was after peeking into Dantë's room. She's looking at me as if she also wrestles with demons on a nightly basis. Like she may actually have a saint's heart beating in that sinner's chest. "I need to think."

Dantë nods and turns away. I grab his hood, stopping him mid-stride. Reminiscent of when we were kids, I lean my brow against his.

"Are you sure you want to keep going?"

"Why wouldn't I?"

Carefully, I say, "You know why."

Dantë's red eyes anchor to mine, allowing me to see every individual thread of maroon and vermilion and rose weaving through his haunted irises. "No, I don't."

"Don't play dumb with me like you did with Poppy. I know the real reason you stalked that Hale girl."

Since hearing him lie to Poppy about Margot still being in his life, I've had my suspicions. He may be helping me for no other reason aside from having my back like any decent brother would. But he's also got some skin in this game.

Margot was the love of Dantë's life until the day she abandoned him after he handed her a priceless heirloom. Grief has been eating him alive day in, day out. He lost his best friend, the person he wanted at his side for the rest of his life. Even after a year without her, he's been clinging to the shred of hope that she'll come back and prove to him she isn't the thief she turned out to be.

But she hasn't. And he's desperate for answers.

Desperate enough to tread back through the underworld to find her.

"Tell me where I'm wrong," I say when he remains deafeningly silent. "You stalked Remiel to see for yourself how much of a risk you'd be taking in hiring her to trace Margot. When you realized your precious hacker was affiliated with the Morgensterns, you bailed."

Danté drops his gaze, avoiding my probing stare. "I told you it was recon. You're the one who jumped to conclusions about my rivalry with her as Halestorm."

"Conclusions you didn't deny." I lean back so he can fully appreciate my irked frown. "Now, you're what? Helping me slay the dragon for the treasure beyond?"

"I'm not the only one benefitting from this. You want that dragon dead, too."

"I want justice. Hundreds of innocent lives could be saved if this monster dies." I jab a finger into his chest. "*You* want the inconvenience removed for your own personal gain."

"Can you blame me?" He swats me off and drags a tattooed hand through his hair. "Margot took Mama's ring and ran. I *need* to find her. I..." He stalls, tugging his hood up to shade his downturned lashes. I don't speak, giving him space to think through what I can only imagine is a warzone of emotion. "That ring is the only piece of our mother we have left, Brontë. I need to get it back. I can't do that without finding Margot. If anyone can track her down, it's Remiel."

I close my eyes and see our mother's glimmering opal ring. It was her mother's, her grandmother's, and so on. A true Bourbon heirloom handed from generation to generation through the noble French bloodline. Stolen by the same person who broke my brother's heart.

"*He's your brother, mon petit chérubin,*" Mama used to say, her hazel eyes bright with pride. "*Take care of him. Always.*"

I vowed to protect him. Never have I broken that vow.

I'll be damned to every circle of hell if I do so now.

My eyes open and lock onto the note. "Time to best a devil, then."

MAELSTROM

POPPY

September rain drums the glass as Emi's aquamarine eyes bore into mine. "The fuck did you just say?"

Perching on the edge of her bed beside Hades and patting the purring bobcat runt's gray head, I chirp, "I said I left Brontë a note."

From her lamplit desk, Emi's mouth gapes wide open. "Have you lost your goddamn mind?"

Maybe. "No."

"Do you have a death wish?"

Probably. "No."

"Let me get this straight. You broke into Brontë's house. Uncovered his plan to *murder* you, turn you into a book, and *sell you on Etsy.* Then you left him a fucking *note.*"

My lips purse. "When you put it like that, it sounds like a terrible decision."

"That's because it *is* a terrible decision, Poppy!" Emi explodes, startling Hades. He jumps as if she shot him in the ass and bolts for the stairs leading down to the café. "What on earth were you thinking?"

"I was thinking I need allies rather than enemies, Emi," I snipe, growing tired of defending my rash decision. I didn't regret it for a single moment these past few weeks. Until now. "I was thinking I would at least try to avoid bloodshed. I was thinking I have much, *much* bigger problems than a spiteful coroner with a very questionable hobby. I need friends, Emi, and you're supposed to be one of them. Do me a favor and act like it."

"I *am* your friend, Pops. I'm just"—she nibbles her bottom lip and idly taps her keyboard to light up the reactive keys with bursts of bright red—"I'm worried about you."

"I can take care of myself."

"Of course you can." She scoffs flippantly. "Because you're a Morgenstern, which automatically makes you invincible."

"Remiel." I lance her with an icy glare. "Don't."

Emi hisses out a defeated sigh. "So, what did you write in this suicide note to the psychotic coroner?"

"I gave him my number and threatened to turn him over to the feds if he doesn't assist me."

"Judas Priest." She drags a hand through her long, raven layers. "Do you think he can actually help?"

"Yes. No. I don't know." I flop onto my back and stare up at the angry clouds dumping their torrential tears onto the world. "I wanted to get ahead of him. Offer an alliance to keep him off my back so I can deal with this sabotage shit in peace."

A pause. Then: "Still no leads?"

"Nope."

"Anything I can do?"

"No. My cyber team is on it. The further you remain away from this, the safer you are."

"That's not necessary. I can take care of myself, too."

"I know."

Emi, like Fiona and Cas, doesn't work for me or my family. She does know how to defend herself, though. How to kill, if needed.

As her shoulders droop, I add, "You could look into Cas and Fiona." I highly doubt they're involved, though; Castor isn't the conniving type, and Fiona is too busy to rip her nose from her phone for longer than two seconds.

Emi blows out a slow breath. "So, I may have already done that."

I close my eyes, sighing. "Of course you did."

"I didn't find anything, if that's any consolation."

It's not. "Mhm. Top notch initiative, Emi."

Fabric rustles, and the mattress shifts with added weight as Emi lies beside me. We didn't grow up together. I imagine if we did, we would've shared countless hours like this. Lying beside each other and whispering in the dark.

We became fast friends after she showed up at Beelzebub's with a rental application in her hand for the apartment space above the café. Ghosts swam in her eyes when she spoke of her past. She lost her parents to a tragic house fire. She doesn't speak of the years in between losing them and finding me. Since then, she's been working as a self-employed hacker to fund her dream of becoming a professional gamer.

To achieve that dream, she needs to be rid of her criminal life. There is no such thing as dipping a toe into the underworld; it consumes the soul until nothing is left. The less involved she is with this turf war, the better.

"Talk to me, Pops." Emi elbows my ribs, waiting for my eyes to open. "How bad is it?"

Petrichor and electricity fill my lungs as I breathe in the storm and breathe out the maelstrom within. Trying to figure out how to describe the shitshow my life is quickly becoming, I settle on: "We don't have much time left."

"You say that like you're a dying animal."

"Well, that's what we are, Emi. A living beast on its last leg and very little breath remaining to give."

Her gaze grows somber. "I heard you when you said you don't want me involved. But if I can help in any way, promise you'll ask?"

I don't want to, but if only to make her feel less like I'm benching her, I nod. "*Hai*, I promise."

It's at that exact moment my phone buzzes.

I glance down at the screen illuminating my pocket. Freeing my cell, I note the unknown number. "What are the chances it's a telemarketer?"

Emi grimaces, eyeing the device like it'll grow fangs and spit venom. "Significantly lower than the chances it's a coroner with a personal vendetta against felons to whom you willingly gave your number as part of your final wishes."

My heart bashes against its cage, an unnerving reaction. I shouldn't be nervous. Or am I excited?

Before I can debate which is worse, I accept the call. "Hello?"

"*Bonjour*," Brontë's smooth and silken baritone rumbles in my ear, louder than the thunder rolling outside. It's what I've always imagined Lucifer's voice to be—equal parts sinful and damning. His is the voice of temptation. "I'd like to discuss your proposition. Are you available to meet tonight?"

I lurch up, fixing my tousled fringe. "I'm free all night."

Emi cringes, mouthing, *Gross.*

I flip her off, and she flips me off in return.

Brontë, mercifully, ignores the unintentional insinuation. "I'm on the road. I can be at Beelzebub's in fifteen."

"*Parfait!* See you s—"

He hangs up.

I slump, grumbling, "*Au revoir*, you fucking prick."

The unseasonably cold air on this early autumn night nips at my exposed skin with boreal breath and rime-ridden teeth as I step outside and squint through the wall of pouring rain into the parking lot.

Thwip flaps my butterfly knife as I flip it free from my pocket. A precaution, just in case shit goes south with the coroner who's not only been stalking me for ten years but also wants to turn me into bookshelf décor.

Maybe I really do have a death wish.

Ten minutes of freezing my ass off later, Brontë's cobalt Corvette glides into a spot. The purring engine shuts off, and out steps the coroner who has no business being the paragon of tall, dark, and handsome.

A pity he's not a doctor. McSavory would've been the perfect nickname.

Hiding my knife behind my back, I wave with enthusiasm. His frown twitches as he draws the hood of his work jacket over his head and treks toward me. His fists are clenched in his pockets. I swear I see the outline of a gun gripped in one.

The hairs on my nape stand on end. Fear strokes my most primal senses awake. Maybe Emi's concerns were valid. What if Brontë came here to kill me, just as he'd been planning all along?

Dread erodes my stomach. My arm drops with my smile. Instinct pushes me back a step as my thoughts siphon to a single bleating plea: *kill.*

I flick the wings of my knife open.

My arm cocks.

And then a hand clamps around my throat.

KEROSENE
BRONTË

I did not come here to kill Poppy. I came here to make a bargain.

Yet every step I take feels like I'm walking toward the gallows.

Frigid rain slaps my hood with fat, cold droplets as the storm bellows a warcry in the night sky above. Adrenaline floods my system with memories. Throwing me back in time to a desert ranch. Tossing cold metal in my grip. Blaring a deadbeat soldier's slurring commands in my ears—

Thunder smacks me back to the present. I squeeze the Kimber in my pocket to ground myself. The gun is for my own protection, nothing more. If all goes as planned, there won't be a single need to use it.

I'm halfway to the café's entrance when I hear the scuff of boots on stone followed by a choked gasp.

My head snaps up.

Poppy isn't there.

The roaring world goes silent, and my training kicks in.

I quicken my pace, careful to avoid drawing attention from anyone on the street or in the café. Slinking to the edge of the building, I peer around the corner. Through the blinding sheet of rain, I distinguish a dumpster nestled against a brick wall graffitied with an ominous demonic skull grinning around a mouthful of fangs. Almost like—

The dumpster rattles as something slams its opposite side in an offbeat rhythm.

I lurch into motion.

As I move, the past blurs with the present. Brick blends to barbed wire and back again. Cobblestone shifts to mud then reshapes when my soles don't sink. Thunder morphs and rises to a howl as I round the bend.

I don't know what I'm expecting to see, but it's certainly not a man in black with a gaiter pulled up to his lightless gray eyes as he chokes the life out of Poppy. Her boots pound a desperate beat into the dumpster as the man squeezes her purpling neck. His grip is so tight, not a single sound escapes her bruised and bloody lips. Her wrists are pinned beneath his knees. A spray-painted butterfly knife lies on the ground, just out of her reach.

Wrath. Fury. Rage. None hold a flame to the maddening inferno burning through my veins at the sight alone. Of that vile, villainous, *powerful* woman flat on her back and kicking her legs as uselessly as an ensnared hare.

"You should consider yourself lucky, *printsessa,*" the man croons with a thick Russian accent, dragging a hand glinting with brass knuckles down the center of her chest. "It was only a matter of time before someone was going to do to you what was done to us. You should be grateful I got to you first. This way, you won't have to suffer at the hands of some other ugly mug, *da?*"

Poppy flails without purchase, kicking that dumpster like it's hell's gates. She finds me looming in the dark, and the raw plea in her eyes dumps kerosene into my blood.

I *detonate.*

In an instant, I grab the man by his hood and throw him into the brick wall. Under his surprised yelp, I hear Poppy's rough coughs and choppy breaths.

Alive, is my only rational thought. *She's alive.*

I send a fist sailing into the man's stomach. He lets out a garbled curse and doubles over, spitting blood.

Faster than an adder, he strikes back.

Speed was never my friend. I sidestep, but not quick enough. Brass slams my jaw. I reel back, tasting salt and iron. Another immediate blow to my temple sends me stumbling. I blindly draw my gun, flicking the safety.

"Mine," hisses a pink streak blurring by.

Poppy hammers the man with a front kick, audibly cracking bone. He wheezes, clutching his chest, and then she has her blade at his throat and his mask pulled down as she snarls, "Blackguard bastard!"

Lightning flashes against the man's manic grin. "Would you not have done the same if you were me?"

"No, Vlad. Vows mean something to me—to *us.*"

"Vows of dead men mean nothing," Vlad spits like a viper. "The Volkovs were meant to rule this city. It *never* belonged to the Morgensterns."

"We trusted you. *I* trusted you."

"Your mistake, not mine."

Poppy shakes her head, her chin strangely wobbling. "What about Kai? Nik?"

Vlad merely laughs like a madman.

"You forget that I know you better than you know yourself." Poppy sneers, her knife drawing a thin stream of blood as she presses her weight into the blade. "You're too stupid to be working alone. Who else is involved?"

Vlad runs his tongue along his toothy grin. "See you in hell, *printsessa.*"

Faster than she can react, he grabs her wrist and wrestles the knife from her grip—

Bang!

The gunshot is muffled by a thunderclap. Blood splatters the wall, smeared with chunky brain matter. Vlad doesn't make a sound as gravity yanks him down to the ground.

Baby blues swing to me. My smoking gun automatically trains on the arrowhead fringe marking the bullseye between them.

A stilted silence limps by, louder than the storm.

With those glacial eyes leaking mascara tears and rain washing blood down her face, Poppy Morgenstern looks like a true angel of death. Her luminescent irises are stark against the bloodshot whites, adrenaline still pumping a chaotic current through her veins.

Fear is easy to read in most people; pinched features, stiff movements, erratic breaths. Hers, though, is sketched in every line of her trembling silhouette. This little devil with a Hadean heart isn't just scared; she's terrified out of her goddamn mind.

Bruises circle her slender neck in purple rings. My stare slashes to the man who made those marks on her delicate skin. What book should his hide be wrapped around? *Misery? Bag of Bones?* Or is *Carrie* the ultimate form of justice?

"Brontë," Poppy croaks, tugging my focus back to her as she looks at me the same way she did when I was asleep. Like she understands—no, like she *sees* me. "I need you."

I need you. Those three words drop upon my head like a meteor slamming to the earth. She asked for my help, and I came to discuss my price. Not wave a gun in her face.

Slowly, I flick the safety and lower the weapon.

The relief in her eyes threatens to pulp my chest as she breathes, "*Merci.*"

I nod then jerk my chin toward the dead assassin. "Mind if I take him?"

Poppy glances between me and him, him and me. Her pink lips purse into an oddly adorable pout. "You're not going to eat him, are you?"

"I'm not that kind of psychopath."

"What kind are you, then?"

I brush past her, chuckling quietly. "My own special blend."

PETIT DIABLE
POPPY

I've learned three things about Brontë Bourbon: he's bitter, broody, and unbearably beautiful.

Brontë is a living replica of a literal deity—deeply bronzed skin; charcoal hair trimmed to a faded undercut rebelling from its slicked style to frame sharp cheekbones; tattoos of angels and demons starting just beneath his aggressive jawline and disappearing beneath the deep *V* of his black tee. Most mesmerizing is his smolder. *Fuck,* it could crack any chastity belt.

He's the kind of man built to make mothers hide their daughters.

Brontë slides out a spine from the bookshelf beside my bed, where I'm cuddling Jezebel as we tolerate his unwelcome perusal of my room. "You're a vamp girl?"

"Not at all. I'm an Anne Rice girl."

He pulls another vampire fiction novel by a different author. "You sure?"

"*That* is a very unique fantasy where vamps have wings."

The bastard spies another, smirking as he drawls, "Who taught you more French: Lestat de Lioncourt or Gabriel de León?"

My teeth grind. He's too perceptive for his own good. "Are you done stalling?"

"I'm not stalling." He slips the books back into place and leans against my desk in an attempt to look casual. He looks as comfortable as a priest in a brothel. "I'm waiting for you to start."

"I don't know where to start." I rake my fingers through my soggy hair. It still looks like pink seaweed streaked with the blood of a traitor.

Thankfully, most of the evidence of Vlad's death was washed off by the storm before we came in through the back and headed upstairs. Kahula didn't even notice; the baker was too busy cleaning up for the night and singing along to Dove Cameron's *Lethal Woman*. Emi, on the other hand, did not miss the blood on me as we passed her room.

I'm *so* not looking forward to that particular interrogation...

"Do you start a book at the end or the beginning?" Brontë retorts, his tone as lifeless as a flatline. Sarcasm, I'm learning, is his first language.

"I think you missed your calling in stand-up, *monsieur*."

"Unfortunately, that involves dealing with the worst kind of people."

"The cheerful?"

"The living."

I snort, and he almost—*almost*—cracks a smile.

An awkward silence ensues. He watches me as I watch him. What does he see? A woman or a monster?

Candlelight twirls through his multi-hued irises, blooming the ochre, burning the evergreen, charring the speckled patches of sunshine. All surrounded by enviously thick lashes and several creases at the edges betraying a life of laughter.

I can't help but wonder if he laughs most with the living or the dead.

"Sit." I point to the plush wingback at my desk. "You look uncomfortable, and it's making *me* uncomfortable."

I'm surprised when he doesn't deny my assumption *and* does what I ask.

Shirking off his damp jacket and hanging it on the back of the closed door, Brontë lowers onto the seat. He rolls his sleeves, revealing a scrawling portrait of more ethereal beings inked on his arms. Arms that are roped in thick muscle. His eyes flick briefly to my pink skull mask wedged between books on my nightstand.

"I just have one question." Impressed he's capping his curiosity, I nod for him to continue. "Are you in a cult?"

I blink then bark a laugh. "What kind of question is that?"

"The valid kind. You draw pentagrams with your victims' blood and say shit like 'by the stars.'"

"Tradition passed down through each Morgenstern generation since the day some distant ancestor supposedly made a deal with the Devil." I wave off his blank stare, eyes rolling. "We're an empire, not a cult."

"Fair enough." Brontë drags a hand over the bruises blooming along his temple and jaw from Vlad's brass knuckles. Then he draws a folded note from his pocket. *The* note. "Perhaps you can begin by explaining what this means."

It's as good a starting point as any.

Brontë listens better than anyone I've ever met. Not once does he interrupt. He embodies patience, entirely calm and unbothered up to the yawning end of my long-winded monologue. Exhaustion has steadily pushed me down to the mattress, where I'm now sprawled on my stomach beside a snoring Jezebel.

"So," Brontë says, leaning his elbows on his knees and scanning me as if assessing through a new lens, "you really are a princess."

"That's not exactly a normal response to someone telling you they're a rising crime lord."

"I've seen your kind before."

I shouldn't be intrigued. I may have given him a slice of my history, but he owes me nothing in return. Certainly not his childhood story that clearly didn't involve a cute puppy or surprise trip to Disney.

I can relate.

Snuffing my curiosity, I get to the point. "Then you understand the importance of my mission. Whoever this saboteur is that Vlad had been working with, they must be stopped before innocents are caught in this war."

Brontë inclines his head. "How can I help?"

The ultimate question I've been mulling over for weeks. I straighten, folding my legs beneath me and linking my fingers in my lap.

"As a coroner, you have unlimited access to specific databases I don't. I need you to find out what you can about any casualties within the city, including those brought on my own hand."

"So we don't overlook any of your victims who could've been connected to this saboteur."

"Exactly. I don't care what the cases were closed as. Even if it's not murder, you and I both know most deaths are covered up by lies and red tape. From this point on, you're also going to be monitoring future deaths for the same information."

He nods, catching on quickly. "Find the roots, cut out the cancer."

"Permanently."

"What about the remaining Volkovs? How do you plan to assess if they've jumped ship like your Brutus lying in my trunk?"

I blow out a long breath, my shoulders falling. "Nik and Kai are my own demons to drown."

For just a moment, I let myself glimpse that faraway dream of my future as queen of Salem's underworld. In it, I wouldn't need to worry about the Volkovs turning their backs on me. Because I wouldn't employ people like them to begin with.

I blink the vision away before any traitorous tears can rise to the surface.

Brontë searches my eyes, though what he's looking for, I don't know. I'm still shivering. My throat and face have their own separate pulses of raw, aching pain. I'm craving a bath, but I can barely keep my eyelids from drooping. I'm edging dangerously on crabby the longer he sits there and stares at me.

My teeth graze a split in my bottom lip, and I taste blood. "This is the part where you tell me if you're in or out."

"No. This is the part where I tell you what I expect in return for accepting this deal after saving your life and owing you nothing."

Clever *and* beautiful, a dangerous cocktail. Sexy as hell, too. "Name your price. I'll wire half the funds now, half when we're done."

"I don't want your money, Poppy. I want your hacker."

"Which one? I have dozens...for now."

"Not a Morgenstern hacker." Brontë taps a tattooed knuckle against my desktop screensaver displaying a photo of me and Emi at last year's Comic Con. "Your freelancing friend."

My frown furrows years into my skin. "What do you need her to do?"

He unlocks his phone and flashes a photo of a familiar tall blond. She's a bombshell with chocolate eyes and serpentine curves, absorbing the all-consuming embrace of his twin brother.

"I need her to find Margot. Dantë and I will take care of the rest ourselves."

Emi's help is a small price to pay, yet it's the most he could've ever asked of me. This is exactly what I was trying to avoid, isn't it? Pulling Emi deeper into the abyss? Hacking on her own terms is one thing;

but this, searching for someone who may not want to be found, could lead her down a rabbit hole with no escape.

I shake my head. "Emi isn't on the table."

"Then find yourself a new coroner willing to play criminal."

"I could force you to help me. I found your pretty skeletons, remember?"

"Indeed, you did. On camera, might I add. Let's not stop there, though, because you spent the past hour admitting to me, a public official, that you're a crime lord's daughter with an entire necropolis in your own closet. Who will a jury believe, hm? The criminal or the coroner who's been cleaning up her messes for the last decade?"

I bristle, but he's not wrong. I have dirt on him, and he has dirt on me. Our swords are poised at each other's throats. A single wrong move, and we're both dead.

"If Emi doesn't want to help," I warn, "you'll get someone else."

He doesn't hesitate. "Deal."

I shift forward, offering my hand. "Allies, *monsieur?*"

Like a Victorian Era gentleman, Brontë curls his fingers around mine. They're warm and calloused and unexpectedly comforting. My heart stumbles into an uneven rhythm as he lifts my knuckles to his lips and presses a soft, almost reverent kiss to the knobs of bone.

"Allies," he murmurs against my skin, "*Petit Diable.*"

MISERY

BRONTË

"**W**hat's in the box, *monsieur?* Booze? Drugs? Random body parts?"

"Technically?" I tuck the package into the crook of my arm and swipe my ID badge from the dash. "All three."

Poppy's eyebrows elevate as she tugs off her helmet and sets it on the seat of her sleek silver Kawasaki Ninja parked in the empty lot beside my car outside the medical examiner's office. "That's...cryptic."

I snicker. "Were you going to say creepy?"

"No."

"Lie."

"I'm not lying."

"Mm. Another lie."

Her arms cross, her brow flatlining. "What makes you think I'm lying?"

I greedily take the invitation to drink her in. The setting October sun gilds her silhouette like an ethereal aura, and I'm reminded of why she's been living in my mind like a fever dream for weeks. Her bittersweet scent is still lodged in my nostrils from the night we made our bargain. Her fear, too, is still seared behind my eyelids.

For weeks, rage has been coursing through my veins. Rage at myself, for aiming a loaded gun at her head. For giving her a reason to fear me. If anyone deserves to be skinned alive and slapped onto *Pride and Prejudice*, it's me.

Poppy isn't the cold-blooded killing machine I first thought her to be. She's a *person*, with friends she loves and an entire city she's trying to protect. She isn't a villain or a vigilante destined for evil. She's playing the cards she was dealt to the best of her ability while ensuring her world of shadows doesn't eclipse the rest of us.

Since that night, cold regret has suffocated the hot wrath. Shame's knife has sunk deep into my guts, tormenting me with the memory of those baby blues shining with terror in the face of death.

"Your voice goes up an octave at the end," I drawl as I step past her. "It's impressive, actually, for anyone to be so bad at lying."

With an impressively dramatic eyeroll, Poppy sighs. "Why are we here, Brontë? Your message was incredibly *cryptic*."

Well, she's pissed.

Très bien. I'd rather her ire than her terror.

My grin drops as reality banishes the surreal haze I seem to lose myself in around her. "You'll see. Did Emi kill the cams?"

She checks her phone and nods. "We have fifteen minutes."

"Waste not," I say, heading for the back entrance.

Poppy watches with curiosity as I swipe my badge to unlock the door then pans her gaze over the empty and lightless office, following as I lead us toward the descending stairs. When I drop off the box at Quinn's station in the forensics lab, she lobs me a quizzical look.

"Payment for a friend's favor."

I offer no other explanation as I lead her to the morgue. The rebound book is, after all, for Quinn's help in investigating Poppy. Her breath clouds in the frigid air as she surveys the stainless steel autopsy tables, the wall of cold lockers.

"Creepy."

"Truth." I chuckle at her vitriolic lour. "Well, *that's* a face."

"Ten minutes." She taps her wrist. "Waste. Not."

Finding my penlight, I fit on a pair of medical gloves and unlatch the locker I've been dreading reopening. "*Venez ici.*" She cocks a bemused brow, and I sigh. Her vampire books must not have taught her much French beyond the basics. "Come here."

Poppy obeys as I pull out the slab, studying the sheet concealing the corpse beneath. "Who is it?"

I toe a rolling stool toward her. "Sit."

"I'm not a dog, fuck you very much."

"*S'il te plaît, Petit Diable.* Sit your royal ass down."

"What does that mean? '*Petit Diable.*'"

"Little Devil."

A scoff. "Hilarious."

"*Merci.*" I point my penlight at the stool. "Now."

Poppy plops down, grumbling, "Yes, Master," like a dejected Igor. *Angels save me.*

I peel the cloth back, exposing the ashen flesh of a young woman with bright green hair. All emotion drains from Poppy's face. Her throat bobs, hands wringing in her lap.

"Jett..." She examines the post-organ removal sutures criss-crossing up the cadaver's chest. "What happened?"

I pull the sheet farther down, revealing the pentagram carved into the woman's abdomen.

Poppy's eyes are as dim as a sunless sea. "When?"

"Today—around noon."

Those baby blues lift to me, a frostbitten fire burning within them. "Tell me everything you know."

As I lean against my car now parked beside Poppy's motorcycle outside Beelzebub's and breathe in cherry smoke, Poppy inhales a sapphire cocktail from her vape and exhales pale blue mist up at the stars. It smells like her sweet, nostalgic scent of cotton candy.

"Bax is going to lose his shit," she says, "when I tell him that not only is Jett dead, but she was found in a fucking dumpster. That girl was like a sister to him."

"Your people are searching the city's cams," I remind her. The street chemist's death, while grim, is a death that no one with a badge aside from Scull will care to investigate. "It shouldn't take long for them to find the killer."

"I know. I'm just tired of this guessing game."

"You're certain it's not another rogue Volkov?"

"At this point, I'm not certain of anything."

That's it, no further explanation.

"Now who's being cryptic?" I tease, earning her middle finger. "What's happened since we last spoke?"

Poppy eyes me sidelong. "You don't have to do this."

"This...?"

"*This.*" She gestures between us. "Pretend you care."

"Am I that transparent?"

"Brontë," she huffs, rubbing her temple. "The only thing you care about is our bargain."

That should be the case, but it's not. I genuinely want to know what's been the cause of those sleepless bruises beneath her lashes. I don't blame her for not trusting my intentions, though. I did have a gun aimed at her head last time we crossed paths.

I wouldn't trust me, either.

That knife of humility lodged in my innards digs deeper. I welcome the pain along with misery's familiar company.

"Believe what you want, *Petit Diable*. Either way, I'm here until this"—I lift my dying cigar—"burns out. So, you can either open your pretty little mouth and talk. Or stand here and brood decades from your rapidly dwindling youth. Your choice."

Poppy swings a slow glare toward me. "No wonder you get along so well with the dead."

"Why? Because they aren't as easily offended as the living?"

"No. Because they aren't alive to know how abominable you are."

I shrug, wisps of gray smoke wafting from my nostrils. "Truth."

For a moment, I think she'll yank on her helmet and peel away. But she doesn't. She remains rooted, straddling the bike and staring at the stars with a dose of longing. Like she wishes she could escape to any other world, no matter how far.

"Have you ever seen a cat play with a mouse, *monsieur?*"

"*Oui.* Sadistic hellions until they get bored and eat their entertainment."

"Since the seventeenth century, my family has been the cat. For the first time in centuries, we are the mouse struggling beneath the paw." She leans her arms on the handlebars of her motorcycle and blows out a heavy sigh that ruffles her sharp fringe. "Poaching our people was only the beginning. They've since moved to sabotaging our operations. The cams around every targeted location are tampered with exactly when shit goes south. Day after day, it's been disaster after disaster."

"Have you tried setting them up? Staging a coup and slaying the snake once it slithers in?"

"Of course I've tried to trick the bastard. You think I'd be bitching about it now if any of the attempts had been successful?"

"Easy, *Petit Diable*. Only trying to help."

Blue smoke seeps from her sigh. "I know."

"Sounds like you have a mole, though."

"No shit, Sherlock."

"And Dantë said *I* need to get laid," I mumble, crushing the cigar beneath my boot.

Her arctic gaze snaps up. "The fuck did you just say?"

"I said, what is that?" I deflect, lifting a hand to trail my fingers through the cloud of cyan smoke. "Smells nice."

A beat of silence passes. Her left eye twitches.

Then she cranes her neck and guffaws at the sky. It's a laugh befitting someone who belongs in a straightjacket. *By the angels,* it's so goddamn beautiful.

A corner of my mouth tugs up despite my best efforts to keep it down. "What's so funny?"

"The—B-Bax—it's—" She sputters through cackles that sound like crows fighting over a fresh carcass. "Fairy Farts! It's Fairy Farts, and you think it smells nice!"

Makes zero sense to me. A chuckle still escapes from listening to her ridiculous laugh and seeing her luminescent smile brighter than any star.

Then her pocket buzzes. And that bright beam burns like a wick, melting her mouth into a sober line as she lifts her phone with a slight tremor in her hands.

Clarity strikes me like a bullet to the chest, leaving me breathless. She never asked for this life, this hand of spades. Her father dealt them to her. I'd wager every last penny to the Bourbon name he never asked if she wanted to keep her hearts instead. He just took them away, robbing her of every dream she ever had.

Because of him, she will never have a normal life.

I immediately want to pulverize whoever is on the other end of that text. Especially if it's Alexander Morgenstern.

Eyes wide, Poppy breathes, "*Kuso.*"

"What?" I bark, not bothering to sound pleasant.

She tosses the phone to me. "Notice anything familiar?"

I play the clip featuring a hooded man tossing Jett, dead and bloody, into the alleyway dumpster she was found in. He's tall and lean, his physique similar to the assassin stored in my studio. "A Volkov?"

She nods. "Malakai."

I toss the phone back to her. "Looks like you found your mole."

Poppy grins, and it's the most infernal expression I've ever seen on a woman. "Cats eat moles, don't they?"

My own smile mirrors hers. Her wickedness is contagious, her allure all-consuming. Even if she didn't choose this life, she's certainly embraced the silver linings. Her passion is punishing the corrupt, in which we have in common. "Enjoy your meal, *Petit Diable.*"

"Oh, I assure you, *monsieur.* I intend to savor every last bite."

DEMONS
BRONTË

"**A**re you fucking kidding me?" Dantë barks, his shout echoing in the otherwise silent kitchen. "You've been at this for *weeks,* and all you have is old news of Margot falling off the face of the fucking planet?"

Emi bristles, squaring her shoulders. "Would you rather I make something up to make you feel better?"

"*Excusez-moi* for being a little disappointed. I expected more from the best."

"Funny, that almost sounded like a compliment."

Dantë pinches the bridge of his nose. "There must be more you can do."

"I did all I humanly could. I'm a hacker, not a witch."

"Could've fooled me."

Emi scoffs. "Your brother should've eaten you in the womb."

My twin opens his mouth for another damning riposte, and I clap his shoulder, squeezing in warning until he winces. "Brother, might I suggest you take a breath and let this lovely woman explain?"

Dantë rubs his eyes. "*Désolé,* Remiel. This isn't an easy pill to swallow."

Emi clears her throat, pulling a stack of papers from her shoulder bag and setting them on the island. "This is a compilation of Margot's digital footprint: emails, texts, online purchases, social media posts, etcetera. She was active up until last year, when she submitted her resignation at St. Aurelius's and disappeared."

"Fled," Dantë corrects her quietly, sifting through the papers. "She *fled* last February. On Valentine's Day."

"Which leads me to my next point."

Emi draws her laptop, fingers spidering across the keys. She twists the screen, showing us a soundless clip of Margot flashing Mama's invaluable opaline ring at the camera as Dantë kisses the edge of her sunshine smile.

I watch him from my periphery. Utter agony radiates from his gaze as he watches himself play on a loop with her in his arms.

"This was Margot's last post," Emi says softly. "Uploaded the morning she went missing."

"Margot didn't go missing." Dantë drops the papers with a heavy *thump*. "She *ran*."

Emi closes her laptop and clasps her hands, holding his hellfire glare as if it doesn't burn. "Why would she run?"

For a full minute, Dantë has nothing to say. Emi looks at me, but I busy myself with brewing a fresh pot of coffee while my brother considers how deep a grave to dig. Then: "Because I didn't tell her about my"—a darting glance to me—"*our* past until after I proposed. She was...afraid."

"Of?"

"What we did to survive."

"Survive what?"

"I can't say."

"Can't? Or won't?"

"With all due respect," Dantë growls with zero courtesy, "it's none of your fucking business."

This time, Emi falls silent, backing away from the line in the sand. I can already see her forming theories. Theories she'll undoubtedly share with a certain little devil mercilessly hunting down the Volkovs, two of which have proven to be working with the anonymous saboteur behind the fall of her empire. My brother's gatekeeping is born of self-preservation, but the last thing we need is to be placed on the suspect list or worse—mistaken for spies.

"Our past is ugly, *mon amie*," I say, handing her a steaming mug, "riddled with enough demons to send any topsider like Margot running."

Emi nods with a level of understanding only another survivor of the underworld's darkest pits would possess. "There's another explanation for Margot's digital absence. You're not going to like it, though."

The ensuing silence is a guillotine, the implication slicing through the air.

"No." Dantë shakes his head in immediate denial. "I'd know if Margot was dead."

The sun sinks behind the clouds, the shadows growing long. None of us say it, but he wouldn't know. That gut feeling brought on by the death of a loved one is romanticized in fiction. In reality, there is no such cosmic warning. Margot could've been dead all this time, and he would've been none the wiser.

Emi sets down her untouched coffee. "I'm sorry, Dantë. I've done all I can."

He doesn't answer. His stare is frozen on the pile of papers that may as well be a mountain of bones.

"*Merci*," I say, escorting Emi out the front door.

When I return, the papers are in the trash, and my brother is sitting on the sand outside, watching dusk roll over the sea like he once did every night with the woman of his dreams. Without closure, he'll be staring at that sunset forever.

Never moving on.

Turning from the windows, I pluck the papers from the trash and head downstairs to the studio. Vladimir Volkov's hide is finally dry and ready to be wrapped around Oscar Wilde's *The Picture of Dorian Gray*. The custom order came in on the same night of his death, and he seemed vain enough to earn the honor of eternally embracing a narcissist's tale.

There's a mark on the skin that I must've missed during the psychedelic haze of flaying the organ from his bones. My thumb skims over the scar—no, *brand*. Angling the slab in the dim light, I decipher the raised outline of a demonic skull, horned and fanged.

The memory of a matching symbol flashes behind my eyes in the form of graffiti on the brick building beside Beelzebub's. With it, fractured pieces of my past skip through my skull like stones tossed over water. I focus on my surroundings, refusing to be lured beneath the surface.

I know this symbol. It still haunts my nightmares.

Dropping the slab, I fish my phone from my pocket and dial Poppy. Her phone must be synced with her bike, which sends an automatic reply saying she's busy driving.

"*Putain,*" I hiss, snapping a photo of the symbol and texting it to her before dialing another number.

Emi picks up on the first ring. "Brontë? What's—"

"Where's Poppy?"

"Oh, uh...I think she's on her way to Indigo. It's a local tattoo parlor that doubles as a bar."

"Send me the address."

There's a pause as she types and sends a text. "Is everything—"

"*Merci, mon amie.* Truly."

I hang up and charge upstairs for my keys, praying I'm not too late.

HELL'S GARDEN

POPPY

If Beelzebub's is hell's library, Indigo is hell's garden.

I lift my hand, fingertips grazing the soft petals of blue bleeding hearts and baby's breath and sapphire roses weaving through the overhead rafters. Every candlelit surface is kissed by deep sapphire floral patterns and potted plants all ranging from sky blue to midnight violet.

Slipping my mini Glock into its holster at my hip, I nod to the mountainous bouncers and weave through the crowd singing and swaying to the live indie band playing beside the bar. Circe Castellanos, a curvaceous woman with rich brown skin and electric yellow hair in a blue lace jumpsuit, saunters over and leans her palms on the counter with a secret smile.

"Evening, boss. Here for dinner?"

I nod, but I don't return her grin as I order a drink. The high of solving Jett's murder died the moment I realized it wasn't a win. This is exactly what happened to the Volkovs when our families were at war. The Morgenstern empire is as stable as a house of cards. We've already lost significant forces, significant power.

How much more can we lose until we fall into our own tomb?

The only sliver of light on this dark day is that Circe, my friend and the most coveted informant in my arsenal, found Kai. I trusted her with the intel of my family's disarray and Kai's hand in the scheme. She snatched him from whichever gambling den he'd been pissing away his time and money in. The backstabbing mole is safely stashed in the freezer, patiently waiting for my arrival after having undergone several beatings by the largest bouncers here for his insubordination.

I'm in no rush to meet with him, though. Perhaps his balls will do me a favor and fall off while I sit here and enjoy myself.

Relishing the bourbon's burn, I ask, "Have you been able to find Nik?"

Since Vlad and Kai have shown their true colors and turned against my family, I've placed a bounty on Nik's head. If anyone can sniff him out, it's Circe.

But she's shaking her head, snuffing my confidence. "No such luck."

"*Kuso.* Do you have *any* good news up your sleeves?"

"The opposite, actually." Circe grimaces, leaning closer and lowering her voice. "Do you remember the arms dealer, Vanessa Crowe?"

I know everyone who works for my family, especially when they've deserted us. "*Hai.* She was the first turncoat. What about her?"

"I broke into her apartment, and I've never left a place faster in my life. Dirty dishes rotting in the sink. Mold *everywhere.* It's like she hadn't been there in months."

"Not a surprise. Vanessa probably used her brain and moved."

Circe shakes her head. "You know the webs I weave. I pulled every string to find her and came up short. It's like she never existed. Same goes for the others you mentioned. I don't think they've defected, boss. I think they're dead."

I wasn't in a particularly good mood before, but now?

Now, I'm pissed.

I knock back my drink and plop the empty glass on the counter. "About that dinner..."

Flagging a pair of bouncers, Circe leads us to the hallway hidden by a blue velvet curtain behind the bar. She unlatches an industrial door on the left wall, revealing the frosted innards and my mole handcuffed to a metal chair coated in ice.

Malakai, spitting blood from his last beating onto the frozen floor, glances up and blanches. "Jesus."

"Wrong Christ," I croon as the guards grab his chair and drag it to the next room.

Circe's tattoo parlor is a neat and tidy space. On the far wall, a screen streams an underworld news broadcast on mute, subtitles scrolling rhythmically. A neon sign above the entrance door across the room reads: *Fuck therapy, get a tattoo.*

"Leave us." I wave a lazy hand toward the hallway. "Make sure no one gets lost looking for the bathroom."

Circe follows the bouncers out, her chortles echoing in the dark.

Prowling in a slow circle around Kai, I take my time making him nervous. I never had a problem with him. Aside from inheriting the same pompous attitude as his cousins, Kai does what he's told without much bitching. He avoids looking at me with those Volkov-gray eyes, his fear prominent without his cousins present.

Fear—and guilt.

I pause behind him and noisily prep a tattoo gun, watching goosebumps pebble his nape. "You turned your back on me then murdered Jett. Why?"

"Y-you killed Vlad."

"Vlad killed himself the moment he attacked me." I test the needle, smirking as he twitches. "Whose shadow are you cowering under now?"

The beat of the music pounds through the silence.

"I know you're not as foolish as Vlad." I trail the needle over his shoulders. "Answer my questions, or I choose where you get your next tattoo."

Kai glares back at me with pure hate. "Fuck you, *printsessa*."

I grab his jaw, forcing his head back and hovering the needle above his left eye. "Care to repeat that?"

"Fuck. You."

"If you insist. Take a deep breath now. This is going to hurt a little."

I jam the needle into his eye and pull the trigger, carving through the lid when he squeezes it shut. His snarl rises to a scream as I break the skin and pierce the sclera. He thrashes in my grip, inadvertently shredding his own eyeball.

"That's for Jett, you piece of shit," I spit, tugging the needle free. Blood squirts from the gore. Vessels dangle limply from the tattoo gun's tip as I hang it over his other eye. "Tell me who you're working with."

Malakai laughs. I realize why a moment before I hear his metal cuffs clang against the floor. He grabs my arms and wrangles me back against the wall, knocking the tattoo gun from my grip. I knee him in the groin, scrambling for my Glock as he curls in on himself.

I aim at his face at the same time he rams his shoulder into my gut.

"This is for Vlad." His hands snare my throat, slamming my skull into the wall. "Deep breath. This is going to hurt."

My head crashes against the hard surface again and again. It feels like a jackhammer is splitting my brain in half over and over until my vision blackens—

Kai is suddenly wrenched backward. Gravity pulls me down as my blurry sight tracks another silhouette tackling the assassin to the floor. *Crack, crack, crack,* his cranium claps as my savior bashes his head on the unforgiving linoleum. The assault stops when Kai's brains are splattered around him like a gruesome halo.

Karma is truly a savage bitch.

I blink my swimming vision clear, unsure of what I'm seeing. "Brontë?"

Those beautiful hazel orbs find me, an inferno of rage burning within them. He abandons Kai, kneeling by my side with a blood-stained scowl. "This is the second time I've saved your ass, *Petit Diable*. It's getting inconvenient."

I snort and immediately regret it when pain ricochets from my neck to the backs of my eyes. He reaches for me but pauses.

"May I?"

"Such a gentleman." My grin falters into a wince. "Be my guest."

With more care than I've ever been shown, Brontë wraps an arm around my chest and folds a hand over my nape. His skin is warm, his touch gentle as he shifts me forward and prods the back of my head.

"No open wounds, but you probably have a concussion. You're going to feel like shit for a few days after it wears off."

"Fan-fucking-tastic." I squint at the open entrance door he must've come through. "Why are you here?"

Brontë eases me back against the wall and pulls Kai's pulverized corpse over to my side. He reminds me of a cat bringing a dead rat to another cat, and I nearly giggle as he crouches, ripping the assassin's shirt open. The laughter bubbling in my throat sinks when I see it—the demonic skull branded on Kai's right pec.

My lungs stall. We aren't just fucked.

We're fucking *doomed.*

TRAITOROUS
POPPY

I stare at the demonic skull in my text thread with Brontë, head pounding and mind reeling as he drives me home.

"Is that what I think it is?" His knuckles bleach on the shifter and steering wheel. He's been tense since we left Indigo, and his discomfort is beginning to chafe my suspicion. Noting my slitted stare, he adds, "I've heard of cults branding their members, but it's different seeing it with my own eyes."

I catalogue his careful wording for later dissection. He didn't say he *never* saw something like this before. But my brain is still splitting in two, my critical thinking skills suffering alongside it.

"This is the mark of a cult named Leviathan," I divulge. "If my family is the crown of this city, Leviathan is the church. Grandpapa Lucian told me stories about them when I was little. Their origins go as far back as our own. They are an organized operation spearheaded by nine individual Masters that specialize in their own respective subdivisions composed of Magi and Acolytes. The Volkovs were once members of Leviathan's assassin guild, but they disaffiliated with the cult once they had enough power to wage war with us. I'm surprised Leviathan took them back. I'm even more worried about why."

"Do you know who the Masters are?"

"No one does. Finding them is an impossible feat anyway. They're a true shadow organization that doesn't exist anywhere. No recording, no camera, and no book will have any documentation on them. The only reason I know is because of my papa and grandpapa, who were told the same by their forefathers. Leviathan was once close friends with the Morgensterns. Since then, though, the connections have faded."

"Until now."

"Right." I peel off my sweaty jacket and lean my aching head back, lifting my cell and dialing Papa. "Now would be the part where you pray for me, *monsieur.*"

My father answers, listening to my report with growing agitation. When I'm finished, he hisses black curses. Glass shatters in the background, taking an axe to my bleeding brain. I hear Mama's curt tone before the phone is passed to her.

"Where is the last Volkov boy, Poppy?"

"I don't know, Mama. No one has seen or heard from him. I'll keep trying—"

"No." A single syllable, yet it's sharp as a scythe. "You will not *try* anything. You will do as commanded. Find Nikolai. Bring him to us. You cannot fail."

"*Hai,* Mama. I—" The line goes silent, and I gape at the screen. "She hung up on me."

Shame pushes me deeper into the seat as white noise swarms my skull. I attempt to swallow several times, but it feels like I've traded places with my targets. Like I'm the one gagged and destined to die.

The first tear balances on my lashes. It may as well be my soul tiptoeing the edge of a knife. I'm breathing like I just sprinted a marathon, fingers forming talons in my hair.

You cannot fail.

Brontë says something I don't hear as I dial another number. My heart clamors to the beat of my wrath as I bounce my leg and rake my nails over my scalp.

"Pick up, you fucking coward." When I'm unsurprisingly pushed to voicemail, I inhale the calming scent of bourbon and cherry smoke. "Nikolai Volkov, if you ever gave a damn about me, call me back...please."

I send texts to what's left of my cyber team, the sticky grit of Kai's blood on my fingers smearing over the screen. Anxiety rises alongside bile in my throat as the fear of failure burns in my bones like corroding acid.

Brontë is still talking, but all I hear is: *You cannot fail*.

My gaze floats down to the dragon tattoo on my arm. Its stare traps me like a spiderweb.

"You cannot fail," it coos.

My lips numb, and my mind goes dark. Dark as a locked room.

The world around me fades in and out. Until I can only see that dragon and its jaws opening wider and wider to devour my black soul—

"Poppy." I glance up to see Brontë watching me from the driver's seat as he parks us outside Beelzebub's. The sight genuinely shocks me. I didn't even feel the time pass. "What's wrong?"

Kuso. This cannot be happening. Not now, when I need my mind to remain sharp and focused. Panic attacks haven't haunted me in years, since I started self-medicating with my vape.

Should I be seeing a therapist? Probably.

But who am I going to talk to about all my problems as a crime lord's daughter set to inherit a crooked kingdom without earning myself a pair of silver bracelets and a wardrobe of orange jumpsuits to match?

"Nothing is wrong." The lie tastes like ash, and his nostrils flare as if he can smell it. But I'm already plastering on a plastic smile. There's one more thing I need to do while I'm thinking clearly enough to get it done. "Now that the mystery has been solved, you're hereby released from our bargain. Keep your pretty mouth shut, and you won't have to worry about dropping the soap."

I wave with a forced flourish and open the door.

Brontë *lunges* across me to whip it shut. The locks slam down like prison bars.

In the span of a blink, I'm trapped in a car with a man I barely know. A man who, not so long ago, wanted me dead. A man who killed a trained assassin tonight with his bare hands. A man who seems to have no qualms taking lives without batting an eye. He's so close, I can taste the smoke on his breath and feel his body heat wrapping me in thawing warmth like a hot fire on a cold night.

With lethal calm, he demands, "What are you doing, Poppy?"

I jiggle the handle with a sweaty palm, but it doesn't budge. "Trying to leave so I can scrub death from my pores and cuddle my cat. Maybe squeeze in a chapter or two of a steamy romance before bed."

"That's not what I meant." He leans back, resting a thick arm roped in dangerous amounts of muscle on the center console. "You're not even queen yet, and you're drowning."

I bristle, going from nervous to disgruntled in a heartbeat. "What?"

Brontë angles his jaw, studying me like he can see through every layer of my skin. "Have you considered not taking your father's place?"

I rub my aching temple, repeating, "What?"

"You're working yourself into the ground, and you can't even see it." He points to my white-knuckled grip around my phone. "You're clearly struggling to keep your head above water. At this rate, even if you do manage to conquer your little cult problem, you're going to sink faster than you can swim."

"You have no idea what you're talking about."

"How would you know?"

"Because you don't have the faintest inkling of what it's like to live in someone else's shadow, nor do you know what it's like to be a criminal beyond your little Etsy shop of horrors."

Brontë's eyes burn with hellfire and brimstone. "First of all, don't ever condescend me. It's petty and immature and disrespectful as fuck. Second, don't sit here and pretend like you know me. You don't."

This gives me pause. No, I don't know him. Only the snippets I've been able to glean from breaking into his house and violating his privacy. What other skeletons are in his closet besides his questionable hobbies? Judging by the ghosts haunting his darkening gaze, he may have more specters in his shadow than me.

Chewing the inside of my cheek, I mumble, "Sorry."

As if the entire universe is listening, Brontë asks quietly, "Have you thought about turning your back on it all? Refusing to take the Morgenstern crown and living a relatively normal life?"

"Not an option."

"Why not?"

"Because—" My retaliation stops there. My gaze drops to my scarred hands.

I never questioned my future. A future that could become someone else's.

What would the king of Salem say? What would he *do* if I told him no? Me, his only child whom he raised to continue his legacy that was his father's and his father's father's and so on? I know what he'd do: he'd never speak to me again.

A single tear carves a traitorous path down my cheek.

Brontë tracks the teardrop all the way down to my chin. It wobbles then slips free and crashes to my lap. He lifts a hand, reaching for me. His fingertips feather my hair, a mere flirt with the strands like he's testing an invisible line. He touched me earlier, but not like this. He inches closer, his hand seeking my wet cheek. His skin barely brushes mine. It's such a soft, *reverent* touch that I flinch like it'll sting.

His arm falls, his jaw ticking. "Our deal isn't done, *Petit Diable.*"

"You helped to unmask Leviathan, and I lended Emi. We both upheld our ends. Unless I missed something...?"

"You still have a rogue Volkov on your hands, and I still have a thief to find. Our bargain has only just begun."

I bite my bottom lip, tasting iron. To turn down his help now would be foolish. I don't trust him. There's too much being left unsaid to put my faith in his intentions. But he's declared himself my ally and saved my life. Twice.

Right now, I need more friends than enemies.

My gaze drifts out the tinted window and to the mockingly bright city lights beyond. "If it'll keep you from wrapping me around my favorite book."

"I don't want that, Poppy."

"You did."

"Not anymore."

There's too much in that single statement to unpack while concussed.

Tugging on the door handle, I rasp, "Mind letting me out of this cage now?"

Brontë exhales through his nose but immediately unlocks the car. "Stay awake for a while. Monitor your symptoms. If you start to feel worse, call me."

I nod and dash out, warmth quickly bleeding from my bones in the moonless night.

An hour later, I peek through the washroom windows brimming with frost. He's still there, his 'Vette rumbling in the lot. The cherry of his cigar blazes red from behind the windshield, gray smog filtering from the car like a living beast. I sit at my desk, pretending to read while cuddling Jezebel.

He doesn't leave until I blow out my candles.

I watch his car's taillights fade into the night, mindlessly rubbing the dragon on my arm and shivering like I've been left outside for too long, abandoned in the cold. When I fall asleep in bed with Jezebel purring beside me, I dream of Grandpapa Lucian teaching me the origins of our family. Of the Morgensterns helping people rather than harming them. He even takes my hand and leads me back in time to seventeenth-century Salem. Showing me my ancestors as they brewed potions and crafted crystals for the townsfolk.

When I wake up, I wish it hadn't been a dream at all.

SEMANTIC SATIATION
BRONTË

There's a term for when you've read or repeated something so many times it loses its meaning: semantic satiation. A fancy way of saying the brain has grown so tired it temporarily forfeits any attempt at connecting the dots between what it sees and what it knows.

That's where I am with these goddamn papers.

Sighing a white cloud in the morgue's chill, I ignore the cadaver lying beside me and sift through Margot's life now chronologically organized in a binder. Since Emi reported her lack of findings, I've been searching for anything she may have missed. As always, though, I land on the very last page with blurry vision and a kink in my neck.

I've read over this the most: Margot's resignation letter. It's framed with such cookie-cutter prose, it's perfect—*too* perfect.

Which was Margot's entire personality.

Setting the binder aside, I boot up my office laptop and scour medical records of the city's victims of crime. Since making the initial deal with Poppy, I've been searching every shift. Now that we know the face of her saboteur, I'm looking for anything potentially leading to the cult sweeping through her empire and destroying her future like a god's almighty hand.

Leviathan may be a faceless entity, but it's composed of humans. Humans make mistakes. No one is truly flawless.

Poppy once mentioned casualties during her family's turf war with the Volkovs. Her grandfather had been the king of Salem at the time, which was around the beginning of online recordkeeping.

"Don't tell anyone," I warn the old man who died in his recliner with 1970s porn videos playing on his living room TV. "This isn't exactly legal."

He remains blessedly unmoving.

Hours slip by. I nod off twice.

Nearing the end of my shift, I close my companion into his locker, clean up, and carry the laptop back to my desk. I have enough time to search a few more cases, so I click into the next in my queue.

The autopsy report is two decades old and describes the death of a man whose body had washed up on the bay shore, his throat slit. I scan through the gruesome photos, pausing with bated breath when I spy the Leviathan brand on his chest.

My eyes narrow at the name. "Soren Bonaparte?"

Quickly, I find the file of Sebastian Bonaparte—the criminal whose hide has wrapped a dozen copies of the same classic novel now sitting in homes across the globe. I'm a thorough man. There wasn't a single mark on his skin. I don't find any evidence of branding in the post-mortem photos, either. The remaining report contains the same information Scull initially provided: relatively young, professor of occult studies, employed by St. Aurelius's Liberal Arts.

My brow furrows. I flip to Margot's resignation letter, addressed to St. Aurelius's Liberal Arts. My brother's runaway fiancée worked at the same academy as a criminal who was more than likely related to a dead member of Leviathan. A member who was murdered during the Morgensterns' war with the Volkovs.

I immediately dial Emi.

"*Bonjour, monsieur,*" answers a voice that isn't hers.

"*Petit Diable?*"

"Disappointed?"

"Not at all." Poppy has been recovering this past week, resting as per my instruction. My world, though, has strangely dimmed in her absence. "Where's Emi?"

"Masturbating in the bath. May I take a message?"

I choke on a swallow, dragging a hand down my stupid smile. "I found a lead on Margot. Possibly Leviathan, too."

"Thank fuck. I'm going insane in this bed."

Insane. The lighthearted jest reminds me of our last encounter, when I'd been dropping her off at Beelzebub's. Something wasn't right with her on that ride back from Indigo after speaking with her parents. She didn't hear a word I'd said, like she wasn't even next to me. She was just staring at her tattoo, gaze glazed as if in a trance.

I'd be lying if I said it isn't starting to scare the ever living shit out of me. If she keeps throwing fuel onto the flames of her impending burnout, there's a high chance she'll start to unravel into panic attacks. Maybe even hallucinate. Possibly hurt herself and others she doesn't truly mean to harm.

Just like my father.

"Well?" Poppy snaps, cutting through my thoughts. "That's your cue to tell me more, *monsieur.*"

As I catch her up on what I've found, my mind wanders back to that night, turning over every word she spoke and expression she wore for the signs I so clearly missed—the stress, the anxiety, the episode of complete dissociation.

Slowly, I reach a harrowing conclusion: Poppy isn't drowning; she's trapped at the bottom of a crumbling empire as the weight of expectation crushes her into oblivion.

"Brontë," Poppy barks, startling me. "Are you still there?"

Angels, now *I'm* the one dissociating. "*Oui,* still here."

"I asked if St. Aurelius's would have a storage area for staff that are no longer employed."

"Like an archive? I would think so."

"*Parfait.* Are you free tomorrow night for a little adventure?"

Checking my work schedule, I frown at the graveyard shift penciled in for tomorrow night. Easy enough to switch, though. A few of my colleagues owe me favors for covering their past shifts when I didn't have a life outside work and the studio.

"Depends," I tease, if only to keep her on the line a moment longer. "Does this 'little adventure' involve breaking-and-entering?"

"Is that a problem?"

It should be, but the fact that she's asking for my help means if I agree, I'll be with her if shit goes south. Or worse—if she's attacked by her anxiety and gets caught by campus security.

"Not a problem," I say. "I'll pick you up at eight."

Poppy chirps, "It's a date," and promptly hangs up.

"Angels above, bless my soul." I sigh, dragging a hand through my hair and suddenly fiending for a smoke. "I have a date with a fucking devil."

LA FIN
POPPY

Brontë strides beside me in the dark and musty archives of St. Aurelius's Liberal Arts. Our phone flashlights pan the tall racks stuffed with unorganized boxes thrown down here without a care for order. His footfalls are as noiseless as mine, which made trespassing onto the grounds of St. Aurelius's easier than it would've been with anyone else.

To my chagrin, his past remains an enigma. Emi is confident the Bourbon brothers have criminal histories after her last visit shed a sliver of light on Margot's disappearance. Too much of my past week has been spent obsessing over countless theories and one blaring question:

What happened to them?

I've been dreaming of him, this maddeningly mysterious coroner. He's in my every thought, as permanent and permeating as ink bleeding on a page. Staining every crevice in my mind. I *need* to know more.

Emi bought us all night for this mission, feeding a pre-recorded loop through the cams. We have until campus security's shift changes in the morning to find what we need and get out. Now may be my only chance to get answers straight from the source.

"Did you go to school, *monsieur?*"

Brontë cocks an eyebrow. "Of course I did."

"How far? College? Graduate?" At his escalating frown, I shrug. "Just making small talk."

"I'll answer yours if you answer mine."

A harmless deal. He knows enough of my secrets already to put me behind bars for life. "I'm listening."

"What was school like for you?"

My head tilts as I consider, watching motes of dust swirl in the beams of light. "I've never stepped foot inside a classroom. Knives were my crayons, people were my canvas. My peers were mostly other Morgensterns. I didn't make any noteworthy friendships until after I moved out. At that point, there was no use seeking a degree. I already had a PhD in cold-blooded murder."

"Yet you were overpowered by two out of three Volkovs."

"I have to have *some* kind of Achilles' heel, don't I? Otherwise, I'd be perfect, and perfect is boring." He snickers and I elbow his ribs. "Your turn."

"I'm originally from Texas but attended university here in Salem."

"Texas? You don't have an accent. How long did you live there?"

"That's *two* questions asked out of turn, Poppy."

I scoff, pausing mid-step and flinging my light in his face. "You already know the highlights of my childhood. It's only fair that you share yours."

His jaw flexes, clearly reluctant. "It's not pretty."

"Thank all the stars for that. Pretty pasts are as boring as perfect people."

Brontë sighs, tapping my phone with his. "Lower the interrogation lamp, Nancy Drew. I'll spill."

We fall back into step, gazes roaming the shelves that are as disorganized as a hoarder's home. Minutes crawl by as he considers his story and how to spin it. I watch him from my periphery. His shoulders are high, his movements stiff.

"Not easy, is it? Trying to figure out where to start."

"No, it's not."

"Do you start a book at the end or the beginning?"

"Who taught you such wisdom?" He snorts at my beaming smile. "Back to the beginning, then. I was born in a small Texas town called Valentine. Dantë and I are sons of Noah Abernathy, a Marine with a Purple Heart for taking shrapnel to the chest shortly before we were born. Our half-sister, Virgil, is three years older than us. She shares the same mother, Genevieve Bourbon. We never knew V's father. Only that his death drove Mama from her own home in France when V was still in diapers. Mama had been a scholar in religious studies, but she got sick when the three of us were young. When she died, she took the best parts of my father with her. He was your stereotypical trauma-case-turned-widower: drunk by dawn, out cold most of the day, ruthless by dusk. On the worst nights, he'd throw us into homemade mazes with rabid bloodhounds, handing us limited rounds and testing our survival skills.

"One night, while V was at a friend's house, Dantë knocked over a picture of Mama by mistake. Next thing I knew, our father had him by the throat. A single squeeze separated my brother from death, and I acted on instinct. I grabbed the shotgun our father had left on the kitchen table with his empty bottles. I didn't even give him a warning before I aimed at the back of his head and blew his brains all over the walls. It was on me, on Dantë...it was everywhere. When V got home, the three of us ran. Took our mother's name, traveled across the country. Eventually, we built a new life here in Salem and found Mama's family overseas. We visit them when we can, usually around the holidays." He shrugs. "*La fin.* The end."

I stare at him, unblinking as we trek down another cluttered aisle. "I have so many questions."

"I'll answer one."

"…That's it?"

"That's it." Brontë chuckles at my disgruntled huff. "Unsatisfied, *Petit Diable?*"

Very. "No."

He grins mischievously. "Lie."

Unexpected heat blooms low in my belly. *Why is that hot?*

"One answer is better than none, no?" When my frown gouges lines into my cheeks that I'm sure will leave permanent creases, his shoulders shake with a throaty laugh. "That face."

I scoff, sifting through my mental list and landing on a crucial plot hole. "What happened in the time between Valentine and Salem?"

His lighthearted laughter fades into the oppressive shadows. "My siblings and I got ourselves involved in shit no one ever should."

My interest piques. "Like what?"

"I'm not answering that."

"Why not?"

"It's your turn. Not mine."

A lesson my father taught me long ago: deflection defines guilt.

I stomp on Brontë's boot, halting him. "Are you afraid I'll find out you got yourself involved with shit like Leviathan?"

Victory sings in my veins as he flashes his teeth at me in a silent snarl. "Don't, Poppy."

"Don't what?"

"Don't push me. Not on this."

"Why? What are you hiding?"

"Nothing you need to concern yourself with."

"Is that so? Because it seems to me that *you* could be another mole."

"I'm not."

"Bullshit."

Brontë inhales a long breath and exhales through his nostrils. If he were a dragon, smoke would be billowing from his mouth. His rage is a wildfire, sinful and scorching. It fuels my own, my fingertips heating as blood pumps into the farthest reaches of my body.

"Nothing to say for yourself?" I taunt, my grin growing serpentine. "Was that story bullshit, too?"

His pupils slowly expand to encompass the colors. His rising wrath is a deep, dark void of black fire. I want to see it *ignite.*

"Let's skip to the end of this book, shall we? You show me your brand, and I'll make your death swift. Maybe I'll try my hand at bookbinding. Wrap you around the Devil's Bible. An ode to mommy dearest—"

Brontë grabs my throat, forcing me backward. I gasp, shoving the butterfly knife from my pocket under his chin. A trickle of blood slides down the rainbow blade from his stubble to my trembling fist. His fingers pulse, his nose brushing mine as his lungs heave with adrenaline.

It takes me a long beat to realize his hold on my neck isn't as tight as it should be.

"I am not your enemy, Poppy," he whispers, rogue strands of his hair tickling my brow. "I've saved your life *twice* when I could've taken a seat and watched you die. I bear no brand, nor am I associated with Leviathan. Your skull is as thick as a fucking brick wall, but you're not stupid. Stop mining for gold in a trench full of nothing but bones."

I gulp, my body trembling with an unhealthy dose of relief and excitement. Relief, because he's proven my theories about his intentions wrong yet again. Excitement, because I now know how to crack his icy exterior and burrow under his skin.

How fucked up is it that I crave this man who turns corpses into books to rip my pants down and choke me while he fucks me in the dark?

"Don't," Brontë warns again, like I'm a cat pawing a cup toward a table's edge. This time, though, he's not hostile; he's disturbingly somber. "Don't look at me like that."

"Like what?"

"You know what."

A teasing grin toys with the edges of my lips. "Your hand is around my throat, *monsieur.* How else am I supposed to look at you?"

His mouth opens for a retort, but it closes when his eyes flick over my shoulder. "What are the odds?"

My eyebrows pinch as he guides me aside then releases me. I rub the phantom feel of his fingers on my neck as he lifts the lid off a box labeled: Lovecraft. Chills slither up my spine.

What *are* the odds we find Margot's belongings by pure chance?

Brontë rifles through manila folders and knick-knacks the sorority advisor left behind. Most of it is meaningless: a name plaque, potted succulents still clinging to life, pastel pens and colorful highlighters. Then he plucks an object woven with twine, raven feathers, animal bones, and blood.

Drawing an invisible pentagram over my heart, I breathe, "Stars bless me."

"The fuck is it?"

"A death sentence." I take the poppet, shivers wracking my frame as the bones prick my skin. "I've only ever heard of these in Grandpapa Lucian's stories. Leviathan sends them to those who they want dead, marking their prey before hunting them down."

"Why the hell would Leviathan target Margot?"

"Lions don't concern themselves with lambs until they grow claws and teeth."

Brontë blinks. "Are you still concussed?"

I roll my eyes. "You know what I mean. Leviathan wouldn't have bothered Margot unless she was a threat."

"Margot was harmless."

"No one is harmless." My chin tilts as I consider the possibilities. "You mentioned before that Sebastian was related to a Leviathan member. Maybe Margot learned about the connection and got herself mixed up in cult business?"

Brontë's expression steels over as he scans the stacks we have yet to peruse. "We'll cover more ground if we split up."

Hours and miles of walking later, we find nothing. My feet are dragging as we meet at the exit with sagging shoulders. Tapping his phone light off, Brontë reaches for the door.

Before he can touch it, the lock slides loose, and the handle turns.

I trade my phone for my knife, but then Brontë throws me over his shoulder and sprints for the farthest reaches of the room. Plopping me down in the corner conveniently located behind the messiest shelf in here, he flattens himself against me, pancaking me to the wall.

"Ouch! What are you—"

Brontë claps a hand over my mouth, a finger to his own lips as footsteps methodically pace the stacks. Light flickers back and forth, keys jangling noisily over the faint sound of music and off-pitch humming. A badge glints from between the shelves.

Security. We must've stayed past shift change.

If we're caught, Leviathan will be the least of our worries.

My heart rebels against the fear leaking into its chambers. I can't stop shaking, my breath bursting from my nostrils in audible blasts.

Brontë, reading me like a book, gives me an incredulous look. I shake my head, unable to contain my growing fright. I've avoided the back of a cop cruiser my entire life. It's not the police I fear. It's the crown on my head painting a target on my back in the cement blocks after.

Slowly, his hand moves from my mouth to cup my nape. His eyes don't stray from mine as he lightly massages the tense muscles. I wince as he works a knot free, and his other hand curls around my fist clenching the knife. He thumbs my knuckles, sweeping in soothing strokes. He's as close as he could possibly be, yet he finds a way to get closer by dipping his chin and pressing his cheek to mine. His warmth caresses me like a blanket, wrapping me in comfort.

My lashes flutter as my nervous system relaxes. Years could've passed, and I wouldn't feel it. All I know is the darkness and *him.*

I hear the door close. I don't move.

"Poppy?" Brontë peels back. "Are you all right?"

No, I'm not all right. I thought staying in bed for a few days while nursing a concussion would've lessened the chances of another panic attack happening.

But I was clearly dead wrong.

The admission is prancing on the tip of my tongue. I should tell him about my losing battle with anxiety. Not to necessarily confide in him, but to warn him that my slipping mental state could become a liability neither of us can afford while on these covert, high-stakes missions.

"I..." My brain falters as I glance over his shoulder and spy a familiar name scrawled across a box: Bonaparte. "This is getting too weird."

He follows my stare, grunting in agreement. "Up jumps the devil."

Unlike Margot's box, Sebastian's is empty.

How quaint. Another dead end.

——◆——

As Brontë drives me home, his focus periodically shifting from the road lathered in dawn's darkest blues to the Leviathan poppet in my lap, my phone buzzes. I croak a zombified, "Hello?"

"Long night, *printsessa?*"

My world goes gray. "Nik?"

Brontë brakes too hard at a red light, aiming an apologetic glance at my scowl.

"I heard Kai is dead," Nik says as casually as if speaking of the weather. "I heard it was you and your sidekick coroner who did it. Is this true?"

No point in lying when that's exactly what he's expecting me to do. "It's true. He left us no choice. Is this a courtesy call before you take your shot, too?"

Nik chuckles, the sinister sound scraping over my skin. "Friday, midnight. Meet me at V and V. You remember which room?"

A coffin unearths from the darkest corner of my mind, cracking open and showing me scarlet blood oozing into gray eyes blazing like silver flames as I choke the life out of my phone. "I remember."

"See you then, *printsessa.*"

Click.

I stare at my cell, the screen blurring. Brontë says something, but I barely hear him. His voice is muffled, like I'm underwater. I look up to see him parking us in the lot at Beelzebub's and turning to me. His hand lands on my bouncing thigh, unease in his frown. It's almost like he can *see* the stress eating me alive.

"Talk to me, Poppy."

I shouldn't ask him to help. I don't need it. I've been on my own for so long, serving at Papa's side with no one else as my sword and shield. I'm no damsel, but even I can admit when I'm scared.

Twice, I've faced the Volkovs. Twice, I've almost died.

Nikolai is the deadliest of them all.

"What are you doing Friday night, *monsieur?*"

PHEROMONES
BRONTË

I fucking *hate* nightclubs.

They open past a normal bedtime. They're literally deafening. They're expensive with no reason to be. They're filthy, sticky, sweaty; perfect breeding conditions for germs and viruses and diseases to mingle and spread. Not to mention, they're the public hunting grounds for the true predators of our world: rapists, trafficking mules, murderers.

Voodoo & Velvet is crawling with them like maggots on rotting fruit. I see them now, men and women alike eyeing the crowd hungrily from the shadows deepest in the corner booths and private tables, like they're starving wolves and the rest of us are fresh meat.

The Kimber in my pocket grows heavy as I resist the urge to slaughter them all. Skin them alive and make them watch me sew their flesh onto the perfect book as they sit in their own blood and shit.

Lavender smoke streams behind Poppy as she leads us deeper into the den of vipers. Flashing lights flicker and flit over bodies wrapped in velvet and straps, lace and chains. Pheromones perfume the air with the smell of sin and sex, heady and sweet.

Yet all I see is *her*.

Poppy Morgenstern is a lightning strike in churning waters. Her low-cut, single-sleeved silk dress is the same bloody shade of scarlet as my suit, standing out with stark, electrified beauty. Half her pastel pink locks twisted into twin space buns are held in place by spray-painted shuriken stars. The rest of her sleek tresses stream down the curve of her exposed spine, framed by delicate gold chains hanging in strategic intervals from her nape to her dimpled tailbone.

Goddamn, I could watch those little divots for the rest of my miserable life. They pop and fade and pop again with every sway of her hips, distracting me from the marvel of her apple ass and her toned legs wrapped in gladiator sandals from her elegant ankles to her succulent thighs. Her upturned eyes are lined with thin wings of kohl, her tempting lips stained red like she's been kissed by a bloody rose. She isn't a demon or a devil or a succubus or even a goddess. There is no word for her species, because she's the only one to have ever existed.

She's the only one that ever will.

Poppy leads us over to a guarded set of descending stairs, reaching into her purse and passing wads of big bills to each of the hulking bouncers. They unhook the thick rope and wave us on. Halfway down, the pounding bass recedes to a distant rumble. A smog of cigarette smoke greets us, ushering in a menthol migraine splitting my senses at the seams.

We slip through a set of heavy black velvet curtains at the bottom of the steps into a long hallway lined with private lounges. Poppy steers us into the last on the left, and I try not to react to what I see.

It's a little difficult to remain composed, though, when there's a stage on the other side of a glass wall showcasing a naked woman on a dais covered in black roses. Her chocolate tresses pool on the floral floor as she lazily rides a man worshipping every inch of her.

This isn't just a private lounge. It's a voyeurism room.

The woman wears a black-feather mask to conceal her eyes, but I see her lashes flutter shut as she slides her fingers down to where she ends and he begins. She flicks her clit and lifts her soft, supple body to show off the thick wet cock impaling her over and over again, along with the glow-in-the-dark strap-on he wears to delve into her ass and magnify her pleasure.

An ache threatens to tent my trousers—

"Brontë."

Poppy catches my eye with a fiendish spark in her baby blues. She fills two glasses with rich amber spirits from a bar cart and pats the only piece of furniture in the room: a plush velvet loveseat designed to swallow carnal sin.

"You look uncomfortable, *monsieur*, and you know what that does to me."

I force myself to move, unbuttoning my jacket as I settle into the seat. Poppy's stare drops to my exposed abdomen, bare beneath the coat as per her request, roaming the tattoos and muscles that clench beneath her shameless perusal. I let my own gaze slide over the sliver of soft, beige skin trailing between her breasts that are magically held in place despite the flimsy fabric draped over her chest. The front of the dress matches the back, plunging all the way down to her taut navel, adorned with those thin metal chains.

I want to snap each one with my fucking teeth.

Poppy hands me a glass. Thank the angels it's bourbon.

Then she plops straight onto my lap.

I let out a garbled curse, the sudden presence of her ass on my dick flushing all my blood south. I have no defense against the immediate reaction of my erection jutting against her tailbone. She goes rigid, the whites of her eyes flashing. I chide myself inwardly, grasping for *something* to fight my own aching need.

Dead pup—

No. Anything but that.

James P. Sullivan.

That helps.

Wookiee.

That helps even more.

I'm Sullivan, she's the Wookiee.

That definitely does *not* help.

Poppy wiggles in place, undoing all my progress. She drapes an arm over my shoulders, casually fixing the collar of my jacket, and settles against me with a contented hum that wraps talons around my skull and drags them all the way down my fucking spine.

"Comfy," she muses, sipping her drink with a shit-eating grin. "You?"

"Peachy," I grit out. She's made herself at home like a cat in a patch of sun while I'm taut as a drawn bowstring straining for release.

Poppy tuts. "Guess I'll just stand."

I have zero interest in showing her the evidence of what she's done to me. So, I snake an arm around her waist and haul her back in.

She lets out the most adorable squeal I've ever heard, burying her giggle in my neck. I turn my smirk into her hair, my fingers slipping to her ribs and *squeezing* until she makes that sound again.

"You stay right where you are, *Petit Diable.*"

When she lifts her easy smile, I nearly lose mine. She's fucking angelic with that smile. And *I'm* the one that put it there.

Her gaze drifts to my softening grin.

Too long. She's been looking at me like this too damn long for me not to notice. I don't know when or why it started. It's like her unease around me dissolved and morphed into desire. It's torture, because I don't know if this is genuine or if it's just her way of mastering her fear.

And I've had enough of guessing.

Carefully, I reach up and trace a finger down the length of her hair. It's as smooth as spidersilk, as soft as poppy petals. She doesn't move, neither leaning in nor breaking away. Watching me like a panther assessing another panther.

"Are you afraid of me?"

Poppy searches my eyes. Her bourbon-sweet breath clouds over my face as she whispers, "I was once, but not anymore."

This may be my only chance to right my wrong.

I palm her jaw and tilt her head up, pressing my lips to the soft hollow of her cheek. It's my apology, the only way I can give it to her. Her heart pounds a battle beat into my fingertips resting at her pulsing carotid, and I pull away.

She fists my lapels, keeping me close. Her saccharine scent intoxicates all my senses.

"I forgive you, Brontë. Bygones?"

"Bygones." I slide my hand through her hair, idly toying with the ends as she traces a fingernail over my tattoos. "You're absolutely lustrous tonight, *Petit Diable.*"

"You're not such an eyesore yourself." She remains close, the tip of her nose brushing mine with each rapid breath I can taste on my tongue. "You need to start sharing those cigars, *monsieur.* They make for the sexiest cologne. Dr. Frankenstein's Wet Dreams, Bax would call it."

I chuckle, daring to splay my palm low on her spine. "I'll share mine if you share yours."

Her lashes flutter in time with her hummingbird heartbeat. "When and where?"

"Hm." I pretend to consider, drawing idle circles over those tantalizing dimples. "Now and here."

She *tsks*, dragging a fingertip down the column of my throat. "That's rather bold of you."

"I'm merely a man who knows what he wants."

"Oh? What do you want?"

I grip my glass too tight to hang onto my own diminishing willpower. "What I shouldn't have."

"Adam and Eve got away with it in the end, didn't they?"

Angels, the urge to give in and capture that tempting mouth with mine is overwhelming. My self-control is on the verge of being crushed in the deluge of hunger as her teasing grin flirts with my own. A snarl slips out of me, and it sounds like a starving beast being taunted with an endless feast.

"So desperate for me," she breathes through my parted lips, drawn by the same polar force I feel in my own bones as she slowly, slowly closes what little space is left between us. "I like it."

A demoralizing sound escapes me, muted by a cry of pleasure rattling the glass wall from the other side. Overtaken by primal need, I lurch forward.

"No time for a quickie, I'm afraid," drawls a lightly accented voice.

Poppy jolts with a gasp, nearly dropping her drink and toppling from my lap. I barely save her in time, banding my arm around her and folding her into my chest.

In tandem, we glare at the intruder.

Nikolai Volkov is standing just inside the door, hands in the pockets of his black jeans, gray eyes on the performing couple now fading under the dimming lights. The wicked scar carving a lightning bolt from his left ear to his temple and slicing his eyebrow in half is what strikes me first. The second is his foreign-blooded beauty. He puts even *me* to shame.

I wouldn't be surprised if he and Poppy...

Realization crests the horizon of my awareness as his focus slides to her, completely skipping me. She didn't want me here to feel less afraid like I thought she did. I know I'm not here to protect her; she can handle being her own white knight.

No, I'm here to make her ex-fuckboy jealous.

Bitter rage rears its spiteful head. I let it shove me back, back into my own mind. Where I hide in the shadows and watch.

WHIPLASH
POPPY

Brontë tenses, all of his limbs locking into place. His attention is magnetized to the assassin. He's not just pissed; he's *livid*.

As am I. For the first time in too long, I was actually enjoying myself.

"You look exquisite, *printsessa,*" Nik drawls. "You didn't have to dress up just for me."

"The only person I ever dress for is *me.*" I sip my drink and drape my arm over Brontë's broad shoulders. "Hope you don't mind the company."

"The more the merrier, no? Brings back old memories."

It does, but I don't admit it aloud. We've been in this room together countless times. Watching the show while touching and teasing each other. Inviting the actors to join us when their performances were done.

Nik dons his cocky grin as my jaw remains shut. "I'm aware I interrupted a moment, so I'll be quick." He strolls over with slow steps, pausing a few short feet away. From the inner lining of his jacket, he draws something ivory and holds it out for me to take it. "Look familiar?"

"Unfortunately."

I take the demonic skull mask, feeling Brontë's eyes shift down with mine. The ice in his limbs thaws. He skims his fingertips over the bone sewn onto a plain black balaclava. Unlike the poppet we found in Margot's belongings at St. Aurelius's, he recognizes the mask.

"Context, Volkov," Brontë growls. "Spit it out."

For the first time since slinking in here, the assassin looks at the coroner. A still moment passes in which neither of them blink. Hell, I don't think they even *breathe* as they remain trapped in this impressively hot yet entirely immature glaring contest.

"We don't have time for this alphahole bullshit." I wave the mask like a white flag between them. "Nikolai, explain."

Nik splits his eyes from Brontë and sews them onto me. "Someone slipped that under my apartment door the morning I called. Vlad and Kai received the same before joining Leviathan's ranks. Along with this." He hands over a small card with a series of coordinates stamped in the middle.

My lips purse. "What is this?"

"By my understanding, it's a sort of invitation. If I go, I'm agreeing to be a member of Leviathan. The coordinates lead to an old graveyard outside the city. I debated going—"

"Shocker," utters Brontë.

Nik frowns. "To spy on them from the inside. I didn't want to make any major decisions without your blessing, *printsessa*."

It takes me a second to fully process his admission. "You're not leaving us for them?"

"Do you really think I'd be here if I was?"

"I don't understand. We killed your cousins, yet you're *helping* us...?"

Nik's laugh cracks like a whip. "Oh, I pray those idiots are getting pineapples shoved up their asses by Lucifer himself as we speak."

Brontë's mouth twitches like he's suppressing his own laugh.

"You're being sincere," I prod, still unsure. Nik was never close with his cousins, but he has no family left. Because of me, he's the last of his bloodline. "You *actually* want to play double agent?"

Nik's grin fades with his militaristic nod. "You have my word, for what good it's worth from a Volkov." He says that last part bitterly, with a hint of self-loathing I don't miss.

"How do we know you won't fuck us over?" Brontë demands.

"You don't, Bourbon. Get over it."

Brontë snickers, the crystal in his grip cracking with a distressed *chink.*

To me, Nik adds, "I'm not asking you to trust me. Whether or not you do changes nothing. Either way, Leviathan will pay for what they've done."

I set the mask and invitation aside, sipping my drink and relishing its burn. "Why are you more committed to my family than your own?"

Nik approaches the bar cart and pours himself a knuckle of vodka. "My cousins were vermin that did not understand the meaning of a promise. Our grandfathers made oaths to the Morgensterns. Those oaths were never meant to die with them." He downs his drink in one swallow then plops the glass back down. "Vlad and Kai did what they thought our fathers were too cowardly to do. In my opinion, they got what they deserved."

I have no reason not to believe him. Unlike his turncoat cousins, he hasn't made a single move to attack me. My allies are scarce. I can't let my pride stand between us.

"We'll look into the street cams, see if we can identify the person who paid you a visit. My concern, though, is what happens if you decline the offer. Leviathan is unpredictable."

Nik's scarred eyebrow lifts expectantly. "Which brings us back to my proposal."

Brontë toys with the mask, sharing a somber look with me. I know what he's asking himself: What if Margot didn't run away? What if she's dead? This isn't about my family or some lost heirloom anymore. This is about slaying a monster before it can slaughter any more innocents.

But I can't fight back without an army of my own.

I glance at the invitation. No matter what history I share with Nik, I can't afford to lose him. He's my best assassin. I care more about protecting his life than risking it. I was never skilled at strategy, but I know when to fall back instead of charging forward at the expense of my most precious pawns.

If I had the strength, I'd stage a coup. Storm those coordinates, battle Leviathan to the death. But I have no warriors. The last thing I can afford right now is losing what little power I have left.

"No spy games." I knock my drink, letting it scorch the dread from my stomach. "Lay low until I say otherwise."

"As you wish." Nik bows his neck and moves for the exit.

"Nikolai." He halts, casting a questioning frown over his shoulder. "Your family was once part of Leviathan. Do you know anything that can help us?"

"I wish I did, but you know as much as me. There were no stories told to us as they were to you. Shame, I suspect, silenced my kin from sharing the greatest failure of our forebears who abandoned their sacred vows to seek power over yours."

I nod, heavy with defeat. "Don't go home. Leviathan knows where you live. Crash with Circe at Indigo. Don't tell anyone else where you are. I'll clear your name with Papa and pull the headhunt for you."

An arrogant grin pulls his mouth into a lopsided smile that once took my breath away. "Careful, *printsessa*. Your heart is showing."

"You should count your lucky stars that I still have one. Or I'd kill you where you fucking stand."

Nik's expression sobers. With a final dip of his chin, the door shuts quietly behind him.

I sag against Brontë, my body caving to gravity and the exhaustion of my pounding headache. "That was…illuminating."

"Indeed." In a sudden yet fluid movement, he rises, forcing me to stumble back onto my feet as he aims for the door.

"Wait!" I catch his elbow, turning him half around. "Where are you going?"

"Home."

I sputter, confused. "But we came together."

"Uber exists for a reason."

"We need to talk about Margot and Leviathan. What's our next move?"

"I'll talk to Emi about Margot. You can take Volkov's stalker." His chin jerks toward the invitation. "It wouldn't hurt to scope that out, too."

"Don't you want to help?"

"You don't need my help."

"We work better together, don't we?"

"We're not a team, Poppy. We're not even friends." He shrugs me off and swiftly buttons his jacket. "Don't mistake this alliance for anything more than it is."

I blink, whiplash cracking me across the face. "I'm sorry, was I hallucinating when we almost kissed?"

"No."

"Then what changed? Not half an hour ago, you were all over me."

"Pheromones. Tricky little bastards."

I scoff, crossing my arms. "Why are you pissed? Was it Nik?"

"No."

"Was it me? Did I say something?"

Brontë pinches the bridge of his nose with a nettled sigh. "It's late, and I have back-to-back graveyard shifts at the morgue this weekend. Are we done here?"

"No, we're not done until I say—"

My purse buzzes.

I hiss a curse, whipping out my phone. It's Bax, reporting a fire cooking his lab and everything in it. By the time I'm done calming him down and doling out orders, I turn back to Brontë, ready to peel his layers until I get to the core of his wrath before it festers any more than it already has.

But he's gone.

And I've never felt more alone.

MUTILATION

BRONTË

Decay, pungent in its sweet rot, slithers up my nostrils in droves with the metallic fetor of rusting iron. Scene lamps filter weak patches of dim light onto the sea of evidence markers circling a nude woman who stood no chance against the monster that did this to her.

"Fucking Christ," gripes Scull against the medical mask he pulls over his nose as if it will block out death's stench. "I know we've had our fair share of unpleasant shit, but this is downright *odious.*"

I couldn't agree more.

The woman is staged in a steel chair within an abandoned chemical factory, her wrists bound behind her by pink feather cuffs. Her head is thrown back as if she died screaming. Her throat is missing, and an object is lodged within her gaping mouth. Her femoral arteries are severed. Blood, dark as an aged bottle of merlot and dried to a mahogany crust, cakes her from the roots of her curls to the tips of her toes. A pentagram is carved into her abdomen, deep enough for her entrails to seep out in fetid ropes. Another is drawn around the chair from the pool of gore.

I don't miss the parallels. Half the wounds are a perfect replica of Poppy's victims. But this wasn't her doing.

This was Leviathan.

I pull a pair of nitrile gloves from my pack and click on my penlight. "Introduce us, *mon ami.*"

The detective shakes his head. "You know as much about Jane Doe as me, Bourbon."

"Jane Doe?"

"Mhm. The anonymous tip came in from an untraceable number. No witnesses, no camera footage. Still waiting on ID confirmation from the lab."

Stuffing down my rising unease, I draw pliers from my bag and pull the obstruction from the woman's throat. Dangling in the dim light is Leviathan's signature curse.

Scull snickers. "What is that? A voodoo doll? Does our vigilante think they're a witch now?"

Ignoring him, I pinch the corpse's hair between my fingers and smear the blood. The hair beneath is a familiar shade of red. In an instant, I recognize her.

Fury burns my blood to ash. This isn't a random murder.

This is a message.

Leviathan is coming.

⚔

My knuckles rap urgently on Poppy's bedroom door. Inside, something heavy *thumps* onto the floor. Expletives hiss as fabric shuffles. An audiobook playing quietly over the speakers pauses just before the door swings open to reveal a droopy-eyed Poppy. She's in a dusky pink yukata printed with powder blue baby's breath petals and butterflies seeking their nectar, cradling to her chest a book with a tattooed man wearing a stag skull on the front cover.

"Brontë?" She blinks away a fog of confusion. "What are you doing here?"

"I called. You didn't answer."

"I fell asleep reading." Her uptilted baby blues slowly scan my scrubs, then the dark hallway behind me. "What time is it? How did you get in here?"

"It's three a.m. I picked the lock on the back door." Ignoring her gape, I gesture to the room. "May I?"

Poppy widens the door for me to step inside. I pat Jezebel's head in passing then open a window to the early December chill. Fishing a lighter from my jacket, I ignite a cigar and take several deep drags.

"Are you going to tell me why you're here? Or should I grab a chair and wait until you're done sulking?" Poppy pauses, her reflection pouting. "I might be dead by then, actually."

I sigh. "We have a problem."

"Could you be any more vague?"

I watch the dark sea writhe like a live beast beneath the full moon. A silence stretches between us, loud as a soundless scream. I wonder if she hears the scythe hanging over her head, swinging in the breeze as it waits to come crashing down.

"Brontë." She snags my reflection's vacant stare. "What happened?"

Exhaling a long smoke stream through my nostrils, I wordlessly pull the autopsy report from my jacket and hand it over. Her scrunched nose straightens as she sifts through the grisly scene photos.

"F-Fiona?" Tears line her lashes. A storm of disbelief, grief, and rage rises to meet my gaze. "What is this?"

"You know what it is. Leviathan murdered a member of your inner circle. Worse, a friend. To add insult to injury, they made it look like *you* did it. Killing Fiona is Leviathan's way of shoving your face in the dirt, Poppy. If your family's history is a roadmap, you know where this leads—your family's doorstep."

Poppy curses, snatching her cell from her nightstand and making a call. From what I gather, she's ordering her cyber team to check the scrubbed cams for anything the police may have missed. Cherry smoke burns the noxious acid from my gut as she speaks in hushed tones, her fluffy slippers wearing a line through the floor as she paces back and forth for what feels like an eternity. When she hangs up, her shoulders couldn't be any lower.

"No bread crumbs to follow?"

"No." She steps close enough for me to breathe her coffee and cotton candy scent spearing through the bitter cherry smog. "*Merci, Brontë.*"

"For?"

"Bringing this to me." When I don't respond, she rests a hand on my arm. I stiffen, but I can't seem to make myself brush her off like I should. "I know how much of a risk you're taking in helping me."

"I'm merely doing my part."

"You and I both know that's not true. You could've easily done nothing and let Leviathan come for me. Would've made your decade-long hunt for me worth the wait."

I ignore the pang in my chest. If we'd never met, that's exactly what I would've done.

"As I said, we made a deal. This is me upholding my end. Nothing more, nothing less."

"You're upset."

"False."

"You're lying." Her nails curl into my sleeve, sharp as talons. "At least have the balls to look at me when you do that."

My molars grind as I meet her bloodshot eyes. "Happy?"

She beams a fake smile. "Ecstatic."

Then the little devil steals my cigar and flicks it out the window.

"The fuck was *that* for?" I growl, baring all my teeth.

She bares hers back at me with twice the ire. "Because you're being a broody bastard and walking around with a stick up your ass!"

"That's rich, coming from the woman who thinks the rest of the world is here to serve at her fucking feet!"

Poppy recoils as if I've slapped her, crimson dusting her cheeks. In rushes the guilt—

Sharp pain lances across my face in time with a blade slashing a streak of rainbow through my right cheekbone.

And out that guilt soars.

"Fuck!" I bark, palming the deep gash as she hisses like a cat spitting its hate.

"Insult me again, and I'll sever your vocal cords so no one will hear you scream while I flay you alive."

Guilt seeps back in as tears slip down her cheeks. I wrench myself away from her contagious fury and storm out before I can convince myself that I deserve what she's done to me, that I caused her more pain she didn't need.

But I did. I *know* I did.

And that only stokes the flames higher.

STRANGERS

BRONTË

Blood trails behind me in the studio as I paw through the shelves for the isopropyl alcohol above the slop sink. After splashing the fresh gash with water, I dump the solution onto a rag and slap it to my throbbing cheek.

An inferno ignites the cutting pain to a burning affliction. I brace a hand against the sink and gasp into the stained basin. Unbidden teardrops blur my vision as the searing agony grows and doesn't fucking stop. I slam my eyelids shut against the torturous burn.

All I see in the darkness is *red*.

It paints the canvas of my father's flesh. Streaks down my brother's face. Coats my own like oil. Cold metal scorches my hands. A gunshot blasts my eardrums. Beneath my stampeding heart, I can still hear the distant howls of the hounds, braying from their cages as the grim reaper comes for their master.

Years flash behind my eyes. I see blood slickening my hands. I feel skin slipping from sinew. I hear screams of the living destined to join the dead.

I shake my head in a feeble attempt to clear it. Play Mozart over the speakers, the ebony and ivory notes chasing the memories back to where they belong. Pat my weeping wound and dig in my pockets for a cigar. My nerves are so shot, I fumble the lighter three times as I try and fail to flick the flame to life.

"How John Constantine of you."

The lighter slips from my useless fingers, metal clanging a cacophonic clatter. "*Putain.*"

A snicker sounds from behind me. "Relax, *monsieur.* I haven't actually come to collect your soul."

I fix a glare on the little devil that must've followed me here as she picks up the lighter and thumbs the trigger. Fire leaps between us, ochre light warming her arctic mask.

"There," Poppy chirps when gray streams from my nostrils, snapping the lighter shut in my face. "All ready for hell."

"Cute." Blowing smoke at her smirk, I approach the worktable, finding a needle and surgical suture. My hands quake so badly, I'm barely able to thread the eye.

"Sit," Poppy murmurs, her gentle hands pressing firmly on my shoulders, coaxing me down to the stool. "*Parfait.*"

She takes the needle and thread then steals my cigar. Holding up a finger against my protest, she lifts her vape in invitation. "Go easy. Bax is notorious for brewing his batches strong."

Like a drowning man desperate for air, I take the deepest breath I can.

Vivid colors flood my tongue. A kaleidoscope of flavors collide in my throat. Sugary sweet, like rainbow sprinkles. The hit calms the tremor in my bones, soothes the bucking beast in my breast.

"Angels." A lavender plume curls from my long and tranquil exhale. "What *is* that?"

"Unicorn Cum." Poppy chortles, pocketing the liquid magic and threading the needle. "No cock will ever compare."

A chuckle slips out. "I suppose not."

"Speaking from experience?"

"I've had my share."

Poppy grins, hollowing her cheeks on the cigar. "You should trade these for a vape. Would work wonders for that chip on your shoulder."

"How much does that cost?"

"For you?" A shrug. "Your soul will do."

"Just my luck."

Chortling, Poppy passes over the cigar. With a careful pinch and sharp poke through the tender flesh of my cheek, she starts the first suture.

Keeping my focus on my bloody hands twitching in my lap, I remark, "You know what you're doing."

"I'll take your blatant shock as a compliment."

"Not many people know how to properly stitch aside from doctors."

"And soldiers."

"Touché. Your father taught you well."

"Actually, it was Nikolai who taught me."

Against my better judgment, my interest piques. "Your sworn enemy was your mentor?"

"Our grandfathers were enemies, not us. We grew up as friends." She dabs a rag to the numbing gash on my face then resumes the stitches. "Nik and I had a lot in common: both born criminal heirs, both raised to kill. As we got older, our friendship grew into something more."

"Let me guess. He was Romeo, and you were his Juliet."

"*Hai.* That is, until my family won the war against his family and made them bend the knee." She takes a long breath, her hands remaining steady as she sutures with clinical precision. "We were at V and V. He stole my phone and locked me in a storage closet. The music was too loud for anyone to hear me. I was soaked in my own piss by the time I was found the next morning. When I saw him again, I left my mark on him. To this day, Nik hasn't apologized for what he did. No one knows aside from us. Well, except you."

I don't dare reply, unsure what to say or how to say it. What Nikolai did to her wasn't where her distress started. But it could've been where it all began to snowball and roll downhill until it became an avalanche that buried her beneath decades of trauma.

"I want to know what I said or did to upset you so much," Poppy goes on, looping the final stitch. "I'll respect your boundaries if you don't wish to tell me, but it's been bothering me, Brontë. Whatever it is, I'd like to apologize for it. If you'll let me."

The last dregs of my anger drain from my system. "I know you were using me to make him jealous."

"Hm." Poppy squints, cutting the thread with her butterfly blade. She dabs the drying blood from my face and neck with the rag, taking care to clean my hands, too. Then she flattens the knife under my chin, forcing my gaze up to hers. "I have no need to make Nik jealous. Such behavior would imply I care about what he thinks, and I don't. But you, Brontë Bourbon"—she steps closer, wedging herself between my spread knees—"I care about what *you* think of me. The reason I asked you to be there that night was because I *wanted* you there. I felt solid with you. I, um...I have a lot of stress, which is why I have the vape. I don't know how, but your presence is becoming more potent than any smoke. You kept me rooted to the present instead of spacing and getting lost in the past while a demon from mine was five feet away."

Remorse floods my system. "Do you still care for him?"

Poppy heaves an impressively hefty sigh for someone so small and rests a palm on my chest. "A part of me will always care for Nik. But I care for you more."

As she holds my stare, I see these past months reflecting back at me from her ocean eyes. We still hardly know each other, yet what we have feels almost like friendship.

But not quite.

No, this is companionship. A connection shared between kindred spirits. We're alike, her and I, two predators circling each other in a cage. I'm a fool if I pretend otherwise. But Poppy is still a criminal. Even if she does ever forfeit her birthright, she'll always bleed black.

It's maddening, this magnetism. I want—no, *need* it to end. Before it turns me into the person I was before I fought to earn my halo and wings.

"In case you were wondering," Poppy says, her gaze dropping to follow her forefinger tracing my tattoos, "the street cams outside Nik's apartment were—surprise, surprise—*scrubbed* the night Leviathan dropped by."

I nod stiffly. "Did you scope out the graveyard?"

"No. Been busy losing a war."

"Fair enough."

"Has Emi found anything more on Margot?"

"Nothing but dead ends."

"How is Dantë taking it?"

"He doesn't know."

"I see." Her palm splays over my heart, and her tone softens as she whispers, "Do you care for me, too, Brontë?"

Of course I do. I've cared for her since I saw her fighting for her life in an alleyway. Hell, before that. Since I felt the scars on her hands as she handed me her favorite book and looked at me like I hung every damn star in the sky.

But this...whatever *this* is, it would never work.

We are from two very different worlds. Poppy is a crime lord's daughter. I am a coroner. She's a criminal, and I work with cops to put people like her behind bars.

"It's late." I savor the cigar like it's my last meal. "You should go. Talk to Emi. Process what happened to your friend."

"I don't want to talk to Emi. I want to talk to you."

"*Bonne nuit, Petit Diable.*"

That face. It's like I've plunged my fist into her chest and crushed the precious diamond inside.

Better this way, I tell myself, even as the beast within bellows its fury.

Poppy drops her hand and steps back. I look at anything but her. She doesn't offer the apology she came here to give, and I don't ask for it.

In less than an hour, we've reverted back to complete strangers.

"*Bonne nuit,*" she murmurs, "*mon ange.*"

Mon ange. My angel.

I have the sudden urge to set myself ablaze and burn myself all the way down to hell.

Poppy's boots leave my periphery. The moment she's gone, the cold slithers in. It permeates my blood, wraps my bones in permafrost, nestles in my marrow like an eternal winter. A violent shiver wracks me, my own body unstable without her infernal fire.

"By the angels," I carp, rubbing an ache in my temple. "I'm so fucked."

MAUSOLEUM
POPPY

Tears smear the dry blood of my dead friend on the floor of the abandoned chemical factory.

Fiona and I weren't close, but her murder still feels like a blade in my gut. I've been so preoccupied dealing with my family's demise, I'd barely spoken to her these past months. A fact I'm confident Leviathan knew before choosing to target her.

That cursed poppet they'd shoved down her throat has been haunting my nightmares. I don't know if Fiona had received it beforehand. From what little I saw of her at Beelzebub's, she never spoke of it. As is the same old theme with Leviathan, any video evidence was expunged.

I've warned my other friends. Castor is lying low with his motorhead crew. Without his lab, Bax is staying with him. Circe and Nik are safe at Indigo, and Emi is sleeping with a dagger under her pillow. They're as prepared for the reaper as possible.

"I'm sorry I failed you, Fiona," I murmur, kissing my fingers and pressing them to the floor. "Keep the devil's bed warm for me, will you?"

I wish I'd feel an impossible breeze. A sign to tell me she forgives me as a final act before moving on to the afterlife. If there even is an afterlife.

But I live in the real world, where those things don't actually happen.

Wiping my eyes with my sleeve, I navigate the decrepit factory with the same familiarity as home. This place is where my father and Grandpapa Lucian once ran Morgenstern operations.

It's also where I made my first kill.

I climb up a rusty set of stairs. At the top is an old office space. I nudge the door open with my boot, the hinges screeching their defiance. The room is small, cold, and lacking any personality: a simple metal desk, a cracked leather chair, a prehistoric computer, dusty filing cabinets, grimy windows overlooking the industrial space. All relatively normal for an abandoned chemical plant.

Aside from the old bloodstains on the concrete floor.

I slip off a leather glove and skim a fingertip over the desk. Tug the chair free and sit. Drag on my vape and breathe purple smoke. Try to understand where it all went wrong.

The Morgensterns have been ruling Salem's underworld since the witch trials, but we weren't always criminals. My ancestors launched a black market under the authorities' noses to help people. They sold herbs to ward off demonic influence, weapons to protect against malevolent witchcraft.

You know, the kind of bullshit people back then lapped up like kids with candy.

Then torches turned into bombs, pitchforks into guns, harmless plants into toxic drugs. Somewhere along the way, we forgot who we are and what we stand for.

If it were up to me, I'd have Bax stick to batching strictly vape juice. I'd sell weaponry to those who wish to defend themselves with something stronger than mace. Enlist mercenaries to hunt the scum of the earth. Hire hackers to steal money from the corrupt and donate it to charities and clinics and volunteer organizations. Dismantle human trafficking rings. The possibilities are endless.

It's not up to me, though. Even if it was, Leviathan has made achieving such a dream impossible.

I am not the heir of an empire. I am the heir of a mausoleum.

Standing, I push the chair back in and give the bloodstains a wide berth as I leave. Just once, I let myself glance over my shoulder to blow a kiss at where Fiona took her last breath. It's a trick of the light—I *know* it is—but I swear I see a figure standing at the office window upstairs, watching me through all the layers of dirt, death, and decades of decay.

FIDDLE
BRONTË

"How many condoms do you need, *crétin?*" I mutter, hefting the trio of boxes sporting the telltale Trojan helmet from the front porch. Of course, a gaggle of elderly women out for their Saturday morning walk spot me and cackle like crows.

I fucking hate people.

Glaring at them as they wobble away, I shove through the door.

Pause. Turn around.

Drop the boxes.

Rip the poppet of twine, bone, and feathers from the handle.

"Fuck," I hiss, crushing the abomination in my fist. "Fuck, fuck, *fuck.*"

Confirming Dantë is still asleep upstairs, I lean against the kitchen island and tap into the house's exterior camera feed on my laptop. I'm not surprised to find them scrubbed clean, a loop of snow falling to the street playing all night.

Leviathan is clever, but not enough to completely blind me.

I find uncompromised footage from the non-cellular trail cams monitoring the property. Checking each SD card is a bitch, but worth it when I find what I'm looking for. The vantage point is from the classic red terracotta roof pitched low over the ivory stucco body of the house, angled to watch the street.

A hooded figure slinks in the cam's periphery, poppet in hand. A blast of wind snags their hood, whipping it back. They catch it in time, but I note the lack of a Leviathan mask. They scan the empty street, briefly revealing their profile concealed by a gaiter before dropping down and disappearing from view. A moment later, they're climbing up the roof again, backtracking their covert route.

I replay the video and freeze it on the sleuth's profile. My heart pounds a war drum in my chest as I stare at a doe eye and a single untamed ringlet. The image is grainy, but I know who I'm looking at.

"Quinn Wildes," Emi says minutes later, fingers flying across her keyboard from the other end of the phone plastered to my ear. "Age: thirty-one. Occupation: forensic scientist. Hobbies: hiking, camping, baking. She's active on social media and has a normal digital footprint."

"Any connection to Margot?"

"Not that I can see from a quick search, but that doesn't mean there's nothing to find. Want me to keep digging?"

"*Hai,*" answers Poppy before I can speak. "Make it a deep hole."

My blood thrums at the sound of her voice. "Eavesdropping, *Petit Diable?*"

"I've been here this whole time, fuck you very much." *Angels,* I miss her fire. "You're friends with Quinn. What do you know about her?"

"Everything." I glance at the paused video on my laptop. "Or, at least, I thought I did."

"Anything will help," Emi says, clicking and clacking away.

"Quinn's a local. Her parents passed when she was still a kid. She was raised by her grandfather, who'd been a retired cop before he passed away a few years ago. She's a fervent justice-seeker, but she sticks to the law. She's pulled some strings for me in the past, though it clearly bothered her."

"What kind of strings?" asks Poppy.

"The kind that led me to you."

Realization sinks deep the moment the words are out my mouth.

I've been played like a goddamn fiddle.

By my own fucking *friend*.

A beat of silence passes, punctuated by Poppy's quiet curses. Then Emi sighs. "Shit."

"What?" Poppy barks before I can.

"Quinn volunteers at an academic library most weekends."

"*Academic* library?"

"Mhm. Want to guess which campus?"

I grab my keys, halfway down the steps when Poppy says, "Stand down, *monsieur*. I'll handle it."

"The fuck you will."

"Don't be a fool. You can't stalk Quinn in broad daylight."

"I can, and I will." I slam the car door and key the engine. "This is personal, Poppy."

"As if nothing that's happened thus far has been fucking *personal*," she seethes, her voice darkening as her fury rises. "This isn't an attack against you, Brontë. It's an attack against *me*. Leviathan is aware we've been working together. They know what you—" She cuts herself off, but I can guess what she was about to admit. *They know what you mean to me.* "They know how valuable you are to my hunt for them."

"Then they won't see me coming."

"Listen to me, you bullheaded prick! We *finally* have the upper hand. Neither Quinn nor Leviathan knows we caught her in the act. If you go chasing after her right now, you'll waste the only ace we have. Besides, Quinn is an active member of the community. People will know if she goes missing, and we don't need the cops breathing down our necks, either."

The leather steering wheel creaks beneath my grip. I know she's right, but I don't want to hear her logic. I want to find Quinn, throttle her senseless, and get answers.

"What do you propose we do?"

"I need to speak with my parents. They're expecting me today anyway for a family gathering in honor of my grandpapa. In the meantime, I can spare some guards to keep an eye on you and your brother."

"We can protect ourselves."

"Oh?" When I don't indulge her unspoken request for me to explain, she asks, "Would you like to come with me?"

"Where?" Surely, not her parents' with a house full of criminals...?

"I'll drop a pin. See you at Morgenstern Manor, *mon ange.*"

Click.

I expel my lungs, dropping my head back. "Angels fucking bless me."

IMPERFECTION
POPPY

Morgenstern Manor is a behemoth structure standing silent sentry over the sunlit bay like a slumbering giant. From here, the city is a portrait of winter paradise. At the arched doors of my childhood home, there are columns engraved with flora and fauna. Statues of gargoyles and pegasuses, angels and cherubs. Gardens, lush and flourishing even in winter's grasp, sprawl around it all like a sacred forest.

"You grew up in a *castle?*" Brontë gapes as the valet parks his car beside my bike in the circular drive brimming with enough luxurious vehicles to fill any motorhead's wet dreams.

Purple smoke trickles from my scowl. "It's just a house."

"My house is just a house. That thing is the Colline du Château of America."

"Which is...?"

"What do you think, *Petit Diable?*"

"A house?"

Brontë suppresses his throaty chuckle, but he can't stop the edges of his eyes from crinkling. Fuck, I missed looking at him. He's in his fitted cargo pants and black tee, his work jacket unzipped to show off the generous *V* of his tattooed chest. The gash in his cheek, pink and puckered, only makes the coroner hotter. The wound I gave him is a perfect imperfection in a masterpiece.

I stare for a few moments too long to be polite. I look away, but not before he notices.

His expression frosts. "Why am I here, Poppy?"

"Moral support."

"Lie."

I sigh a cloud of steam, in no mood to play this game. "My parents are about to learn that Quinn is a member of Leviathan. They will be pissed. You, as Quinn's friend and colleague, are guilty by association. You are here to prove you're an ally."

His brow flattens. "I don't need to prove anything."

"You do if you want to live past noon."

"Is that a threat?"

"It's a promise, Brontë. If you leave now, there's no chance in hell they're not sending me after you to drag you back here for a far less casual visit."

"Drag me back?" He folds his thick arms over his broad chest. "I'd like to see you try."

"I think you already know I'm capable." I glance pointedly at his scar.

"You caught me by surprise, that's all."

"Will you just do as I say for once?" I snap, exhausted and freezing my ass off in the brutal winter wind. "When we're done here, we'll go our separate ways. You have my word, this is the last you'll see me. Emi will continue to funnel updates, but you and I will otherwise never cross paths again. Consider our bargain fulfilled. Deal?"

"Deal."

My eyes burn. It's not his answer that twists the knife between my ribs; it's his lack of hesitation.

I pocket my vape and thumb my damp lashes dry as I lead him inside. Candlelight and merry conversation greets us, the scent of old paper and aged wine on its heels. The vast foyer opens to a sprawling staircase. A vintage Gothic chandelier hangs from the vaulted ceiling. Ornate candelabras line the ebony wood walls, flickering buttery light over servants in swallowtail coats carrying silver platters of drinks and hors d'oeuvres through the growing crowd of suits and gowns. I pluck a pair of wine glasses from a passing tray and hand one to Brontë as I take his arm like he belongs to me, uttering, "Act natural. Mama and Papa should be here somewhere."

To my surprise, he doesn't fight my hold. Nor does he argue.

We circle around the foyer, meeting my aunts and uncles and cousins that flash curious smiles at the coroner while we search for my parents. He's unnervingly skilled at slipping on an easy smile while sharing pleasantries with my family of criminals. When we first met, he was tense and clearly had no interest in being around the living. He'd seemed to have been one of those people who wished to have been born anything but human. There's something different about him now.

Since I cut him deep and gave him that scar, he's changed—almost like I'd cut him free from his unseen bonds. I may have been the one in the mask he'd been hunting for ten years of his life, but he was hiding just as much as me. Is this the real man beneath the antisocial coroner exterior? How long, I wonder, has he been hiding himself away? Choosing to ice out the warmth of humanity rather than bask in it? The man is a lone wolf. Isolated, solitary, fiercely protective of those he loves...overburdened by the responsibility mantled on his shoulders to keep his family safe.

Just like me.

"Impressive," Brontë remarks as we pause in a secluded corner with a snarling gargoyle statue, setting our empty glasses on a passing tray. "Even the kids are sharpwitted and silvertongued."

"They *are* Morgensterns," I muse, only half-grinning. Because most of them are like me when I was their age and already have a running tally of graves they've filled. It sickens me, but I don't let it show. Not here, in front of my own family. "I don't see Mama and Papa. Let's try the library upstairs."

As I steer us up the staircase, passing the oil paintings immortalizing generations of Morgensterns poised in regal gentry, he utters, "Not a cult, huh?"

My eyes roll. "No."

"Where's *your* portrait?"

"Mine will be painted when I inherit Papa's throne." If there's a throne left to inherit.

"When do you ascend?"

"When I find my king or Papa retires. Whichever comes first."

"No arranged marriages, then?"

I toss a glare over my shoulder. "Don't insult us. We're not the Mafia."

Brontë lifts his palms in surrender, mumbling to himself. We reach the top landing, and I let muscle memory lead us down the long hallway lit by more wall-mounted candelabras.

"What about your mother's side?"

I pivot in place, jabbing a finger at his chest. "Why are you suddenly so curious about *ma famille, monsieur?*"

His shoulder hikes. "If I'm going to meet your parents, I should at least know the basics."

"You already know the basics."

"I don't even know your mother's name, *Petit Diable.*"

"Rin Morgenstern, formerly Hayashi. Her kin still live in Japan."

"Do they visit?"

"No."

"Do you visit them?"

"No."

"Why not?"

I huff impatiently. "To put it mildly, the Hayashis disapproved of Mama's courtship with Papa and shunned her for loving a 'demon' and carrying his 'hellspawn.' They cut us out like we were cancer. Never even gave me a chance." My eyes water again. I drop them to my boots before he can see the tears. "Mama said they simply didn't care, but I knew they thought I was evil."

They weren't wrong; I *am* the daughter of Salem's most notorious crime lord.

My stare lifts to a demon on Brontë's throat. Its glare is nefarious, its smile serrated as much as it is vile. It's like looking in the mirror.

Is that why Leviathan is targeting my family? Has this been not a war, but a crusade? It would explain Quinn's involvement; she's a justice-seeker, after all.

How many lives are saved when a crime ring falls?

Warm, calloused fingers crook beneath my chin, tipping my head up. "You're not evil, Poppy. I've seen true villains, and you hold no flame."

It's none of my business what happened to him and his siblings to make him say such things. I'd be lying, though, if I said I'm not more curious now than I've ever been.

The question is prancing on my tongue when he suddenly palms my jaw and leans down, planting a firm kiss to the hollow of my cheek. My lungs fill with his bittersweet musk as he lingers there for a long beat. I don't know how he makes something so innocent feel so sinful. It's agonizing in its torture, succulent in its sweetness.

It only leaves me wanting more.

The urge to capture that tempting mouth with mine is unbearable. I fist my knife to hang onto my own diminishing willpower. I shouldn't want more. He's made his feelings clear. It's why I said what I did, why we need to remain distanced. I can't fool myself into thinking we'll ever be anything more than a criminal and coroner stuck in a reluctant alliance.

But I also can't deny how *right* he feels this close to me.

I want him closer. I want him to push me against the wall. I want his hand on my throat and his body molding to mine as he steals a kiss then another and another.

Brontë inches back, pinning me with his smolder. He doesn't withdraw. Confusion hazes over me as his thumb arcs the height of my cheekbone. He's not looking at me like he doesn't want me.

No, he's looking at me like he wants to kiss me, too.

I lift my chin, my nose flirting with his. His free hand moves to my waist, fingers curling into my jacket pocket to tug me closer. My mouth opens in time with his—

"Aren't you a little old to be sneaking in with a boy?"

We jerk back like a pair of teenagers caught with their clothes off, whipping our heads to see Mama looming in the dim hallway. A thin kimono of glossy black drapes around her elegant curves like liquid ink, the sleeves off-shoulder. Her skin is starlight, and her sleek hair is a curtain of the deepest shade of night. Candlelight dances upon the black and pink ink of the parent tattoo to mine: a Japanese dragon and cherry blossoms twining up her right shoulder. Her polite smile doesn't quite reach her sharp, quicksilver eyes.

"Mama." I bow before the queen of Salem's underworld, motioning for Brontë to do the same. "Pardon the intrusion. This is Brontë Bourbon, a friend. We were on our way to speak with you and Papa."

"We will be down in a minute."

"Actually, we were hoping to speak to you in private."

"What for?"

"We have a lead on Leviathan."

"I see." Distaste leaks from her tone as she turns toward the shadows ahead. "Follow me."

Mama wordlessly guides us to the manor's library, pushing through the double doors and ushering us in. Thick tomes cram the shelves built into the walls. Windows tinted black and spiderwebbing with frost overlook the city. A hearth straight ahead glows with flames blazing bright, warming a lightly furnished lounge area.

Papa is in his leather wingback, a glass of wine in his grip. He's the spitting image of Grandpapa Lucian: rich umber hair, a jawline that could break knuckles, piercing blue eyes set in a perpetual leer. Like Grandpapa, he carries a cold presence with him; like the reaper lurks in his shadow.

Seated in the chair beside him with his own glass is a man I don't recognize. A man with a pistol holstered at his hip and a badge on his belt.

My blood freezes, locking my limbs in place.

Why the hell is my father drinking with a fucking *cop?*

TSUNAMI

BRONTË

Poppy's discomfort is the voltaic charge during an electric storm. Her baby blues dull with apprehension as they flick between her father and the detective beside him.

She's as blindsided as me.

Suddenly, it all makes sense: the decade of her cold cases rotting in filing cabinets wasn't a byproduct of poor policing. It was the doing of a crooked detective secretly working for her father.

First Quinn, now Scull. I'm starting to feel like Christ and Caesar.

Scull's lion eyes mark Poppy first, then me. If he's surprised by my own affiliation with the Morgensterns, he hides it behind a well-crafted poker face. "Never thought I'd see the likes of you here, Bourbon."

"Touché, *mon ami.*"

He drags a thumb over his own right cheek. "Lose a brawl with a butter knife?"

Bravado possesses me as I look straight at Alexander—the man who sentenced his own daughter to living this life with a spade in her chest instead of a heart—and drawl, "Blade kink gone wrong."

Scull chuckles. Poppy stomps on my foot, hissing a rebuke. Rin silently surveys us with a curious curve to her lips as Alexander's gaze rips from Poppy and stitches to me. His attention is as sharp and leaden as an axe.

"I see my daughter still has a habit of letting strays into her bed."

I absorb the blow with a locked jaw.

Poppy tuts, luring his focus back to her. "Why is a cop here, Papa?"

No one else seems to notice how everything glacial about him melts. A part of me is envious of that; my father never looked at me the way Alexander looks at Poppy. He'd hand her the world then claim it's not enough and find a way to give her the entire cosmos instead.

"Detective Scull is a dear friend of ours, Poppyseed. He's assisting us with our Leviathan problem."

"Your timing is impeccable," Rin transitions smoothly, drifting to the bar cart nestled against a nearby shelf and pouring two glasses of sparkling wine. She brings them to us then waves an elegant hand toward a vacant loveseat. "Sit. Tell us about your lead."

As we lower onto the cushions, Poppy bundles her jacket in her lap and fists the fabric tight. Her nerves chafe my own. I slide my arm behind her, fingertips feathering her tattoo. My touch is light, barely there. It's my way of reminding her that I'm here, that she's not alone. Her shoulders loosen, and my chest constricts in response to how comfortable she is around me.

If she knew my secrets, she wouldn't be.

We show them the damning evidence of Quinn's involvement with Leviathan. Watching her slink over my roof with that cursed poppet makes it real again. I'm disoriented and numb from the betrayal, a thousand theories tangling in my thoughts as I relay all I know about the person who had been my only friend. Scull has the nerve to wear pity on his face, as if his own knife isn't lodged in my back. When I'm done and sulking in my own misery, Poppy shares Emi's findings from her quick and dirty investigation this morning.

Rin aims a grim frown at Alexander, who lobs an equally discomforting look at Scull. A silent conversation passes between them. I have a nagging suspicion it's a continuation of whatever clandestine meeting they'd been having before we arrived.

"We appreciate your persistence on this matter," Alexander says, swirling his wine. "Scull will take it from here."

Poppy's spine locks. "What? Why?"

"Because we have more faith in him than you."

Poppy recoils as if she's been slapped. I grind my teeth against the ripostes that are far too dangerous for me to speak. This isn't my battle.

"I know I haven't been able to clean up this mess as quickly as I thought, Papa, but it's *my* responsibility."

Alexander's icy glare lances across the space. "You've done enough. We cannot afford any more of your failures."

"I-I'm sorry, Papa."

"You are not a little girl anymore. Sorry is as worthless as excuses."

Poppy shrinks into my side, bowing under shame's heavy weight. My arm curls protectively around her shoulders, my glower firmly affixed on Scull. His features remain carefully neutral, his posture radiating only slight unease from being in a room full of agitated predators.

"There's no time left, Poppyseed," Rin adds in a hushed tone, like speaking across a deathbed. Firelight smelts her mercury irises as she gazes into the flames almost longingly. "Scull has more resources at his disposal than we do. You're off the case. Permanently."

Rage rises like a moonlit tsunami in Poppy's entire body, ready to decimate everything in her path. A single steely lour from Alexander, though, and it falls just as quickly. She visibly sags, her head lowering submissively.

"*Hai.* As you wish."

Rin ushers us out. Poppy is under my arm, her movements robotic. Her stare is on the floor, baby blues dim as dead flower petals. I fear she's dissociating, possibly spiraling into a panic attack.

But when I drape her jacket over her shoulders, she shrugs me off, grumbling, "Don't touch me."

There she is. Breathing a quiet, relieved sigh, I murmur, "I was only trying to help."

"You have my thanks for that and saying what you did earlier and comforting me in there, but we're done. No more bargains. No more pretending to be friends. The termination of our partnership is effective immediately."

Regret seeps into my bones. I shouldn't have agreed to never seeing her again, but I was pissed at Quinn and pissed at myself for not having guessed her involvement sooner. Most of all, I was pissed at how Poppy and I last left things between us.

"Can we—" I start.

"Done means done, Brontë. Bury your words in a grave where they belong."

My mouth shuts in surrender, and I cast a final backward glance at Scull. He downs his wine in a single gulp, saluting me with his empty glass. A motion conveying our mutual understanding. I have as much dirt on him as he does on me. Neither of us are interested in orange jumpsuits and silver bracelets for the rest of our lives.

As the library doors close, I spy Alexander and Rin sharing a look of unmistakable, undiluted relief.

Clarity chases the wrath from my veins. They didn't mean a word they said about their daughter being a failure. They benched her to protect her from what comes next:

Leviathan's guillotine.

BLACK HOLE
POPPY

There's a reason I don't sell mysteries in my café: I'd much rather shoot or slice straight to the answers.

Yet here I am. Trying to solve the biggest mystery of my life while skulking through the woods toward an abandoned cemetery. Carrying Nikolai's Leviathan mask in one hand, the coordinates from the invitation that came with it loaded on my phone in the other. Jezebel creeps beside me, her big black paws silent on the snow.

Night kisses the sun to sleep, bathing the underbrush in bruised black and blues. Brisk air fills my nostrils with the smell of crisp pine and dead leaves. Above the canopy of tall oaks and towering evergreens, lightning whips the black clouds into a spiraling frenzy. Distant thunder bellows a war cry, threatening to unleash winter's fury. It feels like a warning, the universe roaring at me to turn around and go back home.

But I can't.

I *won't*.

The coordinates on Nik's invitation to join Leviathan's ranks are the only lead I have left. Am I a fool for refusing to respect my parents' wishes for me to keep my distance from Leviathan? Undecided. Their precious detective hasn't found anything more on Quinn. Brontë reported several run-ins with her at work. Each time, she's acted as if nothing is amiss. I told him to back off, refrain from showing our hand. As far as I know, he's listened.

Dread eats at my insides like a parasite, though, as I wait for Brontë to either go missing or get killed. Bile rises in my throat. I swallow it down, banishing the memory of Fiona's mangled corpse before my mind can replace her with him.

We trek along an overgrown path, my cell's flashlight illuminating a wrought iron gate ahead. I halt, reading the rusted script:

ST. AURELIUS'S CEMETERY

The same saint whose academy is stained with Leviathan's footprint.

"Well, I'll be damned," I mutter, breath curling in the cold as I dial the only person I have left to call. "What can you find on the surname 'Aurelius'?"

Emi's keyboard sings my favorite tune as I push through the gate. Jezebel slinks ahead, sniffing the gravestones. The cemetery is a labyrinth of tombstones and mausoleums guarded by statues of snarling gargoyles and weeping angels with broken wings. I can *feel* their eyes on me, tracking my every step.

"Aurelius, a Latin-derived surname originating from a noble family in Ancient Rome," Emi relays. "Felix Aurelius, the founder of St. Aurelius's Liberal Arts in the late sixteen-hundreds, was born in the only American family with that surname. He was burned for heresy after he was supposedly found spearheading a secret society with a select few students who were mistaken for a coven of satanic witches. They were hung around his pyre after being forced to watch him burn. Felix was later elevated to saint status due to his work at the academy having been one of the first to explore teachings of unorthodox religious doctrines."

Founder of an academy. Head of a secret society. Professor of unconventional theologies. All during the witch trials.

Was St. Aurelius the *father* of Leviathan?

"Who were the students?"

"The scanned records I'm seeing in the academy's digital archives are barely legible, but I think I see Harper Bishop, Cheryl Nurse, Leon Redd, and—holy shit. Octavia *Morgenstern?* How is that even possible? She was an only child, wasn't she? You wouldn't exist if she died this young."

"Unless she had a child of her own before her death."

"I don't think so, Pops. It says here that Felix kept detailed records of each student he recruited. There were several entries about Octavia's supposed struggle with infertility."

A chill spiders down my spine. Maybe the stories about my ancestor having struck a deal with the Devil aren't fiction after all.

"It's not important," I say, skimming a thumb over the demonic mask. "I'm going to see what else I can find. I'll be back soon."

"I'll be here, willingly getting my ass handed to me by LuciImHome to keep Fiona's spirit happy."

"You know she wanted you to win eventually, right?"

"Oh, please. That cheeky bitch would've bet on me losing for the rest of her life out of spite for how many times I swapped the mocha in her coffee for Ex-Lax."

Chuckling, I hang up and wander the graveyard. Jezebel lurks around a crypt dwarfing the surrounding headstones. The stone structure is framed by a trio of fallen angels: one sits upon the stout steps and tilts his beatific face toward the moon; the opposite is curled in on herself and weeping into her knees; the last guards the entry with a holy tome in her arms. Carved on a plaque above the door is the name *Aurelius.*

I snicker. "The pompous prick had to have the biggest crypt, didn't he?"

Twigs snap nearby. Jezebel grumbles a low growl.

Fuck.

I tap my cell light off, tuck the mask into my jacket, and dart behind an angel. I skip my mini Glock in favor of my butterfly knife, having no interest in waking any residents living close by with a gunshot that could wake the dead. Jezebel crouches by my side, ready to pounce. Snow crunches twenty feet away. Ten. Five. Imagining a hooded figure in a creepy demon mask, I raise my knife.

The footfalls grow closer...*closer.*

Then they stop.

Firelight casts the shadow of a masculine silhouette across the ground.

Jezebel's growls fade, her demeanor suddenly changing at the same moment I lunge forward and strike. A tattooed hand catches my wrist mid-air, halting the blade an inch from an angelic warrior inked in black.

My eyes snap up, and my arm drops. "*Mon ange?*"

"*Bonjour, Petit Diable.*" Brontë, features lit by the lighter in his hand, hitches a dark eyebrow as Jezebel greets him with a purring yowl. "Fancy meeting you two here."

"Wh-what are you doing here?"

"Stalking you," he says, deadpan, a mischievous glint in his hazel eyes. I can't tell if he's joking or not. "The better question is: What are *you* doing here? Aren't you under strict orders to stay away from all this?"

"I'm an adult who's capable of making her own decisions, fuck you very much."

"As has every victim of Leviathan been thus far."

"Why do you care?" I snipe, my mood souring as every unspoken word between us since our last encounter at the manor comes rushing out. "We're not working together anymore, remember? And it's not like we're friends. You have zero reason to give any fucks about my well-being."

"That doesn't mean I'd celebrate your demise, Poppy."

I scoff and step backward, putting distance between us before I do anything rash like give him a matching scar on his other cheek. My heel catches a sheet of ice.

And I slip.

Too fast, my body pirouettes like a ballerina. My arms pinwheel. My knife tumbles to the ground, bouncing with the tip up as gravity yanks me down.

Stars save me. Despite the books I read, I really, *really* don't want a blade in my ass.

Brontë lunges for my arm, hauling me into him. My face kamikazes off his hard chest as we stumble gracelessly. We slam into a statue so hard, the granite cracks.

And crumbles.

Brontë tucks me beneath his chin as stone crashes around us. I cling to him, and he clings to me. His shoulders take the brunt of the collapse. When the last broken piece tumbles to the ground, Jezebel chuffs. It sounds like a condescending, *Humans.*

I blink down at the angel who fell apart reading her book.

And laugh.

Brontë stares at me in wonder before belting the most radiant guffaw I've ever heard. His laughter is the sound of birdsong during a summer sunset: harmonious and warm and promising a night full of stars.

Thunder rumbles furiously overhead, and our laughter slowly trickles to silence. I'm all too aware of how dangerously close we are: our arms around each other, my cheek plastered to his chest. His scent wraps me in its bittersweet embrace, his warmth thawing the frost in my marrow.

My thoughts inevitably spiral to the past: his healing lips on my cheek, his grounding arm on my shoulders. I backtrack to when he saved my life, twice. Ruminate on when he comforted me at the academy. Skip our visit to Voodoo & Velvet that didn't end as well as it began. Circle to whatever that moment was we shared at Morgenstern Manor, a look of pure want on his face as he held mine in the palm of his hand.

Hot and cold. Push and pull.

Whoever said women are indecisive surely never crossed paths with men in their thirties.

"Brontë?"

"Hm?"

"You can let go now."

"If I do, are you going to fall for me again?"

My unamused scowl carves decades into my cheeks. "Brontë."

"That face." He chuckles, releasing his hold and thumbing his lighter as I snatch my knife from the snow. "So, what have I missed?"

I shake my head once. "You need to leave."

"Why? Whatever news you have now will save Emi the time later."

"We had a deal, remember? You're breaking it by being here."

The residual laughter in his gaze dissipates, swallowed as if by a black hole. He fishes a cigar from his jacket and lights it, breathing gray smoke through his nostrils. "I'm tired of sitting on my ass and doing nothing. I can't fucking sleep. I can't talk to Dantë because he's too busy grieving over a woman who may or may not be dead at Leviathan's hands. Quinn is obviously off the table. Virgil doesn't need this shit on her plate. I have no one else, Poppy. *No one.*"

He may as well have just thrown himself on his knees and begged.

The sky bellows, lightning arcing as ice begins to fall. My lungs expel a long sigh as I gesture to the Aurelius family crypt.

"Let's get inside, *monsieur*. It's a long story."

COMET

BRONTË

"Interesting tale," I say, lighting the last rusted sconce inside the mausoleum as Poppy perches on St. Aurelius's massive sarcophagus. Jezebel remains by the door, already snoring. "I'm confused, though, as to why the coordinates were meant to lead Nikolai here if there's nothing waiting but bones. Where is Leviathan's welcome wagon?"

Poppy puffs on her vape and flicks her knife back and forth in thought, the silence filled by the sleet slamming outside. "Delay in arrival due to inclement weather?"

I chuckle, stubbing my cigar on a shelved Aurelius skull crowned with rotted flowers. "I suppose we waited too long to scope this place out. The invitation most likely came with an unspoken expiration date."

"Mhm. Speaking of the invitation that was in *my* possession and not yours, how did you know where this place is?"

"Nikolai mentioned an old cemetery outside the city. It didn't take many brain cells to find it on a map."

Her baby blues taper on me like she thinks I'm full of shit.

As she should. I'm lying through my fucking teeth.

In all honesty, I already told her what brought me here: *her.* When we were at Morgenstern Manor, I planted a tracker on her. I'd been so enraptured by her undiluted desire to kiss me, I nearly forgot to drop the tiny device in her jacket pocket. Since then, I've been obsessively monitoring her location. When I saw she was here, I left work early and blew through every red light to shave the hour-long ride in half. Haunted the whole time by the entwined memories of her being choked to death and getting her skull slammed into a wall.

But she doesn't need to know any of that.

Shrugging off her suspicion, I step closer and steal her vape to break her concentration. A decadent crimson flushes her cheeks as she watches me drag deep and breathe lavender smoke in her face. Satisfied to have dodged her interrogation, I pass the vape back and lean against a casket across from her.

"So, what now?"

"I don't know." Poppy plucks a skull from the shelf beside her and drags her knife through the layers of dirt crusted on the bone. "The way I see it, we're at another dead end."

I nod, having no words of comfort to offer. She knows she's on the wrong side of a losing battle. Nothing will change that except the death of her invisible foe.

"What are those symbols?" She taps her own knuckles, where ink is mirrored on mine. "Are they runes? Nordic?"

"...You're asking me about my tattoos?"

"I'm sorry, is that not allowed? Are we limited to talking only about my life deteriorating into an absolute shitshow? Or can we take a mental break for one fucking moment while we're cramped in with the dead and talk about something mundane?"

I smear a palm over my smile, amused by her fire that never banks. "Put the teeth away, *Petit Diable.* They're Gothic, not Nordic."

"Do they mean something? A prayer for heavenly protection? A secret phrase to a holy ritual?"

"Why the hell would they be either of those things?"

"You're kidding, right?" She drops to her feet and hooks a finger beneath the sleeve of my jacket, tugging it up to reveal the weeping angel surrounded by laughing demons. "You're *covered* in biblical beings. No one does that to themselves without a reason."

"People get full bodysuits with no meaning all the time."

She drums her knife on the skull with an expectant pout.

I sigh through my nose. "The right spells wrath. The left, pride."

"Two of the seven deadly sins. Sounds like there's a story behind them."

"*Oui:* What doesn't kill you makes you stronger."

"I see." Poppy sets the skull aside and lifts a hand between us, skimming her palm over my chest. I don't make a move to stop her, letting her touch me as my heart thunders in my throat. Her hand halts just atop that raging beast, her skin as warm as hot coals. "What about the angels and demons?"

"An ode to my mother's passion for the ethereal and the everlasting juxtaposition between heaven and hell. Two sides of the same coin."

"Good and evil?"

"Paradise and punishment."

Poppy nods, tracing the designs with a fingernail. She could so easily fist my shirt and yank me down to her. I could frame her face with my hands and kiss her like I've wanted for too damn long. Apologize for saying what I have to the contrary, show her how much I regret knifing her with my words over and over again.

I wouldn't push her away this time. Not after these months of stumbling through the dark and finding my way only when she's near. As I watch her peruse my ink with innocent curiosity, I slowly realize that I'd risk it. I'd risk becoming the person I used to be. She's worth every last drop of that danger.

A tightening knot of want writhes in my core, urging me to take the plunge.

"When did you get them?" Poppy glances up at me from beneath long lashes. "Before or after Salem?"

Suspicion curls its claws into my skull. I know she craves the pieces of my past that I have yet to give. But there's a reason I haven't indulged; Dantë wasn't lying when he said Margot was frightened by our history in this world's underbelly.

"I applaud your attempt at seduction, but you're sorely mistaken if you think I'm dumb enough to fall for it."

She scoffs, confirming my hunch. "You haven't once attempted to hide your familiarity with Leviathan. Now would be a good time to share with the class."

"No."

"I'm afraid that's not an option anymore." Her knife is at my throat faster than I can blink. "I have no other leads but the mysterious coroner who keeps dodging my questions about his sketchy past with the cult destroying my life. Either you spill the tea, or I spill your blood. Your choice."

"Go on, then." My chin tips up in invitation. "Draw the line."

As expected, Poppy doesn't take the bait. "If I recall correctly, you have a brother and half-sister who will surely let me in on your little secret if I ask as nicely as I'm asking you."

Rage floods my nervous system. "They'd kill you before you'd even lay your eyes on them."

"Is that what the three of you were? Killers? Which Master did you work for?"

My canines grind. "We didn't work for anyone."

"No? Murderers-for-hire, then?"

"Poppy, st—"

"Tell me, Brontë!" Tears wet her lashes, the whites bloodshot as she seethes, "Or so help me, I will tie your twin up and cut every fucking tattoo from his skin while you watch."

I don't see red. I see *black.*

I hear the screams of the dying. I taste iron in the air. I feel blood sticking to my flesh. I see the fear and agony in my siblings' eyes as they—

"We were slaves!" I bat away the memories, sucking in a ragged breath when Poppy stumbles backward into the opposing wall. "*Je suis désolé, Petit Diable.* Forgive me, I-I didn't mean to hurt you."

She waves off my concern, patting the dirt from her shoulders. "What do you mean you were slaves?"

I drag a hand through my hair, willing my lungs to slow. "Do you remember how my story in Texas ended?"

"With your father's brains blown to bits. You and your siblings left his corpse in the dust where it belonged."

"*Oui.* Weeks later, we were hitchhiking through Sleepy Hollow and trusted people we shouldn't have. We were drugged and woke up in holding cells built underground. The guards bore the Leviathan brand and wore those demon masks. We were..."

Poppy looks at me expectantly, her foot tapping with inflating impatience.

Just rip it off like a Band-Aid, you fool. "We..."

My vision swims. I close my eyes, clearing my throat as my chin falls to my chest. I don't know which is shaking more: my fists or my heart.

Coffee and cotton candy perfumes the air a moment before I feel Poppy's arms circle my neck, her cheek pressing to mine. "You're safe with me, *mon ange.* I'm not going anywhere, I swear it."

"We were executioners," I confess in a whisper. "We were trained in surgical operation and torture by a psychotic doctor. I was known as Scythe. I skinned people alive. Dantë, Reaper. He broke bones and tore out hearts. Virgil, Nightshade. She brewed poisons. We killed who we were told to kill. The only reason we made it out is because a shadow organization who was hunting them launched an attack and won. We didn't know anything about our saviors, and we didn't stick around to find out. My siblings and I ran in fear of being captured again, but as far as I know, our slavers were killed and their underground hive was destroyed. Upon my mother's grave, I vow this to be the full truth."

Sleet crashes in the silence. I brace myself for her inevitable reaction to tuck tail and run.

But she doesn't.

Instead, Poppy inches back and palms my jaw. "Look at me."

I obey. Her eyes are glossed, her expression agonized.

"Is this why you turn criminals into books? As a sort of...penance?"

"*Oui.* As a sort. Though, it's not a burden. It's a passion."

A small smile graces her lips. "We have that in common, you and I." She rises to the tips of her toes, pressing a firm kiss to my scarred cheek. "*Merci.*"

I nod, and she breaks her hold on me to give me space.

But I don't want space from her ever again.

I snatch her by the throat like she's a comet I'm tearing from the sky. My entire hand covers her slim neck like a collar. She looks at me not with fear, but with a simmering wrath.

I could fall to my knees and fucking *weep* from the sight of that raging inferno.

"Brontë," she warns, flashing her teeth. "I'm not playing cat-and-mouse with you anymore. Let go before I make you left-handed."

Finger by finger, muscle by muscle, I release her throat. Hurt flashes behind the steel wall she thinks I can't see behind. Then I slide my palm over her smooth, soft sternum. Her flesh is hot, borderline feverish with her fury rushing through her veins. Her eyes shackle to mine as I slip my hand beneath her jacket to rest it over her heart. It slams against my touch, fretful as a caged beast desperate to escape its prison.

A beast that looks and feels so much like my own.

"After," I murmur, gently palming her hips and walking her backward. "I got the tattoos *after* finding myself in Salem."

Then I fist her waistband, lift her onto the sarcophagus of a dead legend, and dive straight for her lips.

$$\cdot\!\!-\!\!\bullet\!\!-\!\!\diamond\!\!-\!\!\bullet\!\!-\!\!\cdot$$

DAMNATION
BRONTË

Poppy Morgenstern will be my damnation.

My mouth crashes into hers. She instantly retaliates, biting my bottom lip. I hiss from the prick of pain, tasting rust. She gives it a healing lick and delves for my tongue. I groan like a beast starved for lifetimes, and she arches into me, fisting my jacket and lapping at the roof of my mouth.

I don't know how it's possible, but she tastes even better than she smells: a heady rainbow of flavors from her last vape hit. I palm her jaw, biting her teeth when she tries to take control.

Both of us fight for dominion with every last scrap of our souls. Neither of us yield.

Her knees dig into my thighs, her closed legs sealing me off. I growl in protest. She relents, spreading her thighs and sighing through the long, languid kiss I gift her as I sink between them and meld my body to hers. Her fingers thread through my hair, kneading like a feline in heat. My hands roam the curves of her silhouette and squeeze her ass as I grind against her.

Poppy lets out a breathy moan. Her legs wrap my waist like ivy on stone, imprisoning me in paradise. A purr vibrates from my chest to hers. She echoes the primal sound with a throaty groan. I swallow it whole.

Not enough.

I don't just want to kiss her or fuck her. I want to *consume* her. I want to ruin her for anyone else, brand her with my body, and mark her as *mine.*

"Brontë," Poppy breathes through an open-mouthed kiss that has me seeing entire constellations. "Stop."

Stop, stop, stop, the command clatters through my muscles and bones like an order from the other end of a leash.

It takes every ounce of my willpower to tear myself away. To rip my lips from hers, still my hips, and flatten my palms on the sarcophagus. My breath mingles with hers as her heavy-lidded eyes lift to mine. She doesn't know it, but she has all the power in the world right now to cut me open and bleed me dry.

Then she says, "If anything happens to you because I'm too selfish to stay away, I…"

I loathe the fear in her voice. Fright doesn't belong anywhere near the most powerful woman in the world. "You should be afraid for *them,* Poppy. Not me."

"You're only human, Brontë."

"As are they." I plant a soft kiss to the bridge of her nose. "No more woes tonight. That pretty fringe can only cover so many age lines."

Poppy closes her eyes and controls her breaths as I idly twist a strand of her hair between my fingers. The pastel pink lock wraps the runes on my knuckles like praying hands over a holy writ.

"What are your wishes, *ma reine?*"

"That depends." Her eyelids lift, unveiling those diamond eyes. "What does that mean?"

I kiss a slow path over the vicious arc of her cheekbone before breathing in her ear, "My queen."

Her shudder summons my devilish smile, and I drag it down her thrumming pulse.

"Kneel." She trails a fingertip over the scar on my right cheek. "I want you to kneel, *mon ange,* and beg for my forgiveness."

She could ask me to carve out my own heart, and I'd do it.

"One condition." I cherish the flutter of her lashes as my lips travel up to hers. "No more of that *'monsieur'* bullshit. You call me *'mon ange'* or *'mon roi'* from now on."

"*Mon roi?*"

"My king."

Poppy grins fiendishly. "Deal."

Gifting me with a kiss that defies gravity and flings me into the clouds, she loosens her legs and nudges me down. I lower to a knee, eyes on hers as I peel her waistband past her hips. Kissing her soft skin and relishing her shivers, I inch the fabric lower.

Lower.

Until I have the unobstructed view of paradise beyond her pearly gates.

And a glittering black bat plug firmly lodged in her ass.

Angels fucking take me. It's a miracle I don't blow my load from the sight alone.

"I don't hear you begging, *mon roi.*"

"Poppy—"

"Lucia." She smirks down at me. "My middle name is Lucia."

Of course it is.

"Poppy Lucia Morgenstern, you have my deepest apologies for every lie I've spoken and deception I've enacted. Upon my life and soul, I vow that I am truly sorry to have caused you any pain, seen or unseen."

Her fingers weave through my hair, nails scraping my scalp as she grips by the root and forces my eyes up to hers. "I have an IUD, and I'm clean. Your turn."

The implication heightens my every sense. "I'm also clean."

"*Magnifique.* Now eat this pussy like a good boy."

I swallow as her legs widen, welcoming me home. My fingers bruise her supple thighs as I tip her down onto my open mouth. Her jaw drops as I feast on her pussy like a lion with raw meat. Her head falls back, spine arching. I lick her swollen clit and guide her across my face in a motion as old as time. I growl into her, savoring her shudders as the vibrations wrack her bones.

The sarcophagus creaks as she grips it too tight, her hips undulating with abandon. I kiss her cunt and drink her earthen sap like it's the fountain of youth. I suck down oxygen when I can, not giving a single fuck if I die of suffocation in this sweet oasis.

My fingertips flirt with the plug. When I can count the ridges lining her throat from how far back her head kicks, I tug the small handle. Her pussy clenches around my tongue in return.

"More," Poppy whimpers.

I pull the plug halfway out and plunge it back in. Her neck bows, and her groans turn savage. She's close, but I don't want her to be close.

I want her to split at every perfect seam.

I nip her clit. Blow a whisper of breath on her glistening sex. Swallow her whole. Fill her with my tongue until she comes undone. Her muscles stiffen with her paralyzing orgasm, and I let primitive instinct take over my limbs.

Rising, I yank my Kimber from my jacket. She watches with wide eyes as I free the clip and empty the chamber then drag the barrel down her navel.

"Your knife, *ma reine.*" I tap my carotid. "Put it here."

Poppy obeys, her cold blade kissing my skin.

"If I do anything you don't like, you know what to do."

She nods, chest heaving as I seek her pussy with my gun.

"Ready, *Petit Diable?*" She nods again, and I *tsk.* "Don't be lazy. Use your words."

"I'm ready," she breathes. "Fuck me with your pretty gun."

I bury the barrel straight to the trigger guard as I capture her hoarse cry with a crushing kiss.

"*Fuuuuck,* Poppy," I groan as she moans a curse. "This is *nothing* compared to how it will feel when I'm inside you. But I'm not claiming you here with the dead watching. You need to be patient and wait. Understand?" When she nods, I purr in her ear, "*Bonne fille.*"

"T-translation?"

"Good girl."

She shivers, and I guide her free hand to my belt. Her fingers slip under the waistband, curling around my rigid length. "Oh, God—"

"That's right, *Petit Diable.*" I groan into her mouth as she pumps me to the same torturous rhythm I set for her. "I *am* your god."

"Brontë..." Her spine jerks as I toy with the plug and grind the gun against her clit. "Brontë, I'm going to—"

"You come when I do."

She bites down on a screech of frustration, and I nearly explode from her fury. "Fuck. You."

"You already are. Now shut your mouth before I fuck your pretty tits and paint them in my cum."

"You're paying for this later." She chokes my cock, pumping me from root to tip. "Fucking prick."

My eyes threaten to roll back into my skull and never stop. I thrust my hips, losing myself in the sounds of our gruff grunts and whispered curses.

"Brontë." She sobs, a tear sliding down her cheek. "I can't hold it."

I lick the drop of bliss. "I have faith in you, *ma reine.* Don't let me down."

Her teeth clamp down on my shoulder, more tears spilling from her eyes as she willingly withholds her own pleasure. Never have I pushed anyone this far, but never has anyone been this strong. I am worshipping a deity of another world, and as much as I'm telling her to pray to me, it's entirely the other way around.

"Brontë!" Her entire body shudders as she defies nature to heed my command. "It *hurts.*"

"I'll give you something that hurts." I bite her neck, savoring her gasp. "I don't hear you praying, *Petit Diable.*"

"G-God, let me see heaven."

"Wrong direction."

"Fuck you. Take me to hell." Her blade digs into my neck in warning as her desperation bleeds to wrath. "I want to see every circle on the way down. There, happy?"

"Not quite." I grin as she seethes. "Say my name, Poppy. Say my name, and you can come."

"Brontë! B-Brontë, *Brontë—*"

I steal her lips, tasting her honeyed music straight from her tongue. Her greedy little cunt suckles on my gun. My cock swells, priming to burst. I let out a rabid growl that doesn't even sound human.

"Inside me." Poppy blindly fumbles with my belt and sets me free. "*S'il te plaît, mon ange.* Fill me."

I have less than five seconds to decide my next move. My ravenous gaze bounces from her pussy to her mouth and lands on the bat plug.

Fuck it.

I toss the gun aside, turn her around, pull the bulb, and spread her cheeks, sinking my dick in. Her tight hole devours every inch of my thickening length slickened with precum. Ribbed heat surrounds me on all sides, blindingly tight. I push to the hilt, murmuring praises against her neck as she chokes out Japanese curses.

I rut into her once, twice, thrice. I yank her hair aside and bite her throat. She groans in pure rapture. Her release chases my own, and my cock pulses inside her as stars streak across my vision. I growl into her hair, cupping her pussy and feeding her clit with the pad of my thumb. She moans in tandem with me, our bodies rolling as one, wringing every last drop of pleasure.

Time suspends as the aftershocks rearrange every atom in my body. I ensnare her mouth and kiss her back down to earth. A satiated sigh slips through her lips as she goes boneless in my grip.

"That was...I...holy *fuck.*"

"That was the complete opposite of holy, *Petit Diable.*"

"Good thing we're in a satanic crypt."

I chuckle, dusting a kiss over her drunken smile as I pull out and twist the plug back in. Pearlescent liquid slips past the toy, trailing down the backs of her thighs. I finger my spend, smear it over her weeping slit, grinning as she groans. I force myself to withdraw and buckle my belt, then secure her waistband back into place.

I can't be greedy, not with her.

Poppy remains where she is, her palms on the sarcophagus, her chin skyward, and her eyes closed as she rests her head against my shoulder. I've never seen her this...relaxed. How long has it been since she felt so at ease?

Unwilling to disrupt her moment of peace, I kiss her temple before reassembling my gun atop St. Aurelius's resting place. It's laughably lavish for a sarcophagus designed to hold what I assume is the ashes of the man who was supposedly burned to death: dark bloodstone hewn into the shape of a slumbering angel, his wings broken, his hands folded over an inverted cross cut from a massive ruby in the center of his chest.

I was never devout, but the design seems odd.

Eyeing the deep viridian stone streaked with sinister red, I dig through decades of memory to find Mama as she taught me and my siblings everything she knew about her studies. "Bloodstone, the martyr's stone. Supposedly formed by the blood of Christ mixing with jasper during crucifixion. Believed to protect the beholder against malignant forces." I step closer and skim my fingers over the dusty inverted cross. "Ruby, also a crest of protection. Now why would a dead man need so much security in the afterlife, hm?"

Poppy shrugs, bemused. "Fear of the very thing he worshipped?"

"Fear of his secrets being found."

I press the cross down. It clicks into its own little coffin. Metal audibly grinds from beneath, breaking the seal of the sarcophagus with a sudden hiss of air that startles Jezebel awake. Then it *opens.*

Poppy leaps back, her mini Glock poised to shoot. I snicker and grab a nearby torch. "What are you going to do? Kill him again?"

"*Hai.* If I must."

I sigh, waving away the cloud of dust as I squint into the dark. Slowly, the dirt dissipates.

Poppy's nose wrinkles. "Are those...stairs?"

"Would appear so." I approach the descending steps leading down into a black abyss. "Think it's the stairway to hell?"

"Only one way to find out. Your lead, *mon ange.*"

LEGACY

POPPY

Torch in hand, Brontë wordlessly leads us down the stairs hidden in St. Aurelius's empty sarcophagus. Jezebel follows at my side, her snout never leaving the ground.

"No footprints." My whisper is swallowed whole by the deafening silence. "No one has been here recently."

"Stay on guard, and keep your sights ahead," Brontë murmurs, his gun trained on the shadows below. "Wherever this leads, I don't think anyone was meant to find it."

Down and down into the dark, we venture. All I can hear is the rhythmic crunch of frosty stone beneath our feet and the unsteady breaths leaving our lips. The faint scent of rot sours the air as we pass skulls stacked in the earthen walls, their empty sockets crawling with plump rodents and insects with too many legs.

My calves are cramping by the time we finally step onto flat stone. Brontë's torch pulses weakly as we slowly cross into an enclosed chamber of skulls in the walls and more tombs. Carved in the middle of the floor is a perfectly symmetrical pentagram.

My nose scrunches. "The fuck is this place?"

"It's a necropolis." Brontë lifts the torch high enough for us to see the hundreds of empty sockets staring down at us. "A city of bones."

Shivers shake me from top to bottom. "Fucking creepy."

"The Morgensterns don't have anything like this?"

"We don't bury our dead. We burn them and scatter the ashes."

"For once, that sounds relatively normal."

I scoff, backhanding his bicep. "For the thousandth time, we're not a cult."

"Keep telling yourself that." He grins and nudges my scowl with a knuckle. "There she is."

My cheeks warm, his touch flinging my thoughts back to what we did upstairs. I want to do it again and so much more. But not here, not now.

"Come on." I grab an unlit torch from a nearby sconce and light it with his. "Let's see what the saint was so scared someone would find."

We comb through the chamber, examining every sarcophagus layered in dust for any more hidden doors. Finding none, we stow our weapons and wander the crypt. Jezebel slinks for the stairs, guarding our backs.

"Interesting," Brontë utters, his perplexed tone luring me over to where he's chiseling frost from a plaque above a sealed casket. "This isn't an Aurelius."

I raise my torch, reading aloud, "Leon Redd." My lips purse in response to the familiar name. "He was one of Felix's students that was hanged around his pyre."

"Why would he be buried here?"

"Hm." I approach the next casket, cleaning the plaque. "Cheryl Nurse." The next. "Harper Bishop." Chillingly, there's no casket or plaque for my ancestor, Octavia Morgenstern. "These are all names of Felix's students that Emi said were mistaken for satanic witches. What if they weren't just his students? What if they were actually members of his cult? His cult that was mistaken for a coven?"

"Wouldn't that make them Leviathan's founding families?"

"*Hai*, that's what I'm thinking."

Brontë fans out, naming more than what Emi could decipher from the scanned ledger she'd found earlier. Most are archaic surnames that died with them. "Katerina Volkova. As in...?"

"The Volkovs." I nod. "Explains why the invitation coordinates led here, to show Nik hard evidence that he's a Leviathan legacy. A member by birthright."

He roams farther down and then halts as if injected with cement. "*Putain.*"

Slowly, I join his side and follow his stare to the plaque that reads:

BASTIAN BONAPARTE

Ice chills my veins as I recall Brontë's discovery of a Bonaparte who'd been caught in the crossfire between my family and the Volkovs. But Leviathan isn't destroying my empire because of a casualty that happened decades ago.

They're out for blood—because I killed a legacy.

"I don't understand," I admit. "Sebastian wasn't branded. He wasn't a member."

"Perhaps not. Though, he could've been proving his worth by showing Leviathan what he could do and how long he could get away with it. Earning his way into their ranks."

Acidic guilt corrodes my stomach as realization dawns. "So, this is why Leviathan is destroying my life and my future. The ruination of my empire, the deaths of Jett and Fiona and countless others...it's all *my* fault."

"Don't bear that mantle, *Petit Diable.*" Brontë reaches for my hand, his fingers twining with mine. "You didn't know."

Beneath his words, all I hear is: *Your fault.*

My gaze floats up to the demon on his neck. Its wicked stare traps me.

"Your fault," it croons, licking its teeth like knives.

Unnatural cold numbs my limbs. Shadows crouch at the edges of my vision. A heavy fatigue settles into my bones. It feels like the moment before death sweeps in for its final kiss.

Feline yowls fade in and out. All I see is that firelit demon and its jaws opening wide, wide as a dragon's—

"Poppy," growls an urgent voice. "*Reviens vers moi, ma reine.*"

A hand cups my cheek and tilts my chin up to twin hazel firestorms within an angel's face. He repeats his plea, leaning his brow against mine like I can absorb the phrase entirely spoken in...French?

I blink once, twice. "Brontë?"

"*Merci les anges,*" he breathes, leaning back as Jezebel nudges my leg lovingly. "What the hell was that?"

"What do you mean?"

"You don't remember?" I shake my head, and he thumbs tears from my lashes that I don't recall shedding. "You kept saying 'your fault' like a broken record."

I gulp, trying not to let this scare the shit out of me, too. If anything, though, this is my chance to tell him how debilitating my stress really is. "I have a confession." He waits for me to continue, ever patient. "Since I was little, I've struggled with anxiety. I never told my parents, though I'm sure they saw it plenty before I moved out. When I met Bax, he suggested the vape. His batches for me are already at maximum strength, but ever since this Leviathan shit started, I've been having panic attacks. Bad ones. Worse than I even thought possible."

Brontë nods as if this is of no surprise to him. "There have been a few instances where I noticed something was off. But you never said anything, so I figured you had it handled."

"Well"—I laugh bitterly—"I don't."

"What happens when they come on? What do you feel, think, and see?"

"It's hard to explain. Sometimes, I don't remember. Other times, I do. Like the time we were going back to Beelzebub's after dealing with Kai. I was numb. I didn't have any thoughts. My tattoo was *talking* to me." I drag both palms down my face. "Fuck, you probably think I'm insane."

"No, I don't think that at all. In fact, your episodes sound like mine: mental displacement, repetitious speech, hallucinations."

"You get panic attacks, too?"

"*Oui.* For the most part, I have mine under control. It took years of learning my triggers and honing my coping mechanisms to tame them. They still happen, though, like the night you gave me this." He skims a thumb over his scarred cheek and offers a small smile. "You're not alone, Poppy."

Relief soothes the worst of my fear. But the problem remains that these attacks are only getting worse the deeper into this mystery we delve.

"As comforting as that is, I don't need yet another sword hanging over my head."

"I know someone who specializes in our type of stress, if you'd be willing to see her."

Hope blooms in my chest, beating back the gloom. "Who?"

"My half-sister, Virgil. She's a therapist for people like us. She practices with discretion. You can trust her."

I don't hesitate. "How soon can I see her?"

TOLL

BRONTË

"What's the verdict, V?" I ask my half-sister as she refills a pot of black for our debrief of her evaluation with Poppy.

"You already know my answer, B." Virgil swings a melancholy smile over the shoulder of her black lace pantsuit. Her sepia cheeks plump beneath her hazel eyes crowded by her long mane of ivory waves. "Doctor-patient confidentiality. My lips are sealed."

It takes Herculean restraint to not roll my eyes at the bullshit non-answer.

After dropping Poppy off at Virgil's home on Essex Street this morning, I tended to a few errands, then wasted the rest of the afternoon driving around the city. I couldn't sit still, not while Poppy was being evaluated by the only person I trust.

When we settled in Salem, Virgil pursued her PhD in psychotherapy and opened her own private practice to help people caught in the underworld's clutches. People like Poppy, who is supposedly unwinding from the session in V's enclosed greenhouse attached to the small cottage. Which I can't see from this oversized leather armchair in the living room on the opposite end of the fucking house.

"Keep your impatient ass seated, B." V wears a steely lour as she walks a steaming cauldron mug over to me, jabbing in my face an accusatory finger topped with a black nail that looks more like a claw. "Let her come out on her own."

I sink back down with a hissing sigh. "She doesn't even know I'm here."

"Trust me, she knows. In fact, I'm betting you woke up Deaf Delilah next door from her afternoon nap with how hard you pushed that V-eight up the street."

"There was snow on the road."

"And your first instinct was to drive like a maniac?"

"Has to get plowed somehow."

"Plowed." She snickers, drifting to the kitchen sink and refilling a spray bottle. "You're lucky *you* didn't get plowed."

I'm too on edge to attempt a witty riposte as she tends to her Venus flytraps, black bat flowers, cobra lilies, and all the rest of her carnivorous and poisonous plants nestled in handknit nets from the rafters.

Virgil's home is a historical cottage having once belonged to a supposed witch during Salem's infamous trials. Leather and velvet furniture fill the space. Doctoral plaques and several framed awards hang proudly on the cherrywood walls. Crochet projects are nestled in the standing bookshelves stuffed full with religious texts not unlike those Mama once possessed. Crystals and Tarot decks contrast the old tomes with pops of color. All wearing gold silhouettes from the dim candlelight warming the dull January dusk.

Setting my mug onto the stout coffee table beside me, I rub my brow as candles burn the saccharine scent of warm apple pie up my nostrils. "What *can* you tell me about Poppy, V?"

"Why don't you ask what you really want to ask, B?"

My molars grind. "Will she get better?"

"If she prioritizes herself, possibly." Virgil trades her bottle for a mug and leans against the dining table. "If she doesn't, not a chance in hell."

Fear freezes my veins shut. The thought of that beautiful little devil being tortured by anxiety for the rest of her life...

"How can I help her?"

Virgil sips her coffee, steam curling in her hazel eyes. "You are already doing everything humanly possible. A bit of advice, if you're willing to listen?"

"*Oui.*" I nod, my neck stiff.

"If her hallucinations grow any worse, or she becomes combative during her states of delusion, be prepared for what must be done."

The memory of a gunshot ricochets in my mind. I run a hand through my hair. "I..."

Words escape me when I catch movement in my periphery. I know without looking it's *her*.

Poppy peers into the living room from the kitchen, baby blues brighter than any flame flickering around us. A few days have passed since that night in the graveyard, our time spent resting as we both waited impatiently for this visit. Sleepless bruises blotch beneath her lashes. Her fringe is freshly trimmed, half her pastel pink strands loosely knotted atop her head.

Even exhausted, she's as beautiful as a new dawn.

Virgil gives her an encouraging nod.

And then she's moving.

The moment Poppy reaches me, she beams brighter than any sun. "Good news: no padded rooms anytime soon." She grabs my wrist and hauls me toward the front door, chirping, "*Au revoir,* Dr. V!"

Virgil's chortles echo behind us. When I look back, though, her smile is wan and sallow. As if an unseen force is taking its toll. I recognize what I'm seeing a moment before she closes the door.

Fear. Fear for me as I walk a ruinous path that can so easily lead to my own doom.

"Where to, *Petit Diable?*" I ask Poppy as we settle into the 'Vette and pull out onto the street. "My place or yours?"

"For what, *mon ange?* Are you trying to get into my pants again?"

"I'm not *trying* anything, Poppy. If I wanted to fuck you right now, I'd be doing it."

I don't intend to sound harsh. As much as I'd like to continue what we started in that crypt, there are more pressing matters than sex. We have yet to move the needle on Leviathan since discovering the catalyst to their war with her family. We need to figure out a plan before there are any attempts on my life or my brother's. Or worse, *hers.* I'm surprised they haven't tried anything in the weeks that have come and gone since Quinn's little gift.

Poppy falls silent, her expression unreadable. Her palm slides over my hand on the shifter, her fingers squeezing mine. "I missed you."

For a moment, I imagine myself bathing with that fucking toaster.

"I am the one who missed you." I lift her knuckles, kissing each knob of bone. "Forgive me. There's a lot on my mind, and I know there's as much on yours. We need to talk."

"We do." She sighs, rolling her lips as she squints out the window at the passing city lights. "I've been thinking about what we found in St. Aurelius's tomb. I told my parents about Sebastian, not that it changed anything. Papa knows as much about Leviathan as us. I truthfully have no idea where to go from here."

"What about Quinn?"

"You already know my stance on that subject."

"*Oui.* But we've surpassed the point of pussyfooting around Leviathan. She's a loose thread, and we need to pull it."

"Your pal Scull already did all he could: tailed her, rummaged through the campus library, combed her house from top to bottom. Short of kidnapping Quinn and tying her up for questioning—which will only end badly—she's not worth pursuing. Unless you truly wish to harm or possibly kill your own friend...?"

There's a pang deep in my chest as I imagine putting a bullet in Quinn's brain. "She's not my friend anymore."

"Easier said." Her fingers pulse mine. "Trust me on this, Brontë. Something about her being a member of Leviathan doesn't feel right."

"What do you mean? You saw the same video I did. We caught her red-handed."

"You said she was raised by a cop and does most things by the book unless otherwise requested by a close friend like you. Why would she be willingly involved with a cult whose ideals are the very opposite of hers?"

I shake my head, not entirely following. "What are you saying, Poppy?"

"I'm saying you know what it's like to be forced by Leviathan into doing things you wouldn't normally do. What if she's living the same nightmare you and your siblings were in Sleepy Hollow?"

I never considered the possibility, but there's no evidence to support her claim. "Quinn isn't in captivity like we were."

"No, but blackmail is a powerful weapon to wield and achieve the same results. What Sebastian did to his students is proof of that."

The raging beast inside me doesn't want to hear it, but she could be right.

"I'll try talking to her." Noting her frown, I add, "Calmly and at work, where nothing can happen."

"Fine, but promise me you'll be careful."

"Where's the fun in that?"

Poppy snickers, nibbling on her bottom lip. "There's someone else I want to chat with after seeing his ancestor in the crypt."

"Mm. Does this *someone* happen to be a Russian merc who's lucky to be alive and not sitting beside his cousins on a lonely housewife's shelf?"

"I know you don't like him, but he deserves to know about Katerina."

"You aren't concerned that shedding light on his legacy status will turn him against you?"

"If it does, then"—an audible swallow—"I guess I'll have to kill him."

The prospect sounds as enjoyable to her as killing Quinn sounds to me.

"Or," I counter in a lighthearted drawl, "you can watch as I tear off his balls and shove them down his throat."

Poppy snorts, jutting her chin at the traffic light ahead as she sends several texts. "Take a right. We're going to Indigo first."

"And after?"

"Are you working tonight?"

"No."

"Is Quinn?"

"No."

"Then we can go back to your place." She releases my hand in favor of my thigh, grinning when my dick jerks to attention. "That is, if you think we've talked enough…?"

This fucking woman. Her hunger for me is only driving me feral for her.

At the red light, I pull the e-brake and snare her by the nape, swallowing her surprised gasp with a long, deep kiss that leaves her moaning into my mouth. "*Oui, ma reine.* We've talked enough. Tonight, you're screaming my name when you're not choking on my cock."

Poppy giggles, the sound filling my world with music. "Deal, *mon roi.*"

HARMLESS

POPPY

As Brontë and I climb from his car and cross Indigo's parking lot, I wave at Circe, Cas, and Bax. They're practically bouncing on the balls of their feet by the entrance, the three of them having agreed to keep Brontë company inside the bar while I rendezvous with Nik.

None of them know the coroner I've been spending my time with, and they're more than excited to meet him for themselves. Circe is brimming with spritely curiosity while Cas and Bax look like they're ready to get the new guy hammered to spew his secrets like a frat boy during rush.

"Go on," I insist as Brontë pauses, lingering by my side instead of parting from it. His murderous glare doesn't leave the mercenary lingering in the shadows outside the blue neon glow of the bar's stylish sign, watching us with the same uncertain hesitancy we're watching him. "Enjoy some drinks with the crew while I take care of this."

Brontë's cheeks hollow as he drags deeply on his cigar. "I don't trust him."

"Do you trust *me?*"

"That's not a fair argument, and you know it."

Stretching to the tips of my boots, I kiss the edge of his frown. Instantly, his arms are around me. He holds me so close, I can feel his heart trying to beat from his chest to mine.

"I'm a big girl, *mon ange.* I don't need a bodyguard."

"I know you're entirely capable of taking care of yourself, *Petit Diable,* but your track record with every Volkov so far has been less than ideal."

"He won't hurt me."

"He could."

"Let's not forget you were once planning to turn me into a book. Yet here I am, in your overprotective embrace."

"I'm not overprotective. I'm just protective enough."

"Says the man crushing me with a hug."

He nips the arch of my ear. "I'm exerting dominance."

I snort then bite the sensitive spot beneath the corner of his jaw. His answering growl reverberates through my bones, making my toes curl. "You can exert dominance all you want later. Do as I say, and go inside. I need to do this alone."

Brontë sighs cherry smoke through his nostrils. "If he tries anything, he's getting shot in the head. Period." He gifts me with a single harsh kiss that will definitely bruise my lips before releasing me and stalking toward the trio at the entrance.

Stifling my shivers in the absence of his heat, I close the distance between me and Nik. Trying to focus on the chill of the night and the muted bass pounding from inside the bar to keep my thoughts from straying to the hundreds of possibilities this meeting could end badly.

"Your guard dog isn't pleased with being dismissed," Nik remarks, smug as Brontë casts a final warning glare over his shoulder before disappearing inside with Circe, Cas, and Bax. "Does he lack faith in your abilities?"

"Do you?" His imperious smirk fades. "That's what I thought."

"What sparked the need for a private chat, *printsessa?*"

Keeping my hands close to my knife and gun, I tell him of St. Aurelius's Cemetery and his family's connections with Leviathan's founding father. He listens with clinical detachment, his features betraying no emotion.

When I'm done, Nik turns his gaze to the night sky and asks, "Why are you telling me this?"

"I thought you'd want to know."

"Bullshit."

"Pardon?"

"This is a test. You wanted to see if I'd switch sides based on learning I'm a Leviathan legacy."

"That's not true."

"It's at least partially true." His gunmetal eyes drift back down from the stars and drop to my hand anchored to my hip an inch above my gun. "You think I'd turn my back on you from a single sliver of archaic history as if it means more than you ever did?"

A pregnant silence passes as my brain struggles to catch up. "I..."

"This endless mistrust continuously stems from the biggest mistake of my fucking life." Nik drags an agitated hand over the jagged scar stretching like a lightning bolt from the back of his scalp to his left eyebrow. "What I did to you was wrong, Poppy, and I know that. I did it because we never would've worked. You're a Morgenstern; I'm a Volkov. I'd been acting on instinct and made a split second decision that will haunt me forever."

I stare at him, dumbfounded. "I don't understand. What is this? A confession?"

"It's the explanation I never gave you. I'm giving it to you now in the hopes you stop fucking insulting me by questioning my loyalty."

The puzzle pieces finally begin snapping into place. "You did what you did to me because you *wanted* me to hate you? Because of some stupid war between our families that hung over our heads our entire lives before mine beat yours? Do you hear how childish that sounds?"

"Don't get pissy. You should be thankful we weren't another shit retelling of *Romeo and Juliet*. What you have now is a far better fit."

A broken shard with his name on it still lodged in my heart dives deeper. Before I realize I'm moving, my blade is at his throat.

"This isn't an explanation," I spit, unbidden tears blurring my vision. "This is a pathetic excuse for a pathetic man who's running from his demons rather than facing them. Face me, Nik. Hear me now and hear me true: You didn't just hurt me when you locked me in the dark. You *shattered* me."

There, a flicker of anguish. "I know."

"No, you don't. You don't understand that I *loved* you, Nikolai Ivanovich Volkov. I loved you with everything I had to give, and you tossed me into a fucking closet like I was nothing but a broken toy you didn't want anymore."

I never told him I loved him. But I did.

Though, I've stopped counting the time that's passed since the moment I met a certain coroner who cauterized that old wound shut.

Shame drags Nik's chin down. "I know, *printsessa*. I'm sorry."

It's the first time he's ever apologized for what he did.

I flatten my blade beneath his jaw, forcing his somber stare to mine. "I forgive you, Nik. But next time someone offers their heart on a gilded platter, let yourself be loved. No matter who they are. You deserve it as much as the rest of us." He nods, and I withdraw my blade. "You have my apology for doubting your devotion to me and mine. Get inside, get wasted, and make bad decisions. That's an order."

Nik chuckles, slow and slightly sadistic, but it's benign. Harmless. As he's been to me all this time. To think I almost killed him out of pure rage when I gave him that scar.

Guilt, heavy and destructive, crashes through my cranium as he walks away. Deafening white noise rises like a wave, numbing my senses. My vision darkens. My limbs lock. I sag against the building.

Then I see a demonic mask before my knife rips from my fist and spears into my stomach.

ABYSS
POPPY

By the time I register I'm on the ground, my gun is in my grip as I absorb what I'm seeing.

A woman with blood—*my* blood—on her gloved hands staggers backward. She's in strange robes, almost like a nun's but tighter, her hood pulled up. Her Leviathan mask hides her features, but I don't give a fuck who she is as I train my gun on her head with a violently shaking hand.

POP!

The shot echoes through the night, missing her forehead by *inches.* It grazes her hood instead, carving a bloody line through her ear. She yelps and bolts, fleeing down the street, her silhouette outlined in the blinding headlights of oncoming traffic.

I fire three more shots. *Pop, pop, pop,* they sing.

She zigzags, avoiding them all.

Snarling, I surge up and fall back down, screaming as my own blade twists into my guts. My vision blackens before bursting bright white again as agony rages from my belly and bellows out my throat.

Time crawls, the pain numbing. I can't feel my fingers. My lashes flutter as my eyes roll. The black blur lining my peripherals grows. It reaches for me with spindly, starless talons. Promising a touch as arctic as eternal winter only until I reach the dark abyss.

As I stare at death coming for me with a smile on its horrific face, all I can think is, *Which circle of hell will I spend eternity in?*

Shouts. I barely hear them over the ringing in my ears and the roaring in my blood. Fear closes my throat, choking me. All I can see is a single dark figure rushing toward me. Broad hands palm each side of my jaw, their warmth chasing the cold.

"Don't you dare, *Petit Diable*," Brontë growls. "No one gets to kill you but me."

My snort comes out as a cough tasting of copper. "D-don't threaten me with a g-good time."

Several people hover behind him—my friends. Bax, pacing and nearly ripping out his golden surfer curls. Cas, on the phone as his obsidian eyes flit fearfully to me. Nik, holding Circe back as she keeps reaching for me.

Brontë tears my jacket and prods the bloody skin surrounding the blade jutting from my abdomen.

"What are y-you doing?" I rasp.

"Assessing." He barely touches the knife, and I let out a shriek as pain bolts through me like lightning. "That's staying in."

"Is it b-bad?"

"No." His voice shakes. He's fucking terrified. "You'll need stitches. Come on, let's get you up."

He bends my legs over his arm, folding my middle around the blade, and my answering scream nearly blacks me out.

"Shh," he whispers in my ear. "You're going to make my migraine worse than it already is."

"F-fuck you very much."

"That's going to have to wait, I'm afraid."

Brontë lifts me with him as he stands to his full, dizzying height. My head lolls, and I glimpse the pool of blood splattered across the pavement like a grisly child's painting.

"By the f-fucking stars."

"Don't look." He gently coaxes my head against his shoulder, shielding me from the sickening view. "It's just a scratch."

My eyelids lift slower with my next blink. Exhaustion settles into my bones like a warm blanket in the dead of winter.

"Poppy, don't…"

Brontë's voice fades out and tumbles back in as I'm jostled in the passenger seat of his car. He grinds gears, hissing curses as we soar through red lights.

"*Mon roi?*"

He glances at me, panic blackening his wildfire eyes. "Stay awake for me, *ma reine.*"

I try, but sleep wraps me in its cocoon and drags me down into the endless dark where I hear him murmur, "*Je vais te ramener à la maison, Petit Diable.* Always…"

MOZART

BRONTË

Poppy's childhood bedroom is a graveyard of dead dreams.

The musk of old parchment and incense smoke lingers in the air. Ebony wood bookshelves crammed with old romance books and knick-knacks similar to those at Beelzebub's decorate each wall. Tinted windows shield an unparalleled view of the moonlit Atlantic. Feathered quills and leather bound notebooks rest on a desk beside the crackling hearth across the room, untouched.

I wonder if that's what she wanted to be when she grew up: a writer. I can picture her so clearly, wrapped in a blanket and drinking coffee by candlelight while escaping her shadow life in the middle of the night.

"How is she?" Dantë asks as he enters the room, patting Jezebel lying at the foot of the bed and handing me a mug breathing steam.

"The same," Virgil answers from the chair to my right, still nursing her tea.

Emi's tired gaze lifts to my brother as he lowers into the wingback chair beside hers and passes her a fresh mug. "But at least she's not..."

Dead. She doesn't say it.

She doesn't need to.

We all know it's still a possibility for the woman fighting for her life between us.

I sip the bitter black brew, squeezing Poppy's limp hand. With sore eyes, I watch her chest rise and fall in stable, rhythmic breaths.

The gauze on her lower abdomen audibly crinkles in the quiet space beneath the metronomic chirping of medical monitors.

For days, her heartbeat has lulled me asleep and lured me awake. Nightmares feast on my fear, torturing me with the sound of gunfire and Poppy's screams. Of being utterly powerless as she fades away.

I miss her so deeply that the roots of my heart ache with every broken beat.

There isn't much I remember beyond operating, stitching her up, and bringing her to the only safe place I knew. Vaguely, I recall debriefing Alexander and Rin on what happened. Emi brought Jezebel over before showing us the feed from the street cams outside Indigo.

All of it was completely scrubbed.

Since then, I've been sitting here, at Poppy's bedside. Hearing people come and go. Not quite registering their presence. Pumping my veins with caffeine, humming my childhood lullabies to her when no one else is around. Praying.

I don't believe in a single higher power, but rather what Mama told me and my siblings when we were young and afraid as she laid on what would become her deathbed.

"*The angels watch over us all, mes petits chérubins,*" Mama said as we clung to her, desperate to keep her from leaving us forever. "*Whether you believe in them or not, they will always believe in you.*"

"*Petit Diable,*" I whisper. "*Reviens vers moi.*"

Poppy remains as unresponsive as marble.

It doesn't matter how many times I say it, my plea falls on the flat surface of a frozen ocean. I can't reach her from my side of this glacial wall. I keep banging my fist against it anyway. I made her a promise, and I'll fight any god or devil to keep it.

Emi's sudden sob cracks the silence. Tears that only stopped an hour ago pick back up again.

"Remiel," Dantë murmurs, reaching for her. "Come here—"

"I-I need some air."

Emi surges to her feet and bolts. Her footsteps clamor down the hall, fading into the manor's silent heart. My brother remains stuck halfway out of his seat, trying to decide if he should risk making her feel worse by staying behind rather than offering comfort, or risk crowding her space when she clearly wants to be alone.

Damned if he does, damned if he doesn't.

"Give her a chance to breathe," Virgil advises quietly. "If she's not back in ten minutes, go find her."

Dantë plops back down with a heavy sigh, yanking his hood up. Fatigue smears purplish bruises beneath his lashline. He's been sitting here nearly as much as me. Feeding me caffeine. Caring for Jezebel. Working with Emi and Virgil to keep everyone updated on Poppy's status.

There was no more hiding from him when I arrived home with the princess of Salem's underworld bleeding out in my arms, barking at him to help me save her life. After stabilizing Poppy and bringing her here, I told him everything from the day I continued to look into Margot without him to the attack on Poppy at Indigo.

Not once has he snapped. I owe him so much more than I can ever give him.

"*Merci*," I say. "I wouldn't have been able to do this without you." I shoot a grateful glance at Virgil, who's been clearing her schedule to be here. "And you."

She rests a comforting hand on my arm, her peach lips tipping up. "Always, brother."

Dantë nods in agreement and scans Poppy, a silent pain in his carmine eyes. "We were supposed to be done with this shit when we got out."

"Seems Leviathan has roots everywhere," V utters, her gaze distanced. "If only we'd stayed long enough to know who saved us instead of running from them, too."

I nod. "Agreed."

If any of us had connections with the group who demolished Leviathan's limb in Sleepy Hollow, we'd have called in the cavalry by now.

"Maybe this is divine punishment for the shit we did." Dantë sighs, leaning back and resting his head against the chair. "To children in collars and chains. To men and women drugged out of their minds and foaming at the mouth. We did nothing to stop any of it. We *thrived* in it."

"We were young, scared, and vastly outnumbered, *Petit Fantôme,*" V says softly. "If we hadn't donned those personalities and garnered the kind of reputation we did, we would've ended up collared, chained, and foaming at the mouth, too."

A tear trails down Dantë's porcelain cheek. "Do you think Margot is still alive?"

A stilted silence weighs down on us, casting our memories in blood and shadow.

"For her sake," I murmur as Poppy's steady heartbeat keeps me grounded, its music as powerful as Mozart, "I pray not."

SECRETS

BRONTË

Poppy has not yet woken. Instead of remaining a useless heap of anxiety at her bedside, I'm covering a graveyard shift for a sick colleague.

Lightning whips the black clouds above as I pull into the lot and park beside the only other vehicle here: Quinn's old moss-green Wrangler. I haven't given her a single thought since Poppy convinced me to talk to her rather than strangle her.

Locking my car, I flash my penlight through the Jeep's windows. The leather interior is perfectly clean and devoid of any damning evidence. I stroll across the pavement at a stiff pace, swiping my badge at the entrance and weaving through the empty office space. Downstairs, I skip the morgue and head straight for the lab.

I hear them before I see them.

Sighs and moans, heady and breathless, reach my ears. I halt at the lab window and duck at the sight of two half-dressed, writhing bodies. Peering over the counter, I squint into the dark room and decipher the silhouettes.

There, bent over a table of beakers and test tubes, is Quinn. Behind her, his broad frame flexing beneath his business attire as he grips her curls and rails her with mighty strokes, is none other than Detective Shane fucking Scull.

What in the actual fuck? Is he who she's been seeing this entire time?

Having too many theories and not enough brain cells to process them all while the pair fuck like rabbits in heat, I slip back to the morgue and wait it out. A grueling hour later, their footsteps and voices grow near.

Fisting the Kimber in my jacket pocket, I step casually into the hall and act surprised when we spot each other. "Oh! *Bonjour, mes amis.* To what do I owe the...pleasure?"

Scull subtly tucks his pistol back into its holster as Quinn plants a hand on her chest, gasping, "You scared the shit out of us."

I scan the floor. "No, I didn't."

Quinn huffs a nervous laugh as Scull crosses his arms. "What are you doing here, Bourbon?"

"Working. What are *you* doing here, *mon ami?*"

"Working."

"Mm. So late?"

"Sin never sleeps."

I stifle my urge to snort. "Touché."

A moment creeps by as Quinn's freckled face reddens by the millisecond.

"Well, this has been sufficiently awkward," Scull remarks, glancing at Quinn. "Appreciate your help with that case, Wildes. I'll be on my way."

I'm insulted by how dumb he thinks I am. "In what cruiser?"

Quinn's mouth tightens as Scull utters a curse and drags a hand down his face. "What do you want, Bourbon?"

"What do *I* want?"

Scull's jaw flexes. "To keep this to yourself."

"This, as in your secret relationship that will surely get you both fired for conflict of interest?"

"Don't play games with me. I think you already know you won't win."

My eyes narrow, my temper rising. "Does your girlfriend know who you really work for?"

"I don't know what you're—"

"I do." Quinn clears her throat, her big blue eyes flitting between me and the man old enough to be her father. "Let me talk to him, Shane. Pick me up in the morning?"

Scull nods without another word, shouldering me roughly as he passes. *Fucking alpha complex.*

"Brontë?" Quinn notes my wary frown, wringing her wrists. "Let's grab a bite while we catch up. My treat."

⸺◈⸺

Sitting at my desk under the morgue's dim lights, I pick at the pizza Quinn called in for delivery.

Waiting.

Quinn nibbles on her crust, apprehension written all over her face. I offer nothing but a cold mask of indifference with a heavy hint of disgust.

"Back in May," she begins, a nervous hitch in her voice, "do you remember when you found a strand of Poppy's hair and gave it to me for testing?"

"*Oui,*" I grind out, failing to conceal my irritation at her passive confession that she knew, even then, who I'd been chasing. It makes sense; as Scull's lover, she would've known anything about the Morgensterns he decided to share. Which, apparently, was everything. "I remember."

From her tote on the floor, she pulls a familiar object crafted with raven feathers, animal bones, and blood-crusted twine. Along with it, a card not unlike Nikolai's invitation, creased as if she spent countless hours folding and unfolding it. She slides it across the desk. Instead of coordinates, it's printed text—a letter.

"It basically says that I'm an accomplice for not only assisting you in your illegal pursuit of a known vigilante but also acquiescing to your request in prioritizing evidence without official authorization from law enforcement. They threatened to turn me in if I didn't deliver the second poppet that came with mine to you. I took this to Shane and explained the situation. He told me to do as I was instructed."

I skim the text, all of which matches her testimony.

Interesting. No note was left behind with Margot's poppet, nor was there any correspondence attached to mine. What Quinn is claiming doesn't fit Leviathan's pattern.

It doesn't mean she's lying. It means Leviathan knows how to remain unpredictable.

Poppy was right: Quinn was being blackmailed.

There's still one major problem, though.

"You kept this from me, Quinn. I thought we were friends."

"We *are* friends, Brontë."

"Friends don't keep secrets like this."

She scoffs and jabs an accusatory finger at my glare. "You have no right to judge me. Imagine my surprise when Shane told me that you weren't only working with Poppy, but that you're *with* her. That the vigilante you'd been so hellbent on bringing to justice is now your—what? Lover?"

"How often do I see you?" I parry, unwilling to let her turn this on me. "How many times could you have told me about any of this? You're so self-absorbed, you can't even see how much of a hypocrite you're being, or how much you're hurting me right now."

Tears crystallize her long lashes. "You're hurting me, too."

The crack in her voice slices me to the bone. A heavy weight presses down on my neck. It feels like shame's thickest blade, sinking deeper than any knife ever could.

Quinn sniffles wetly. "Maybe we were never friends after all."

"No, I suppose not."

Quinn says nothing as she gathers her belongings and heads for the doors. Not once does she look back. At the threshold, she pauses and tilts her head to show a quarter of her shaded profile as she debates saying what she ultimately chooses to voice.

"I'll put in a request to switch around my shifts so I'm working when you're not. Probably best we stay out of each other's way from now on."

"Couldn't agree more."

The doors shut behind her with a final, mournful note.

POWERLESS

POPPY

I inhale the faint scent of incense smoke and old books fused with snow and sea brine. Without opening my eyes, I know where I am.

Home.

Not Beelzebub's, but the place I called home for eighteen years before I put what distance I could between me and my ancestors' everlasting shadow.

Morgenstern Manor.

A barbed tongue tickles my face, and I swat it away. "I don't need a bath, Jezebel."

"*Petit Diable?*"

My eyelids snap open.

I'm in my room where I grew up, swathed in a sable yukata printed with pale pink cherry blossoms. Empty chairs surround me. The fire in the hearth is low. Jezebel purrs as she flicks her snout up to lift my chin. Clinical monitors map my pulse. An intravenous morphine drip is in my arm. A hand squeezes mine, and my gaze clashes with twin hazel firestorms.

Memories flood my system, and my heart kicks. "*Mon ange?*"

Relief strikes his beautiful features like a meteor crashing to Earth. Tears in his eyes, he kisses my palm, but it's not enough. I fist his shirt and pull him toward me, albeit weakly. He climbs onto the bed, slinging an arm over my shoulders and tucking me into his side as I sob against his chest.

I could've died.

I could've fucking *died.*

My father may have raised me to be fearless, but death never stopped being the ultimate nightmare.

Brontë wraps me in his warmth, his arms strong as steel. He dips his head to meld his cheek with mine and hums a song into my ear. It sounds like a French lullaby. I don't know how long we stay like that: me, snotting all over him; him, holding me like he'll never let go. Eventually, the maelstrom of emotion passes, leaving me drained and barely conscious as I nuzzle the hollow of his throat.

"How are you feeling, *ma reine?*"

"Like I took a knife to the gut." I smile as he lets out a hoarse chuckle. "High as the fucking moon."

"Enjoy it while it lasts."

"I intend to."

He thumbs my fringe aside and kisses my brow. "Do you remember what happened?"

I wish I didn't, but I do. "I squared things with Nik and then had a panic attack. A woman wearing a Leviathan mask came out of nowhere, grabbed my knife, and stuck me. I fired a shot. The bullet grazed her ear. I fired a few more, but nothing hit."

Brontë stiffens. "A woman? You're sure?"

"She was wearing tight robes and definitely had tits."

"Any other notable features?"

I delve into my mind, playing through the brief bursts of imagery. "Average build, though on the taller side. Ran quick and knew how to dodge gunfire. Beyond that...nothing."

He eases back against the headboard. "Not Quinn, then. She's fast, but she's small like you."

"You sound relieved."

"*Oui.* It means we've hit yet another wall, but...I spoke with her. I'll tell you more when you've had some rest."

"Haven't I rested enough?"

"You were stabbed, Poppy, and you lost a lot of blood. Your body went comatose to heal the worst of it, but you'll still need a few weeks to recover."

"Exactly what we don't have: time."

"We'll do what we can." He kisses my nose and traces his fingers over my dragon tattoo. "For now, rest is your ticket out of this bed."

Rubbing my eyes, I scan the empty room and snowy windows. "How long have I been here?"

"A while."

"How many hours?"

"Try days."

"Days?" My eyeballs bug. "I haven't pissed or shit in *days?*"

"That's what catheters and bedpans are for."

"Catheters and bed..." I wriggle beneath the blankets, and my pulse skyrockets. "Oh, *kuso*—"

"Relax, before you give yourself a heart attack." He gives me what I assume is meant to be a reassuring smile. "Rin and Emi have been bathing and changing you."

"*Changing* me?"

He winces. "Are you hungry? Thirsty?"

"I want to take my own bath," I seethe, "and I don't want anyone's *fucking* help."

Brontë chuckles, curling a knuckle beneath my chin and capturing my scowl with a tender kiss that nearly brings me to tears. "Don't ever scare me like that again, Poppy."

I kiss him, over and over.

Because I can.

And because I don't want to make any promises I can't keep.

⸺◆⸺

Time passes in a haze. My friends visit when they can, even though they shouldn't take the risk. My parents linger when they think I'm asleep, their whispers low yet no less urgent. Brontë only leaves when he must. Dantë or Dr. V watch me in his stead. Otherwise, he's at my bedside. Reading, humming, sleeping. Drinking coffee. Always, *always* holding my hand.

I yawn as Brontë settles into his seat with Jezebel stretching at his feet. "What are you reading tonight?"

"A book." He winks at my scowl. "You wouldn't like it. There's no vampires."

"That's not all I read, you know."

"There's no sex, either."

"Ugh, bor-ing."

Brontë laughs quietly, opening his book and threading his fingers through mine. "Sleep, *Petit Diable.* You'll need it for your session with V tomorrow morning."

Dr. V left it up to me to resume our therapy visits whenever I saw fit. The first day I was awake for more than an hour at a time, I made the call. I can't afford any more hazardous episodes, especially not after that last panic attack crippled me from defending myself and brought me too close to the grim reaper. The next one could literally prove to be fatal.

I yawn again, nestling into the sea of pillows. Brontë smiles softly and leans over to brush a kiss to my cheek, far too chaste for my liking. I snag his shirt before he can straighten.

"Sleep with me, *mon ange.*"

A beat of silence passes, filled by the crackling hearth and the featherlight *tap, tap, tap* of snow against the windows.

"I don't think that's such a good idea, Poppy."

"I meant *actual* sleep. The bags beneath your eyes are sagging worse than an old hag's tits."

"Has anyone ever told you that you're shit at giving compliments?"

I toss him a droll look. "I'm obviously not going to jump your bones with all these stitches keeping my insides from spilling out."

He sighs through his nose, eyeing me. "Can I trust you to keep your hands to yourself?"

"I take offense to your complete lack of confidence in my self-control."

"You *are* a heathen."

"Brontë Bourbon, I'm cold and tired and cranky. If you don't get in here, I'm going to gut you and then crawl inside your stomach to use your corpse as my bed out of pure fucking spite."

"Raziel." He plops his book aside with a half-hearted glare and unlaces his boots. "If you're going to use my name like a weapon, you may as well know the whole thing."

"Raziel." It tastes like ambrosia on my tongue. "Which angel is that?"

"The one who records divine secrets."

"That's actually very accurate. You do like to keep secrets."

He scoffs and tugs the duvet, but I yank it back.

"Strip."

He blinks. "*Excusez-moi?*"

"You heard me. Take off your clothes."

"Poppy—"

"Everything but your boxers. Go on."

Brontë curses under his breath but concedes, reaching between his shoulder blades to doff his shirt in a single fluid motion. Warm firelight and cool moonlight eagerly lick between the deep grooves and high rises of his thick arms and broad chest and rippling abs, caressing his strong jaw and lapping the scar on his right cheek in ways nothing else ever could.

I'm fucking *envious* of that light.

He grins like a cat. "Like what you see?"

Who wouldn't? "Take off the rest, you egotistical brute."

"Egotistical brute? Is that meant to be an insult?"

"Hurry the fuck up, Brontë *Raziel* Bourbon."

His laughter licks up my spine as he continues to undress.

Veins cording his long arms and big hands bulge as he grips his belt and flicks it loose. Hypnotized, I watch him unbutton his pants and unhurriedly unwind the zipper. He lets the thick fabric fall, nudging it aside with one powerful, tattooed leg. His black boxers are tight enough for me to see the outline of his cock swollen halfway to a full erection.

Fuck, he's enormous. It's not natural for any man to have the manhood of a god, is it?

Saliva pools onto my tongue, and I audibly swallow. He climbs in and lowers onto his back beside me, fingers interlocking under his head as he lets out a heady groan of relief. The mattress gasps beneath his weight, wafting his scent over to me on a cloud of bourbon and cherry smoke.

I really, *really* need Bax to replicate that aroma as vape juice.

As I slide the furs over him, my focus locks onto a broken sword inked on his left thigh. I reach across him and—

"Poppy, hands."

I scowl, pointing to the blade rather than touching it. "That's a broken sword."

"Ah, *oui.*" His tense body relaxes. "Narsil, the sword of Elendil. Before it became Andúril, the sword of Gondor."

"I thought Dantë was the nerd," I utter, lying on my side to face him. "What does it mean?"

"After Elrond had it reforged for Aragorn, it became a symbol of—"

"Clarification: What does it mean to *you?*"

A corner of his mouth lifts. "Revival. Harmony. Hope for a better world."

"That's...beautiful." Tentatively, I feather the tip of my forefinger over his scarred cheek. Despite his earlier warnings, he leans into my touch. I take his unspoken invitation to shift closer and trace the raised flesh in a soothing line. "You're more broody than usual tonight."

"Oh, lovely. More high compliments."

I poke the edge of his frown. "What's bothering you?"

"Nothing you should concern yourself with."

"If it's responsible for your rapidly growing age lines, I beg to differ."

Brontë closes his eyes, his chest expanding with a full breath. "It's Quinn. She's been on my mind lately."

My ears perk. He hasn't mentioned her since the night I woke up. "Tell me what happened."

"That's the thing: I'm still trying to make sense of it." He relays his experience of discovering Quinn's secret affair with Scull and her explanation for being involved with Leviathan before their spat ended on a sour note. "When you and I showed your parents the video of Quinn planting that poppet at my house, Scull had ample opportunity to clear the air. Instead, he played dumb and let us believe he was chasing a lead. Why waste everyone's time, including his own?"

My heart skips as the answer clicks—and suddenly, it all makes sense. "That Machiavelli son of a bitch."

Brontë peeks at me from the corners of his eyes. "Machiavelli?"

"*Hai.* The man who wrote the controversial classic about ruling with an iron fist." His expression remains blank. I huff, pointing to the bookshelf above our heads. "It's embroidered in gold. Grab it." When he does, I finger through it, explaining, "Niccolò Machiavelli wrote this entire book dedicated to sovereigns. His ideals were radical but effective: power comes to those who strive to be feared rather than loved. Only those who are willing to rise by any means necessary will succeed in their reign. Especially through deceit and ruling with an iron fist."

"And you have this because...?"

"I'm the daughter of a crime lord. Do the math." I close the book and splay a palm over the cover. "Scull is likely using Quinn as a diversion. He's manipulating her while simultaneously distracting us. It's genius, really. The more he leads us down the wrong path, the longer he has to fulfill his vendetta. I wouldn't be surprised if he set Quinn up from the start."

The revelation washes over him, shock quickly replacing the confusion. "Scull is a member of Leviathan."

"Not just a member."

"A Master?"

I nod. "It's a probable theory, but we still need proof. Do you know where he lives?"

"*Oui.*" He tosses the duvet aside and begins to rise. "He's been spending his nights with Quinn at the office. I'll be back in—"

"No." I grab his arm, my fingernails digging bloody crescents into his skin. "We're not splitting up, *mon roi*. I've told you before: we work better as a team."

"You're a little out of commission at the moment."

"I can handle myself."

"You need to heal."

"Brontë."

"Poppy."

"Stop arguing with me, and let me come with you."

"No."

My right eye twitches. "*No?*"

"Foreign concept?"

White-hot wrath arcs across my vision, and I lurch up—only to yelp in pain and flop down. Brontë utters curses and checks my wound, applying gentle pressure to the gauze on my stomach.

"You are not ready for this," he insists, his tone both soft and hard. "I'll move faster on my own."

"I'm fast enough."

"You shuffle like a penguin to and from the bathroom."

"That's because my calves hurt from not using them."

"Exactly. Your body is in a weak state."

"I'm *not* fragile, fuck you very much."

His glare turns glacial. "Is that what you believe? That I think you're fragile?"

"You just said I'm not strong enough to—"

Brontë grips me by the throat and hauls me onto his lap. I gasp, shoving the butterfly knife from my pocket under his chin. A trickle of blood slides down the rainbow blade from his stubble to my trembling fist.

A slow, knowing grin slants his mouth. "Still believe I think you're fragile, *Petit Diable?*"

My strength—or apparent lack thereof—has nothing to do with it. I don't want him going in alone. Knowing our luck, shit will find a way to go sideways. What if he gets hurt? No one will be around to doctor him back to life.

My chin wobbles as I picture him lying in a bed, unconscious for days. For the first time in my life, I feel completely and utterly powerless.

"Don't go alone."

"I work best alone." Brontë skates his palm over my heart threatening to split in half. "You *will* see me again, Poppy."

I don't argue any further, pocketing my knife and hanging my head. "At least call Emi to navigate any cams for you."

"I will." His arms wind around me, hugging me to him. "When I get back, I'll cuddle you properly."

"Promise?"

"Scout's honor."

My snigger stutters into sobs. He smooths his hands up and down my spine, humming softly. His voice is my anesthetic, and I slowly lose my grip on reality.

"*Bonne nuit.*" Brontë angles my jaw up with a knuckle and kisses me once, deliriously deep. I instantly mourn his lips when they're gone and chase him for another. Chuckling, he obliges and shifts me onto my back and tucks me under the covers. "*Ma reine.*"

"Say that again," I mumble into my pillow. "It's fucking hot."

"And you wonder why I'm an egotistical brute." His grin settles against my lips. "*Ma reine.*"

HELLFIRE

Brontë

Despite living on a detective's salary, Scull resides in a backwater apartment in Salem's slums.

The streets cloaked in night are infested with criminals. Barrel fires litter the alleyways like fleas. Drugs openly pass hands. Metal flashes at hips, guns and knives alike. Serpentine laughter slithers through the air, scaling up my spine.

Keeping my hood up and chin low, I stick to the path Emi advised me to take for the least amount of camera disruption to manage on her end. If Scull really is a member of Leviathan, these cams are likely the most monitored.

Aside from a few feral cats hissing my way, I encounter zero issues in finding the fire escape leading up to Scull's apartment. At the door, I snap on a pair of nitrile gloves, pick the lock, and soundlessly step into the lackluster space devoid of any personality. No wall portraits nor décor of any theme to show what kind of man lives here.

Fitting, for a potential cult leader.

Kimber at the ready, I make quick work of sleuthing through the living room, kitchen, bathroom, and his personal office. Finding only eerily tidied belongings and enough espresso to stock a café, I move to the bedroom.

It *reeks* of sex in here.

Stifling a gag, I scour the dresser and find an absurd amount of panties I assume are Quinn's. The nightstand is a trove of lube, toys, and XXL condoms.

And Poppy calls *me* egotistical.

Discovering nothing out of the ordinary after checking every crevice in the room, I sigh and turn to leave. Perhaps we're wrong about him.

As I head for the exit, I spy a book on a shelf above the sofa—Quinn's rebound *Carmilla*. The cat's eye embedded in the leather watches me like it can see straight through me. I swear it winks as if it knows something I don't.

Keeping my face hidden in shadow should a camera be planted in the cover, I lift it cautiously and pause at the sight of a small metal safe lodged in the wall behind it.

The design is old, with a combination dial standing between me and what's inside. A red dot beneath it blinks at me in warning. Any wrong inputs will undoubtedly alert Scull.

There's no room for error.

Scull is a lone wolf; no family, no noteworthy friends. He's vain, but he's not foolish as to use his birthday. I don't know enough about his past to guess any other personal dates. What else would a member of a satanic cult use to guard his secrets? The devil's number?

...Is it *that* easy?

There's only one way to find out.

I dial the code *6-6-6*. Sweat trickles down my temple as the red light blinks faster.

Then the light flashes green, and the lock slides loose.

Jackpot. Even if there's nothing inside, the code alone is proof enough. What lies in wait, though, isn't what I expect.

Gingerly, I seize the old and weathered tome. It's large, heavy. I flip through the thin and delicate pages, slowly recognizing the Latin script paired with sketches of runes and ritualistic instructions. It's a spellbook.

A grimoire.

A loose page slips out. Written upon it is the Morgenstern family tree. Seven siblings are noted beneath Lucian and Josephine Morgenstern, along with their spouses and children and a few grandchildren. Many I recall speaking with my first time at the manor with Poppy. Black lines slash through every name but three:

Alexander Morgenstern

Rin Morgenstern

Poppy Morgenstern

Misery perches on my shoulder as I realize what this is and what it means.

This isn't only the fall of an empire.

This is genocide.

⎯⎯⎯◆⎯⎯⎯

Poppy is asleep when I return.

Alexander isn't.

I've avoided crossing paths with him at all costs, but what I discovered tonight is too important to let lie for comfort's sake.

Stalking through the manor's library, I find Salem's underworld king where he always seems to be: in a wingback by the hearth, chasing his woes from the bottom of a bottle. He senses my presence, his grip on the wine glass visibly tensing.

"You're disrupting my peace, boy."

"That's my specialty, don't you think?"

Alexander grunts, sufficiently miffed. "To what do I owe the displeasure of this particular vexation?"

I tap into my photo gallery and tilt the screen toward him. He studies the image of Scull's Morgenstern kill list. Not an ounce of surprise shows on his face.

"Where did you find this?"

"In the apartment of a certain crooked detective currently shoving his knife deeper into your back."

I anticipate a burst of rage, perhaps his glass thrown into the fire. Certainly not his sigh of dejected defeat.

"You *knew* this was happening," I bite out, incredulous. "Your own fucking family has been hunted to near extinction, and you haven't told your own daughter?"

"Watch your tone, boy." His arctic glower flicks to me then to the chair beside him. "Sit."

The order grates my pride, but I obey.

"Rin and I have known, *hai*." Alexander focuses on the flames, his gaze glossing. "We've been discussing when to tell Poppy."

"The longer you wait, the higher chances she'll hear it from someone else."

His tongue clicks disparagingly at my unspoken threat. "Spare me. You and I are both very much aware she's in no sound state of body or mind to hear it now."

I snicker. "You're such a fucking coward."

Alexander's attention cuts to me. "Would you care to repeat that?"

"Coward." I smirk at his scowl. "Poppy can handle the news. You're afraid of how she'll look at you when she learns that you've been hiding the systematic murder of her entire family."

"Is that so? How will she look at me?"

"Like you're not the strong, capable father she thought you were."

A crack splits through the glass in his white-knuckled grasp. A familiar rage burns in his irises, so bright they almost glow in the firelight.

Très bien. I need his hellfire for what comes next.

"Tomorrow, you're going to tell Poppy, and then you're going to invite the detective over for a nice, *long* drink."

I've never seen his smile before. It's the kind his daughter wears, vicious and infernally wide. Befitting a predator locked onto his prey. His laugh is worse, the chuckle of something vile from the depths of hell.

"You've impressed me."

"Volkov set a low bar, no?"

Alexander chortles into his glass, gesturing to the wine bottle on the table between us. "Help yourself."

I shake my head, rising to my feet. "Raincheck."

He nods, and I take my leave back to Poppy's room down the hall.

The little devil is now awake, sitting against the headboard and reading my book with a scrunched nose, strangely out of breath. She looks up as I pat Jezebel's head, her frown deepening.

"How can you read this shit? There's no sex."

"I told you." I chuckle as I strip down to my boxers and climb in beside her. "Why are you up, *Petit Diable?* You're supposed to be asleep."

Her demeanor sobers as she sets the book aside. "I couldn't stop thinking about all the ways you could've been hurt."

"Mm. Which one was your favorite?"

Poppy snorts, sinking down with a wince and using my bicep as her pillow. "I'm serious, Brontë."

"As am I. Once you're healed, I intend to make all your fantasies come true. Especially the morbid ones."

"You're so"—she searches the ceiling for the right word—"twisted."

"Says the woman who rather enjoyed being worshipped in a satanic crypt."

Crimson creeps up her neck, flushing her cheeks. I kiss each one, savoring their warmth on my lips. She threads her fingers through my hair, idly playing with the strands as she seems to consider what to say next.

That's when I realize she hasn't yet asked what I found at Scull's. And I reconsider why she seemed out of breath while sitting still in bed.

"Were you eavesdropping?"

"*Hai.*" Her lashes lift, her baby blues hard as diamonds. "I was."

"You heard everything, then?"

"Everything."

"You're quite calm, given the situation."

"I was never close with my extended family. Don't, however, mistake my quietude for apathy. Many of my cousins were children, some babies." The same fire in her father blazes through her veins. "Leviathan will pay for this, starting with this Master who thinks he's a fucking god."

Pride swells in my chest. Banding an arm around her, I tug her closer. "Act surprised tomorrow."

"I will, on one condition."

"Name it."

She kisses the angel tattooed on my heart. "I get to watch you play bad cop."

I chuckle again, capturing her lips and refusing to let her go. I kiss her until she grows tired, tucking her beneath my chin as she dozes off.

Her breaths deepen, and my eyes sting. I haven't allowed myself to feel the relief of knowing she'll wake up again. Not until now, as she's in my arms, her limbs curled around me like ivy on stone.

Alive. She's alive and awake and suffered no cognitive damage after nearly dying in a pool of her own blood.

The weight of nerve-wracking days and sleepless nights spent in endless limbo smacks down like a hammer to my head. I hold her tighter as residual fear shoves its rusted blade in my guts and twists. I fist her hair to staunch the shake in my hands.

Alive. The woman I cherish is alive.

No, not just cherish. I'm not going to lie here and cower from what I feel. From what I've been feeling for so long, I don't know when the arrow struck me.

I am in love with Poppy Morgenstern.

And I will love her long after the seas have dried to deserts and this planet burns to nothing but ash and smoke.

MINE

POPPY

B lood drips in bright red strings from Scull's split lips to the library floor.

"A little more to the left, *mon ange.*"

Brontë cracks his bloody knuckles, a gleeful gleam in his eyes as his arm winds back and slams the detective's jaw with a savage right hook.

"No." I shake my head as Scull spits a red wad onto the growing puddle beneath the chair he's secured to with his own handcuffs. "My left, not yours."

Brontë mercilessly hammers his rage into Scull's face. Heat pulses between my legs, but I force myself to focus.

My *parents* are in here, for fuck's sake.

"I like him, Poppyseed." Papa wears a manic grin as he turns to Mama. "*Koibito?*"

Mama sips her wine. "Reminds me of you. Handsome, violent. What's not to like?"

I tune them out as my gaze rakes over the man being beaten to a pulp. We found his Leviathan brand easily once he drank enough drugged wine to pass out drooling. Since waking, Scull has been dodging questions, willingly subjecting himself to Brontë's unbridled fury like it's his nightly routine.

"Stop, *mon roi.*"

Brontë backs off, wiping blood splattered on his sweaty brow and giving me a curt nod. "*Ma reine.*"

"Take a break and comb through his phone." He does what I say as I return my attention to Scull. "You're one of Leviathan's nine Masters."

It's a statement, not a question. He's not going to talk.

But that doesn't mean he can't give us answers.

Scull glares, bloody drool dripping down his chin as he pants against the pain. He's a single solid blow away from a broken jaw, yet he hasn't once screamed. He's been trained to tolerate agony.

"Each Master leads a specific operational guild," I drone, picking my nails. "Their names—and those of their guilds—are unknown. However, the Volkovs were once the beating heart of Leviathan's assassin guild. You recruited them first, so I can only assume that's your bread and butter."

Scull spits blood at my boots. It's the only confirmation I need.

"Leviathan was once friends with my family. Did you know that your founder, Felix Aurelius, recruited my ancestor, Octavia? That she was a member of Leviathan, too?"

He sneers, unimpressed. "Your point?"

"You were issued the kill order because I killed a Leviathan legacy. My point: *I* am also a legacy. Should that not grant me a hearing with your council to plead my case?"

Scull scoffs, his façade slipping an inch. "You're a Morgenstern. The Crown cannot also be the Church."

"Interesting. You didn't deny the fact that you were given orders." I smirk at his agitated lour. "I was under the impression Leviathan's Masters operated as a unit, though it appears you have a ringleader calling the shots. Who is it?"

Scull bares his teeth but doesn't reply.

Brontë steps forward. I snag his arm, not letting my attention stray from Scull.

"Is it someone we know?"

Silence.

"Quinn?"

Crickets.

"I respect your tenacity, but I'm very impatient. Perhaps some incentive will help speed this up."

I nod to Papa, who downs his drink and disappears into the stacks. A moment later, he drags a chair from the shadows. Scull visibly blanches when he sees who's in it.

I wasn't sure before, but I am now; the lion truly has fallen for the lamb.

"Don't worry, Casanova," I croon, brandishing my butterfly knife and lightly skimming the blade up and down Quinn's unmoving arm. "Your Henriette is fine. She took the chloroform like a champ."

I feel Brontë tensing behind me. This is the second part he didn't agree with, the first being when I stripped Quinn down and searched for a Leviathan brand that wasn't there. Unlike him, I don't take people at their word. Aside from waking up in her lab with a headache and no memory of getting a rag shoved over her face while she'd been working on reports, though, I've promised him no harm will come to her.

"Who's dishing out orders?"

Scull's bruised and bloody mouth remains shut.

"Let me rephrase." My knife edges Quinn's pulse. "Give me a name, or the next case to go cold in this city is a tragic murder-suicide of a corrupt cop and his whore."

"Don't," he snarls, amber eyes blackening. "Don't call her that."

I grip Quinn's curls and tug her head back, exposing her jugular to my blade—

"I don't know! All right? I don't fucking know who the orders come from. We're as blind to each other as you are to us."

"That's literally impossible."

"It's not," Brontë says, handing me Scull's phone. "He's been sending and receiving encrypted texts from several different numbers."

"Burners?"

"Could be. Or fake numbers to conceal the real sender."

"We'll ping Emi. She'll know what to do."

Scull's chuckle slashes through our whispers. "Good luck with that. I already tried tracking the source. You're going to find nothing but a steel wall."

"Forgive me for not trusting a word you say." I adjust my grip on Quinn, scraping the blade over each delicate ridge of her throat. His glare tracks it the whole way down. "Next order of business: drop the hunt."

"That's not up to me."

"How is it not? You're a Master. You command an entire *guild* of Acolytes and Magi."

"They receive their own orders. I merely provide oversight to ensure proper execution."

"Who are they, then?"

"I told you: I don't know."

I dig the knife deeper, breaking the skin as Scull roars—

Brontë grabs my wrist, ignoring my glower. "You invited the Volkovs back to Leviathan. I presume you were also invited to join their ranks at some point. How does that work, exactly? How does one become a member?"

Scull licks his split lip, his unhinged stare stitched to the bead of blood slipping down Quinn's neck. "Candidates are selected at the discretion of each Master. Invitations must first be approved before sending."

"*Magnifique.*" Brontë flashes Scull's phone. "Guess I'll just send in my own application to your boss."

"You're on the hit list, too, Bourbon."

"Yet here I stand."

"Patience." Scull grins, sharp and bloody. "Your turn is coming."

Brontë grins back, twice as savage. "Tease."

"I've heard enough," I say, retracting my blade. "Mama? Papa?"

My parents share a glance and nod in unison. Papa gathers Quinn into his arms and carries her out as Mama says, "We have what we need."

I draw my Glock and train it between Scull's lion eyes. This is the man who oversaw the murders of Jett and Fiona and every single Morgenstern. The man who manipulated an innocent woman into doing his dirty work. The man who betrayed my family while sitting in our home and drinking our wine.

Brontë's hand falls on my shoulder. "Mine."

"Are you sure?"

"He could know something about Margot."

"Fair enough." I lower my gun and rise to the tips of my toes, pecking his cheek. "Make it slow."

"I intend to." He fingers my knife from my grip and flattens the blade beneath my chin, stealing my lips in a fierce, deep kiss. Then he nudges me toward Mama, who interlocks our arms as she leads me out the doors.

We're halfway down the hall when the screams begin.

LOST

BRONTË

"I need clothes, tampons, vape juice..." Poppy tugs at her overgrown roots with a pout, leaning heavily into my side as I walk her up the basement steps of my beachfront home that I've barely stepped foot in these past few weeks. "Hair dye."

I offer a grunt, mentally adding to the list of stops to take before returning to Morgenstern Manor. She wouldn't let me leave without her to check on Dantë after calling him with the news of Scull's demise and his non-existent knowledge of anything to do with Margot's disappearance. In the end, I don't know if the crooked detective spoke true. As far as I'm concerned, that motherfucker lied through his teeth up to his dying breath.

I skinned him alive and, tearing a page from Poppy's vigilante handbook, made him choke on his own branded flesh. Alexander took care of the rest, covering Scull's death with a forged note about leaving town. An easy and clean story, given his lack of family and friends to question the sudden departure.

Quinn, however, is devastated. I have yet to see her at work without tears in her eyes. *A necessary evil,* I keep telling myself as I watch her fall apart without him. I did her a favor, and she'll never know it.

Emi is digging into the numbers on Scull's phone, trying to glean the source. All we can do now is wait.

Reaching the top of the steps, I lift Poppy over the threshold to the kitchen.

And stop short.

Dantë is sitting at the island, an untouched coffee before him. His head is in his hands, the afternoon sun gilding his silhouette like a halo.

"Brother? Are you all right?"

"I miss her." He sniffles as he pulls a red box from his hoodie pocket and tosses it onto the countertop. It's as empty and hollow as a soulless heart. "I can't stop thinking about her."

Too slowly, I realize that today is Valentine's Day. The anniversary of when Margot disappeared. Brutal timing and an even crueler fate, considering where we hail from.

"Oh, *mon ami*." Poppy reaches for him, lurching forward.

And yelps as her stitches pull.

I bark a curse at the same time Dantë's bloodshot eyes widen. Poppy catches herself on the island, palms slamming down. Her victorious grin slips as the ring box flips up, somersaults in a golden ray of winter sunshine, and falls back down—straight into the mug. Coffee splatters Dantë, staining his pristine white clothes a shitty brown.

Hissing, I lift Poppy's layers, peeling the gauze and prodding the sutures. My fingers come away red.

Fucking hell.

"Dantë," Poppy breathes. "I-I'm so sorry."

His jaw twitches. Then he laughs.

It's deranged, the guffaw of a madman who's lost everything and just keeps losing. Poppy sputters and laughs with him. I sigh, wetting a rag and tending to her wound.

As I'm patching her up, she dials Emi with a sly grin on her lips.

"For the love of every angel above," I gripe, "what chaos are you stirring now, *Petit Diable?*"

"Tell me, *mon roi*. Do you start at the end of a book or the beginning?"

"That horse is beyond dead, don't you think?"

Poppy reaches back and slaps my ass with a wink. "How do your own words taste?"

This little devil.

Just as Emi picks up, I lean down to whisper in Poppy's free ear, "I'm guessing not as good as your ass tastes, *ma reine.*"

Her giggle almost makes me forget about that look on my brother's face when we first walked in. He's been wearing it for far too long.

How much more can he take before he's as lost as Margot?

INFERNO
POPPY

"I just sat through *hours* of watching you and Emi swoon over a vampire hunter setting out to slay Dracula, and you're *still* denying being a vamp girl?"

"Technically, the Belmonts hunt monsters, not just vamps."

Brontë waves me off, grumbling to himself as he boxes completed projects for orders that are slightly overdue. I wander through his cold, odorous studio. My nose slowly becomes blind to the smell as I feather my fingers over the jars above the slop sink. I tap the glass, noting the thick consistency.

"What is this?"

Brontë glances over his shoulder. "Paint for sprayed edges."

"It's slightly congealed."

"Been sitting there for a while."

I grab a jar and unscrew the lid, catching a whiff of saccharine rot—

"Don't!" He swoops over, snatching the jar and tightening the lid with a scowl. "Cats and curiosity don't mesh well, *Petit Diable.*"

My eyelids slit. "That's not paint."

"It is." He places the jar back on the shelf. "It's just...homemade."

"What's your secret ingredient? Blood?"

"*Oui,* blood."

I open my mouth and close it. "You're not kidding."

Brontë sighs a cloud of mist. "No. The blood is mixed with a few sterilizing chemicals. Now will you stop touching things and park it? I'll be done soon."

I throw my hands up in surrender and carefully perch on his workstation, idly swinging my crossed ankles. "So, where's my book?"

"Hm?"

"You know, the book I was destined to decorate with my flawless skin."

"Your skin isn't flawless, Poppy."

"Rude."

He snorts and flicks a knuckle against my tattoo. "You're tainted."

"That's not any better." Beneath my breath, I utter, "Fucking prick."

"You should be nice to me if you want your Valentine's present."

"My what?"

Brontë tips his head toward the hall leading to the tannery. "Take a look."

Eyebrows pinching, I hop down and wince when my stitches pull a little. He trails behind me like a looming shadow, seeming almost...apprehensive.

I flick on the light and proceed to stare at the festively wrapped package sporting an obnoxiously large pink bow resting atop his logbook on the workbench.

"What is it?"

Brontë leans a shoulder against the wall. "Open it."

I obey, gingerly lifting the package and ripping the festive paper. "By the fucking stars...this is a *masterpiece*."

It's my copy of *Inferno,* bound in a charcoal hide. Scales are etched into the skin with painstaking precision, painted with cosmic hues that sparkle like stars even under the dim fluorescence. A draconic skull made entirely of pearlescent bone is centered in the front face. Glass reptilian eyes, blue as glaciers, peer back at me. A single silver tear is carved down its razor-sharp cheekbone. The rest is immaculate: glittering gemstones embedded in the hide, edges sprayed with that galactic paint, a quote from within inscribed into the back cover.

"*E quindi uscimmo a riveder le stelle,*'" I recite, swallowing a knot in my throat as I gape at him. "How did you know it's my favorite?"

"There were years' worth of tear stains bleeding the ink." He shrugs, averting his gaze to the floor. "Made an educated guess."

My thumb glides over the scales. "Whose hide is this?"

"It's a patchwork. If you look closely enough, you'll see the seams. Your greatest hits since we met are in there: Sebastian, Vladimir, Malakai...and Scull. Dantë helped with the bone. That's his specialty; not mine."

I stare at the treasure he's just gifted me. He may as well have handed me his heart and told me his soul is mine, too.

A second ticks by.

Two.

Ten.

"If you don't like it—"

"*Damattero,*" I snap. "Don't say another fucking word."

His jaw wires shut.

"You escaped the darkest abyss life had to offer and found your haven here." Gently, I set the book aside and step toward him. "This city is your home and hearth, far away from your personal hell. Until I came along and tipped your life upside down. Yet you're standing here, giving me the most thoughtful gift that you *made* with your own hands."

Brontë bends his stiff neck. I flatten my palms on his chest and tip my chin up, holding his gaze captive.

"Do you want to know what I got you?" He nods, and I tut. "Use your words, *mon ange.*"

"*Oui,*" he murmurs, his lips flirting with mine. "I want to know."

Grinning, I lead him over to the stack of hide beside the chest freezer. "Sit."

Watching him obey my command is an aphrodisiac more potent than any drug.

"Good boy," I purr, fingering his top layers. "Take these off."

His jacket and shirt form a pile on the floor.

Fuck, those muscles could feed an entire army.

"Free yourself."

Brontë goes rigid. "You're hurt, Poppy. We can't; not yet."

I flick my knife open, pressing the blade to his throat. "That wasn't a request."

Hazel eyes flaring with fire, he unbuckles his belt and tugs himself loose. I salivate as beads of gleaming precum slide from his broad head and down the steeled length of his thick, swollen cock. Its curve is deliciously wicked. A weapon of pleasure.

"Fuck yourself, *mon roi.*"

Brontë leans back on his elbows and pumps himself with long, slow strokes. A feral grin curls my mouth up. He groans like a starved animal.

I remove my top. My hair slips over my peaked nipples as I sink to my knees. He takes care to adjust his feet so my joints are cushioned by his boots.

"Such a gentleman."

"Only for you."

My smile widens, nails raking his powerful thighs. "I've been wondering if you'd feel like velvet or silk on my tongue."

"Only one way to find out."

I lick my lips. "Let me taste you."

Brontë obliges, fisting himself at the root and nudging my lips. I kiss his crown then lick a single line from his knuckles to the seed leaking from his slit.

"*Fuuuuck, ma reine.*" His hips buck, his hands curling into my hair. I suckle on the tip, and his head kicks. "Mmm, your mouth is fucking divine."

I groan, taking him deeper and swallowing him down my throat. He grips me tighter, his tenderness gone. My hand delves under my waistband, fingers circling my clit. I'm lapping him up like I'm the desert and he's the rain. He's panting, gripping my nape, and pinching my nipples between his fingers.

He's close, but I don't want him to go without me.

I tap my blade against his neck, and he immediately lets me up for air. "You come when I say you can come."

"I can't just—" I bite his dick, and he growls, "I don't come until you say so."

"That's my good boy, Scythe."

He visibly freezes, and it takes me a moment too long to realize why.

Scythe. His old alias. It just slipped off my tongue as easily as his name.

"*Kuso.* Forgive me, I—"

"Say it again."

I blink. "Scythe?"

"No." He winds a strand of my hair around his finger. "Like you want me to leave my mark on you."

"Why?"

"I want to own my past, not cower from it. Not while I breathe the same air as the woman who embraces her own history and what it's forged her to be." He leans closer, murmuring against my lips, "I want to show you my darkness, as you've shown me yours."

Blinking away unshed tears, I climb atop him and straddle his lap. My legs sink onto the hide of dead criminals. I should be disgusted, but it only turns me on more. In his ear, I whisper, "Scythe."

He shivers as his arms close around me, his mouth seeking mine. Each kiss is deeper, longer, hungrier than the last. I push my waistband below my hips and grab his cock, feeding his length through my seam.

His muscles lock. "Poppy—"

"Shh, relax." Careful not to move too quickly, I roll my hips. Flames spark in my veins, and a whimper claws out of me. The feel of his flesh is fucking inebriating. "Just a taste."

Brontë groans, an innocent man before a noose. He kisses me like he's on death row and I'm his last meal. Palming my ass, he pulls me over him. My wet lips fold around his slick cock, and I swear I feel every pulsating vein.

We writhe, reduced to beasts consumed by lust. He tastes like cherry smoke and midnight sin. He feels like devilry and decadence and the darkest fantasy. He sounds like a demon uncaged.

"More," I plead, shameless. "Scythe, *more.*"

"So fucking sexy when you beg."

His teeth clamp around my neck, his hot tongue chasing my pulse.

Stars blotch my vision as pain entwines with pleasure. Euphoria torches my blood. My eyes roll as my head falls back. My pussy clenches his cock, suctioning greedily.

Galaxies burst behind my eyes.

"*Bonne fille,*" he growls around my nipple. "Such a good girl you are, coming all over me."

"Time to return the favor."

My knife scrapes his jugular, and he gasps as he explodes. I hum as he spills between us, coating my cunt in his spend. His groans are gravel, grinding my sanity to dust. I ride his throbbing length, mewling into his mouth as I come undone again.

Brontë breathes French curses against my chest as gravity drags us down from the stars. I dip my blade in our cum, catching his eye as I lick it clean.

"You taste like candy, *mon roi*."

"Candy." He chuckles, resting his brow on mine. "I'm dead and sitting in hell with Lucifer's daughter."

"Morgenstern *does* translate to Morningstar…"

A warm droplet drips from the corner of my delirious smile. He snags my chin, lapping the spill. I lick his tongue then bite his bottom lip, letting it snap back into place.

"*Fuck*," he hisses. "You're fucking lucky I can't retaliate without ripping those stitches."

I wink. "Happy Valentine's, *mon ange*."

Brontë presses his cheek to mine, breathing me in. "Does this mean you like the book?"

"I just spent the last half hour showing you how much I like it."

"Thank fuck. That thing took decades off my life."

I giggle, kissing his scar. He gently switches our positions and cleans me up before tending to himself. He's quiet as we dress, tossing me lighthearted grins when we catch each other staring. But I know how much it means to him what I think of his gift.

I don't like it.

I love it.

And that scares me more than death itself.

STANDBY
BRONTË

I yawn for the tenth time in as many minutes as Emi fills the coffee bar at Beelzebub's with a tray of fresh croissants and three mugs breathing tendrils of steam in the low candlelight. She has yet to explain why we were called out of bed in the middle of the night to meet her here.

It doesn't take many brain cells to guess, though. She's been working on tracing the source of Leviathan's numbers in Scull's phone for weeks without updates.

Seated on the other side of a half-asleep Poppy sipping her coffee, Dantë watches Emi with narrowed eyes. "Buttering us up for the blow won't make it land any lighter, Remiel."

"You don't have to keep using my full name."

"I like it. It's the name of an angel." His mouth twitches when a rosy blush blooms over her dark cheeks. "Give it to us straight. *S'il te plaît.*"

"All right. I have good news and bad news. Which first?"

"No need to get our hopes up just to piss on them."

Emi blows out a breath and plucks Hades from the floor. "I've hit a wall with the numbers. They're all dummies stemming from a single source, which is cloaked behind military-grade encryptions I can't get past without revealing myself as the unwelcome guest banging on their back door."

I grunt. "Guess Scull wasn't lying about that part."

"Guess not," Poppy agrees around a bite of croissant, sitting straighter. "What's the good news?"

"The dummies are all two-way streets. If you call or text any of them, they'll go to the same place."

I rub a growing ache in my temple. "Which leads us back to nowhere."

"Not necessarily." Emi draws Scull's cell from her hoodie pocket and offers it to Poppy. "You have a direct line to whoever is on the other side of that wall. Might as well give it a ring."

Dantë hovers his hand over hers before Poppy can take the phone. "You don't think Leviathan is suspicious of Scull's disappearance?"

"They'd be fools if they weren't."

"Leviathan is anything but," Poppy remarks, swatting Dantë's wrist and snatching the device. "Let's not keep them waiting."

None of us attempt to stop her. This is the only path we have left to walk.

My palm finds her bouncing thigh as the phone rings and rings and—

Someone picks up. They don't say a word.

But we can hear them breathing.

Grim frowns ping-pong between us before Poppy swigs her coffee like it's liquor and clears her throat. "This is Poppy Morgenstern. It's come to my attention that you're pissed at me for killing Sebastian Bonaparte, a Leviathan legacy. Need I remind you that my ancestor, Octavia Morgenstern, was an original member. As a legacy, I demand the right to be heard. That sick fuck deserved the undignified death I delivered, and I'd spend the rest of my life on a time loop just to do it again and again if it meant keeping the innocents of this city safe.

If that's such a crime, you take it out on me. Not my friends, not my family. *Me.*"

I squeeze her knee as she drags her jacket sleeve over her damp lashes. She tosses me a grateful smile, threading her fingers through mine and holding them tight as we wait.

There's a metallic click on the other end. It's a familiar sound, like a lighter flicking open. Then a strangely demonic voice growls, "Standby for further instruction, Poppy Morgenstern."

The line goes dead.

"Judas Priest." Emi grimaces, clutching Hades to her chest. "Was that the fucking devil?"

Dantë shakes his head. "Voice modifier. Could've been anyone, man or woman."

"Whoever they are," I say, "they're a smoker."

Poppy sighs defeatedly into her coffee. "As are you and me and ninety percent of this city."

Uncomfortable silence settles in like a heavy fog. Candlewicks crackle. Winter wind howls. Somewhere under it all, I can hear it: the reaper's blade sweeping ever closer.

Emi buries her face in Hades's fur, her question muffled as she asks, "What do we do?"

Poppy considers, thoughtlessly thumbing the runes on my knuckles. "Now, I suppose, we wait for the snakes to slither in."

NOSTALGIA

POPPY

"Mama?" I ask as my mother silently pads into my bedroom, silver kimono rippling, candelabra in hand. I'm in my bed, reading with Jezebel while Brontë works an overnight shift. "Is something wrong?"

Neither she nor Papa come in here anymore. Not since they broke the news about the murder of our family they'd been keeping under wraps. I acted surprised when they told me, but I think they were aware I already knew. They probably blamed Brontë, but they've only treated him with warmth and respect.

"Nothing is wrong." Mama unlatches a window beside my bed, sweeping it open to the sprawling metropolis. "It's merely a beautiful night I'd prefer to enjoy with my daughter."

The snowy city glitters like fallen stars caught in the night's net. A cold yet balmy breeze drifts through the moonlit drapes. The bay's breath smells like the saltiest brine. Along the distant horizon, a dense fog climbs from sea to sky, shrouding us from the rest of the world like a guarded secret.

Nostalgia trickles in, as indelible as the ink on my skin. I spent many hours looking out that window, a book cradled to my chest. Later, books morphed to knives, painted with the colors I didn't have in my life anymore.

"You wanted to be a mermaid when you were little. Do you re-member?"

My lips quirk. "No."

"The first stories you ever wrote were about mermaid princesses finding their true loves." Mama's firelit smile is both soft and somber. "They're in your father's study, should you feel inclined to take a look. I read them from time to time, to remind myself of those lighter years." She sets the candelabra on my nightstand and plucks an unlit black candle, holding it close as she lowers onto the bed. "Do you know what I wanted to be?"

My neck swivels. I don't know much about my mother's life from when she lived in Japan. She doesn't particularly enjoy talking of the family who disowned her for falling in love with the wrong man.

"I wanted to be an actress," Mama says, her small smile withering. "I remember telling my mama. It was a different time back then. Daughters were meant to be obedient, not dreamers. She told me that my purpose was to be a wife. But I was persistent over the years. I kept bringing it up, thinking she'd change her answer. Until the moment I was tossed onto the street."

Lips trembling, her teary gaze drifts to the moon. I sit up straighter, resting my hand on her arm. She covers my knuckles with a cold and clammy palm.

"My mother told me I was a disgrace to the Hayashi name. She told me she should've been rid of me while I'd been in her womb. She said I was a curse, an abomination. For the longest time, I believed it. To earn her forgiveness, I turned my back on my dreams. I married far too young. For years, I pleased a man who didn't give a shit about me or his four other wives. My only escape was an opera house downtown I was permitted to visit once a month, chaperoned by his guards. That's where I met your father. We were seated beside each other. He introduced himself and told me he was traveling for business, then proceeded to say I was the most beautiful woman he'd ever seen. He didn't let go of my hand, and I didn't want him to. He killed the henchmen guarding me. We left together, and I haven't once looked back."

She chuckles to herself, tears slipping down her cheeks.

"The first strange Morgenstern custom of many your papa taught me was on the night we arrived here at the manor. I'd cut ties with the Hayashis and was still grieving the loss. He gave me a black candle and a knife and told me to carve my family name into the wax. Burning it signified the death of my former life and the rebirth of my new one."

Mama tucks the candle into my grip, folding my fingers around it with hers. My nose scrunches. "I don't understand. What is this?"

"See for yourself."

Tilting the candle this way and that, I slowly decipher the tiny letters carved into the stick. "M—Mor—Morgenstern."

"I should've never let your father drag you into our world when you were still dreaming of mermaids and true love."

"What? Mama, this isn't making any sense."

"This, dearest daughter, is the option your papa and I should've given you a long time ago. It's yours. For whenever you're ready." She takes my free hand, her moonlight eyes brimming with sorrow. "We were going to wait until you were old enough to understand what it meant to do what we do before handing you the keys to this kingdom. You were meant to be given a choice. Then your papa saw an opening, and he took it. When he brought you to the factory that night, I convinced myself it was for the best. That you'd always live with a target on your back regardless of what choice you would've made. I knew you didn't think you had a voice about your own future at all. But you do. No one can take that from you. *No one—*"

She chokes out a sob I've never heard in my life. I don't ever want to hear it again.

"You're my daughter, Poppy. You deserve to thrive, not just survive. When this Leviathan business is done, and you're ready to leave what's left of this family, give this candle to your father and tell him you're finished."

Too many thoughts war in my mind. What comes out first is: "It's not that easy, Mama. He won't just let me leave."

"*Hai,* he will. Otherwise, he loses me."

At the quizzical lift of my brow, she raises her left hand and pointedly slides off her enormous black diamond ring shaped like a crown. The message is loud and clear. If Papa doesn't free me from the bonds of his succession and let me leave the underworld behind—*if* that's what I want—the love of his life will leave *him* behind.

"Mama," I breathe, my vision blurring as she slides the ring back on. "Papa is *everything* to you. You're soulmates. You can't—"

"Do not tell me what I can and cannot do." Her chin lifts as she shifts her fierce gaze to the sea. "I have already sworn it upon the stars, and so it shall be done should the time come."

"I don't know what to say. This is...unexpected."

"Your father has seen the changes in you since this disaster began. I've seen those same changes since you abandoned your dreams."

I swallow the burn in my throat. "*Arigatō.*"

Mama kisses her fingertips and settles them on my dragon tattoo inspired by hers. "Please, darling, don't thank me for this. I'm your mother. Loving you isn't a duty. It's a privilege and an honor. Forgive me for forgetting that."

I clamp my lips to hide their quake. "*Daisuki da yo,* Mama."

I don't remember the last time I said that. Probably when I was still writing fairytales.

Mama wraps her arm like a wing around my shoulders, tucking me into her side. She smells like incense and honey, bitter and sweet. A perfect mirror of her soul.

"I love you more," she whispers, kissing the crown of my head, "my little Poppyseed."

TRAGEDY
BRONTË

"I'm fine, Brontë." Poppy sighs in my ear as I suture the throat of a woman who swallowed swords for a living and slid her last one down the wrong hole. "For the thousandth time, there's no need to worry."

For days, she's been recovering from an infection in her healing wound. Her fever broke this morning, but my mind won't stop replaying the night she was stabbed. I should be with her, not working yet another graveyard weekend that was dumped onto me at the last minute when my colleague called off sick.

"Just take it easy, *Petit Diable.*"

"*Sooo,* don't fuck myself while you're not here?"

A burst of irrational envy blasts through me. "You are *what?*"

"Mm, anger. Would it help to know it's *you* I'm thinking of?"

"Poppy," I growl, seconds from crushing my phone. "Your body needs rest."

"I'm tired of resting."

"Don't be a brat."

"*Ugh,* fuck you. I'm not a brat."

"Lie."

"Just for that, I'm grabbing my enormous, scaly, purple dragon dildo hidden in the coffee table you've used a thousand times without opening. *Au revoir!*"

"Wait, wha—"

Click.

I sigh down at the corpse. "Are *you* tired of resting?"

The cadaver remains peacefully still.

"My point exactly."

After stashing her back into the case, I tend to the stack of reports at my desk. Trying not to think about what is currently happening in that fucking bed without me.

Fuck that.

I tap into my text thread with Poppy.

> Snoring yet?

> No, but I just came.

> Twice.

> Going on #3.

I shift in my seat with a self-admonishing curse. Being turned on in a room full of dead bodies will make me no better than the necrophiliac intern I had three summers ago.

> You should be sleeping.

> You should be working.

> Not with the thought of a cock that isn't mine buried in your pussy.

> It's not in my pussy...

"Angels, I'd sell my fucking soul for that sight."

> **You're going to regret this if you don't stop, Petit Diable.**

> **Is that a threat or a promise?**

My fingers are flying over the screen when the door to the morgue whips open. Quinn barrels in with an armful of reports, head down and focus on her work as she says, "Hey, Tyler? I have the toxicology results from the poison case that you and your intern have been working on. I think your theory is right. The wife totally killed the husband for cheating."

Shit. I didn't think to check her schedule before covering this shift. She must not have heard about the switch.

"Sounds like the poor bastard deserved it."

Quinn's gaze snaps up, eyes wide. "Brontë? What are you doing here?"

"Covering for Tyler."

"Oh, I uh—sorry. I'll just drop these off in his office mailbox and be on my way, then."

Clearing her throat awkwardly, she turns to leave. But a lonely, shriveled part of me doesn't want her to go. Not again and not like this.

"*Ma chérie.* Wait, *s'il te plaît.*"

Quinn stops mid-step. She doesn't turn around, but her millisecond of hesitation is invitation enough.

"When I came to this city, you were my first friend," I say, struggling to keep my voice even. "You treated me like a person and not just some creepy coroner. You believed in my Etsy shop when no one else did. You were my first patron. Did you know that?"

Slowly, she nods. "*The Vampyre* by John Polidori. An original copy from Lord Byron's contest in the early eighteen-hundreds. You brought it back from the dead when every other book conservator I spoke to told me it was better off locked in a glass case in a dark room where no one would ever see it again."

"A tragedy that would've been, don't you think? If you had listened to them and given up when it truly was worth salvaging in the end?"

Slowly, like a gargoyle entering its first throes of life, she pivots to face me. Unshed tears rim her long lashes. "I never would've forgiven myself."

"Nor I. I'll be damned if I let it happen now."

Quinn doesn't show affection often. So when she rushes over to me and embraces me as tightly as she can, I'm too shocked to return it with anything other than a surprised *oof*.

"I'm sorry." She sniffles into my shoulder. "I'm so, so sorry."

My arms close around her. Every unspoken truth radiates between us. I should've confided in her what was happening between Poppy and I. She should've told me about Leviathan and Scull.

There will always be secrets between us. Some, though, are better left unshared.

After a long minute, she pulls away, wiping at her eyes. "Can I interest you in some pizza? My treat."

"I'll buy if you call."

The smile that dawns her freckled features patches the wound in my chest with her name on it. "Pepperoni?"

"Meatlover's. I'm fucking famished."

"Coming right up," she chirps, dialing the number.

Too much time has passed since everything feels as it should. I know it won't last, but I bask in it for as long as I can.

SHRAPNEL
POPPY

Cotton candy smoke billows from my nostrils as I sloth in a candlelit bath and twirl the black candle between my fingers. Mama's words play on a loop in my mind, louder than the March rain slamming its wrath against the windows. Her gift to me, my proverbial death as criminal royalty, has been crowding my mind. I haven't even been able to think about Leviathan's persistent radio silence. I've been too focused on this stupid candle.

I don't know how long I sit here, spiraling down the rabbit hole. Long enough for Jezebel to nudge the bathroom door open, whiskers twitching as she sniffs the air. As if she can *smell* my emotional turmoil. She sits on her haunches beside the tub and chuffs. It sounds like, *Talk to me.*

I let it all fall out, searching her eyes as if they hold the answer. Those bright, blue oceans are as vast as the possibilities I can't even comprehend without suffering a wave of nausea.

This is the last dilemma I should be concerned about. Although no other innocents have lost their lives since that ominous phone call with whoever had answered, the threat is still there. There's a blade in the wind, and we're merely waiting for it to drop on our necks.

Papa's empire is a pile of rubble, but I'm still set to inherit it.

The question is: What do *I* want?

That noxious wave returns as Mama's words circle me, leading my mind around and around like a carousel that won't stop spinning. *For whenever you're ready,* she said as she handed me both salvation and damnation. The former, because I'll finally be free from the clutches of this depraved life; the latter, because my father will never speak to me again.

"I'm not ready," I croak, my throat burning. "Not yet."

Jezebel nudges my cheek with a gentle purr, offering quiet comfort as I let the tears slide free. That's when I feel it: the unbearable pain of a period cramp.

"You've got to be fucking kidding me," I gripe as little warriors with little swords carve their little warpath through my guts. "*Kuso!*"

Jezebel yowls and darts out the door. I would, too, if I had supersonic hearing and had my eardrums blown out by a shrieking harpy.

Moments later, boots cross the bedroom floor in long, confident strides. They stop short at the door left slightly ajar. "You all right in there, *Petit Diable?*"

"I'm fine, *mon ange.*"

"You don't sound fine."

"Well, I am."

"I'm coming in."

A cramp stabs my innards, and I snarl, "Cross that threshold, and I will flay you alive and make you watch as I bumblefuck my way through wrapping your hide around your boring book."

Brontë's rich chuckle trickles through the door. "Bumblefuck?"

"Mind your own business and go away."

"Not until you tell me what's wrong."

"Nothing's wrong."

"Lie."

"I hate it when you do that."

"Oh, look. Another lie."

I set my vape on the nearby sink counter with a sigh. "What's wrong isn't something you can fix."

The door drifts open. I glance down at the evidence of my misery still dangling between my fingers. Quickly, I wind the candle into my hair as light pours in from the bedroom.

Brontë leans a shoulder against the frame, angling his jaw as he studies me from across the space. He's in his tastefully tight black tee and cargo pants, the charcoal strands of his hair slipping free of their slicked style. His clever gaze flits to my vape then sweeps over the slivers of soapy skin he can see in the dim light.

"You make brooding in a bubble bath look sexy, *ma reine.*"

"I'm not in the mood."

"That's a first."

"I told you not to come in."

"Actually, you told me not to cross the threshold." He toes the wooden panel separating the rooms. "I think my hide is safe from your bumblefucking."

Cheeky bastard. "For now."

He grunts, unfazed. "Talk to me, Poppy."

"I don't want to talk. I want you to leave."

"Lie."

"What do you want from me, Brontë?" I explode, whirling in the tub so swiftly that water sloshes over the lip and slaps onto the floor. "Is it a confession you wish to hear? A truth free of any lies? Fine, here it is."

I rip the candle from my hair and whip it at his chest.

"My mother gave me an out, and I can't seem to decide which path I want to walk. I made my first kill at nine years old, and I lost count of the lives I took before I was old enough to drive. It didn't matter if they were men or women, young or old. I killed them all, because this is what I was born and bred to be. Nothing changes that. *Nothing.* No one, not even you, is going to save me from the damage done to my soul. And if anything were to ever happen to you because of me, I'd eat a bullet so I'd never have to look at myself ever again. How is *that* for the fucking truth?"

I don't know what kind of reaction I'm expecting from him. A snapping riposte, maybe even a draconic roar I know he is entirely capable of making. He doesn't do any of those things. No, he just pivots on his heel and walks away.

I sink under the water and envision strangling myself, screaming into the depths until my brain goes numb. When I slide back up, coughing suds, I glimpse a silhouette leaning against the sink and jolt out of my skin.

Brontë juts his chin toward me. "Finished?"

No longer trusting my forked tongue, I nod.

"*Très bien.*" He proffers a palm. "Out."

I obey, shivering as his warm, calloused fingers close around mine. He leads me to my bed, nudging me forward with a palm splayed low on my spine.

"Lie down."

I dig my heels in, rubbing my cramping abdomen. "I need a t—"

He grabs my nape, snarling in my face, "Lie. The fuck. Down."

That shouldn't be hot, right?

Gulping down desire, I slide onto the fur duvet. He turns to the nightstand, rummaging through a tray of massaging oils.

I immediately want to stab myself for being a raging bitch.

Brontë sniffs a few, waving the vials beneath his nose before uncapping a pair.

"That better not be chamomile and sandalwood." I scrunch my nose the way I know he finds endearing. "They smell like dirty feet."

"It's balsam and lemongrass, my brother's personal recipe for rough days." His words are clipped and clinical, his movements rigid as he gestures to my naked body. "May I?"

I hate that he's asking for permission to touch me. "*Hai,* you may."

Thick oils splash onto my shoulders and down the curve of my spine. I shiver as he dribbles the cold liquid over my rear and down the soles of my feet. He coats his broad hands in a glistening sheen before leaning over me and kneading my shoulders.

I shudder and stifle a gravelly groan into my pillow. "Stars, this is almost better than sex."

I hate that he doesn't laugh.

"No wonder your first instinct is to bite." His thumbs press deep, massaging in tight circles. "You're knotted down to the bone."

A string of senseless curses slips out as he works a particularly tender spot on each side of my neck. "I didn't know muscles existed there to tangle."

"They do, and they are. If I do anything that hurts, or you want me to stop, speak up."

"Mhm."

Brontë slowly works down my spine. My eyelids droop as I gaze into the flame upon a bedside candle and soak in each passing second of relaxation and relief.

"You've been holding out on me, *mon roi.*"

The heels of his palms dip into my tailbone, tight muscle loosening like melting clay. "As have you."

Regret stings my eyes. "Brontë—"

"You spoke your truth, Poppy." His hands skip down to my legs. "Let me speak mine."

His words are short, curt, pained at their sharp edges.

I shut my mouth and wait.

"I knew who you were when we first met, but I didn't know what to expect when I called you to make a deal. It certainly wasn't saving you from an assassin. To this day, I wonder what would've happened if I hadn't called at all. If you'd crawled into bed that night only to wake to Vladimir Volkov crushing your windpipe."

I scoff. "Your lack of faith in me is wounding."

He smacks my ass sharp enough to make me yelp in surprise.

"The fuck was *that* for?"

"Interrupting me." There's a dangerous glint in his hazel smolder as he slaps me again. "*That* was for the sass."

I open my mouth to spit a retort, but he raises his reddening palm in warning. I grit my teeth, my cheeks burning as raw want heats my blood. He smirks, rubbing the thick muscles with a level of tenderness that melts me into the bed.

"We've both done terrible things. That doesn't mean our futures are set in stone. The difference between us is that I made my choice. You have one to make, too. It doesn't have to be today or tomorrow. Take your time, figure out what it is you want and do it. Despite popular belief, magic exists. It's called free will."

Brontë leans down and presses a gentle kiss to my tattoo. I swallow a bout of tears as he finally cracks a genuine smile. It crinkles the corners of his eyes, stretches the scar over his right cheek. It's so beautiful—*he's* so beautiful, so seraphic. I'm completely spellbound.

"No matter what you decide, Poppy Lucia Morgenstern, I will be by your side. Whether you fly to heaven or fall to hell, I will fly or fall with you."

A wall inside me fractures and then ruptures into a thousand tiny shards of shrapnel. I can almost hear it shattering like glass crashing to the ground. I know, right here and now, that the decision I make isn't just impacting me.

It's impacting him, too.

"Where did you learn how to wax poetic like that, *mon ange?*"

"Must be all the boring books I read."

I giggle and kiss him as slowly as falling snow. His tongue rolls with mine, his lips tender and gentle. He tastes like forgiveness and patience. I want to bathe in his virtue, his grace, his divinity.

"You must be exhausted," he murmurs. "I should let you sleep."

"No." I fist his hair. His lashes flutter, a purr rumbling through his chest. "Stay."

"How can I resist when you beg like that?"

"You can't." I kiss the edge of his grin. "Scythe."

His eyes slowly open, his pupils widening and contracting like he's waging some inner war. "How is your wound?"

"Scarring, finally."

"Any pain?"

"No."

Brontë brushes his lips over my cheek. "Then I suppose you won't mind if I fuck you to sleep tonight?"

"I, um..." I shift my hips, face heating when I spy the crimson blotch staining the duvet at the apex of my thighs. "We may have to wait a few more days."

Brontë's gaze snags on the blood. I expect disgust, not...*hunger.* His nostrils flare as he works a swallow down his thick throat, the darkness in his eyes warring for dominance. "I'm tired of waiting."

He rolls me onto my back and climbs over me. His large frame dwarfs me as much as a dragon dwarfs a mouse. But I don't feel like a mouse around him. Even now, with him trapping me in place, I feel like his equal, his match.

"We don't have to." I place a palm on his chest. I don't know his boundaries, especially given his past. Seeing is one thing, but feeling blood on his bare skin could be a trigger I have no intention of pulling. "Seriously, we can wait."

His hazel smolder ignites with a burning flame. "How bad are the cramps?"

"Not that—" He nips my ear, chasing the lie from my tongue. "Bad."

"Hmm." He palms my navel, his long fingers slinking toward my aching core. "I can fix that."

A leashed moan leaves my lips. Still, I push his shoulders. "Are you *sure?*"

Understanding clears his expression. "Oh, I—ah…I have a thing for blood in the bedroom. It's different to me than what you're thinking. So *oui,* I'm sure."

"You have a blood kink?"

"Is that too strange for you?"

"No." I fist his shirt and yank him down to me. "I really fucking love it."

"Thank the angels you're just as sick as me."

I let out a moan, silenced by the pouring rain. "Shut up and fuck me, Scythe."

"Begging already?" He *tsks* as he slips a single fingertip through my slick seam, teasing me with a slow stroke. "I thought you were too proud to beg."

"Not begging. *Demanding.*"

"Always making demands, *ma reine.*" His finger dips into my pussy, delving deep, and I garble a curse. "How does taking a break from your throne sound?"

"Better than Mozart, *mon roi.*"

"That's my girl."

Brontë plants gloriously languorous kisses on my neck. Slowly, he curls a second finger into me, adding a third to stretch me taut.

"Brontë," I groan, clawing his shirt as he winds me tighter and tighter. "I need you inside me."

"Pathetic attempt, *Petit Diable.* You can beg better than that."

His tongue and teeth rake a ravenous path of fire down to my heart. He lingers there for a long moment, kissing the flesh encasing that vital organ with undivided attention. It feels like he's kissing my soul.

"Try again. Make it pretty."

"I will *not* b—" I gasp as he snaps his teeth around a nipple, pinching and twisting. "*S'il te plaît.* I'll do anything you want."

"Anything?"

"If you make me repeat myself just to hear it again, I *will* murder you."

"Such a tease."

He suddenly grabs my ankles and drags me to the edge of the bed. Before my brain can catch up with my body, he snatches my throat with blood-slick fingers and pulls me up.

"Sit like the goddamn queen you are."

I obey, straightening my spine and crossing my legs. I lift my chin and set my features into stone.

"*Bonne fille.*" Brontë chuckles, slips a cigar from his pocket, and tucks it behind my ear like a flower. He skims a bloody fingertip down my chest, trailing a line of scarlet to my navel and drawing a downward arrow under my belly button. "I don't need to explain this, do I?"

I shiver in anticipation but manage to steel my façade. "No."

A devious smile spreads his lips, and it feels like I'm staring into the devil's eyes as he croons, "If you wish for a safe word, you'd better tell me now."

Fuck, what is this man going to do to me?

Nothing that will hurt me.

I know it. He knows I know it.

He just wants to hear me say it.

"No safe words." A smirk twists my lips. "Scythe."

AMBROSIA
POPPY

Brontë settles into a leather wingback by the blazing hearth and studies me the same way a starving panther studies a plump lamb.

My brow pinches. "What are you—"

"I didn't give you permission to speak."

"I don't need your permission, fuck you very much."

"Say the word, then. I'll gladly get on my knees for you. You want control, come and take it from me. Or, you can do as I say, and let yourself be whoever you want. The choice is yours."

Choice. That's what this is: a decision for me to make.

Am I his queen?

Or am I his whore?

"I want you, Poppy. No matter who you choose to be."

Lifting my chin, I remain silent.

Brontë grins, his bloodstained fingers leaving sinfully red smudges on the chair as he grips the arms. "Light the cigar."

I pluck the roll from my ear and light it with a nearby candle. I bring it to my lips—

"Did I tell you to smoke it?"

I lower the roll.

"Mhm. Spread those succulent thighs for me."

My legs separate. His shaded gaze dips to the sliver of flesh his blood arrow points toward.

"Wider."

I lean back on the heels of my palms, stretching my lower limbs until they ache.

"*Bonne fille.* Now, touch yourself."

My left hand—

"With the cigar."

My right hand travels the crease of my thigh. Smoke spirals from the cigar in a veil of gray. I slip my fingers through my seam once, twice before delving two digits knuckle-deep and pushing the warm roll of tobacco into my opening, the cap first. A gasp rushes out of me as heat scorches me from the inside and smoke puffs from my pussy.

His chuckle reverberates through the floorboards. "There she is."

Flames lick up my spine as I stroke my innermost walls. My back bows in time with a long moan—

"Enough."

I stop.

"Bring it here."

I stand—

"No." He points to the floor. "Crawl."

I pinch the cigar between my teeth and lower onto the floor. He drinks me in, a king watching his mistress submit herself to him as he lounges on his throne. When I reach him, I sit back on my heels and proffer the cigar.

"Eyes on me, Poppy." Brontë's warm fingers curl under my chin, tipping my face up. "You bow to no one, *ma reine.* Not even me." An unbidden tear slithers down my cheek, and he dips to steal it with his tongue. "No more of these until I'm buried so deep inside you, you're choking on my name."

I nod as he takes the cigar and drags, the cherry flaring red. The sight of my blood smeared on his fingers and lips melts my core to magma.

Brontë wraps his hand around my throat. "Belt."

Unbuckling the clasp, I pull the leather free. He takes it, replacing his hand with the belt and cinching it tight.

"Can you breathe?"

I nod again. He yanks the belt tighter.

Gasping for air, I claw at the strap.

"This doesn't come loose," he growls, "until my cock is filling your pretty little throat."

I nearly rip his pants to free his stiff dick. I have half a second to marvel at the nine-inch map of delicate skin and thick veins on his broad length before I'm taking him in like oxygen. The belt loosens as I swallow him whole and fist what I can't take in.

A curse hisses between his teeth. His fingers curl into my hair as I suckle his crown and pump his length. "You are absolute nirvana, Poppy."

I moan around him, my eyes stinging with the effort not to gag. He angles me deeper, hips thrusting. It's swift, punishing, and leaves me gagging anyway. He's literally fucking my skull, and I can't get—

"Enough," he barks, releasing me.

He flings the belt aside, startling me. I jolt, clinging to his shirt.

He bares his teeth, snarling smoke. "Down, *Petit Diable.* Or I fuck that tight little ass all night and stitch you up in the morning."

Huffing, I sink onto my heels.

Brontë reaches between his shoulder blades and pulls his shirt. Then he commands me to take off the rest. It should be impossible, his beauty. His entire body is ink and muscle and the power of a warrior turned god, and he's all *mine.*

I pepper kisses down the length of the sword tattooed on his thigh, going no farther than the edge of its broken tip before he's growling at me to back off. My insides squeeze in response. Wet warmth slithers down my thighs. I brace an arm around my middle, wincing through the cramp.

From my secret stash hidden in the coffee table beside him, Brontë pulls a bulbous plug shaped and textured like a dragon egg. "Spit."

I let saliva drizzle from my tongue onto the toy.

"Turn around."

When I do, he grips my hips and lifts my ass, guiding my legs onto the seat to frame him. My forearms are on the floor, my most intimate parts bare to him like a buffet. His hot exhales scorch my skin.

"Fucking ambrosia."

Then he drags his tongue from my slit to my ass, smearing warm blood and thick saliva all the way up my crack. My hips jerk, and he eases the plug into me with a rumbling chuckle.

"There's nothing quite like seeing the perfect princess turn into such a good little whore. Ready for your reward?"

"Mhm," is all I can manage as he grinds his swollen cock against my belly.

Brontë grabs my nape like it's scruff and hauls me up onto his lap. My spine is flush with his torso, his cock a spear against my stomach. Snatching my butterfly knife from the coffee table, he scrapes the colorful blade over my throat as the cherry of his cigar flares as bright as a flame in my periphery.

"Tell me what you want, *mon amour.*"

Mon amour. I know what that means: *my love.*

All I hear is the rush of blood in my ears. A single arrow shoots straight through my heart. Something within me splinters and splits into a crevice.

I slip and fall right in, tumbling all the way down to the graveyard of my soul. Freeing the old and buried parts of me from their coffins: the suffering, the heartache, the fury. They all claw to the surface, demanding to be felt.

And I feel them *all.*

The tears deluge, and they don't stop.

"Poppy." Brontë palms my cheek. "What did I say about these?"

I squeeze my eyes shut, breathing his scent into my lungs and wishing I could hold it there forever. "It fucking *hurts.*"

"Why does it hurt?"

"Because you have the power to destroy me."

Brontë turns his cheek into mine, his scar branding my skin. "I'm not Nikolai."

"I know." I blindly reach for his fingers. His hand twines with mine like it was always meant to be there. "I need you to do something for me."

Smoke billows from his nostrils as he cocks a brow, waiting.

"Is there a rune for 'love?'"

"*Oui.*"

"Carve it." My free hand wraps the knife, dragging the blade down to my heart. "Right here."

"Poppy—"

"Now, Scythe. Live up to your name."

Taming his snarl, Brontë puffs the cigar and passes it to me. "Breathe."

Sweet smoke fills my lungs as the knife tips into my flesh. He ghosts the blade in an intricate pattern over my skin, showing me what hell I'm in for. Then he wraps his arm around my waist and pulls me higher. Until his rigid cock nudges my entrance.

"I'm going to fill this pussy past full," he whispers in my ear, "but I need you to stay still while I work. Can you do that for me?"

"*Hai.*"

"Spread those heavenly lips." I obey, reaching down to split my seam wide. His crown presses into me, blood oozing down his length from the intrusion. I moan as he groans, "Fuck, Poppy. Do you see that? Your cunt is *weeping* for me."

And then he carves the first line.

Pain bolts from my chest, ricocheting in my heart and pounding between my legs as he sinks deeper into me. Pleasure melds with agony, the blade shredding my skin as his cock buries into my soul. A burning sensation coils up from where he pushes into me, stretching me farther than I've ever been.

My body revolts, the pain of being split open above and below unbearable.

"Breathe. I won't say it again."

I bite the cigar, resisting the impulse to escape. My fingernails dig into his thighs. It feels like he's caught me beneath his paw, claws outstretched as he drags me down and down to the pits of hell. His hips tilt, rocking another inch into me and splitting me apart from the inside. The growl that bursts from my throat doesn't sound human.

"You're doing so good, *ma reine.* Just a little more."

I'm nearly chewing the cigar to shreds. Tears leak from the corners of my lashes. His hilt is still a world away. I'm so focused on his cock, I barely feel the quick work he does with the knife. The blade leaves my skin with a stinging bite, and the cigar is plucked from my mouth.

"Look."

I glance down to see his elegant script, the bleeding mark as indelible as scars and as stunning as the man who made them. I feel like one of his rebound books. Only, the story is my own. The ink, my blood. The binding, my bones. The hide, my skin. The rune, my soul.

Brontë grabs my jaw, popping my mouth open with his fingers and breathing smoke through my lips. "I love the sight of your devastation."

He grips my hips and *thrusts* into me, bottoming out and slamming his balls against my clit with an audible slap. My cry is silenced by the pounding rain. Blood gushes from between my shaking thighs. I swear I can see the outline of his cock *pushing* against my navel and bulging the arrow he drew there.

"Oh my God—"

"I'm right here. Now quit your bitching and take this dick like a good girl."

His hips roll, grinding his base against my fingers still spreading myself open for him. Embers of euphoria ignite inside me, blazing through the agony. With painstaking slowness, he pulls me up and up, sliding out inch by heady inch. From root to tip, he's soaked in my blood.

"I loathe you, Poppy," he breathes when he's withdrawn to his crown. "You've ruined me, body and soul, for any other."

I bite my grin, relishing his guttural growl as he slowly slides back in. His bloodstained palm splays on my belly, feeling the bulge of his length invading me. His groan thunders from his chest to my heart.

"Mine. Do you hear me, Poppy? You are fucking *mine*."

In the span of a breath, he goes from gentle to savage.

Brontë strikes like a viper, sinking his teeth into my neck. Stars flicker across my vision, and then he's gathering me into his arms like a knight for his damsel and striding for the bed. He tosses the cigar into an ashtray on the nightstand then drops me onto the furs. He swallows my squeal with his lips and tongue as he spears me with his cock in a single, powerful stroke.

Pure bliss explodes through my veins. My legs knot around his waist, and I cling to him as he ruts into me like an animal lost to primal instinct. I mewl into his mouth. He growls in return, fisting my hair and kissing me like he can't satisfy his thirst. His skin dews with sweat, his muscles twitching and clenching as his hips piston. He bites my breasts, licks the blood he draws like it's nectar. Grabs my ass and lifts me higher for longer strokes and deeper plunges. Fills my mouth with his tongue as he fucks me and tastes me like I'm his final supper.

He's chasing me toward the ledge, but I don't want to fall just yet.

"Brontë," I gasp, tugging sharply on his hair. "Look at me, *s'il te plaît.*"

When he does, desperation flares in his hazel eyes. "Don't ask me to stop, because I won't."

"I want you to slow down. Let me come with you."

His veins pop in his neck as he reins himself in, and his pace gradually slows.

"Such a good boy." I smile, tapping the tip of his nose. "Scythe."

He grabs my other arm and traps it above me, his gaze darkening. His powerful body grinds into mine, sheathing himself inside me at a smooth, languid pace. He's everywhere and yet not everywhere enough. I want him closer—to consume me, inside and out.

I throw my weight forward, toppling him backward until I'm riding him. His knees fold up behind me, his thighs caging me in. He drops kisses down the curve of my neck as he pulls me so close, our hearts collide.

This is what I want. Him.

Forever.

My cheek is against his temple, my moans in his ear, his on my neck, our bodies moving to the rhythmic clap of the headboard against the wall. We are mere beasts, drowning with each other in the fires of passion. I happily burn with him.

Too soon, ecstasy coils in the base of my spine. "B-Brontë."

"Fall, Poppy." His teeth drag along the column of my throat. "I'm with you."

My nails claw gashes into his shoulder blades.

Then I let go.

I'm devoured by an inferno of rapture. He tips me onto my back as if we're plummeting from grace, and then he's crashing into me, forcing us down through the layers of earth to where we belong.

When he comes, it's with a growl that shakes the damn bed.

Liquid heat spills into me. He captures my mouth with his, delving for my soul, praises on his lips as my pussy clamps tight around him and milks him. He doesn't stop kissing me until he's hardening inside me again.

I yelp as he suddenly flips me to my stomach. There is no tenderness in the way he lifts my ass off the bed and punishes my pussy with his cock. My teeth leave marks in his arm when he holds me as I come, pressing me deep into the furs.

I'm going to die in this man's arms.

And I gladly welcome my end.

TWILIGHT
BRONTË

Twilight and birdsong lure me awake. Coffee and cotton candy caress my senses. A steady heartbeat thrums against mine. Poppy's heartbeat.

I peek down to see her snoring on my chest. The duvet pools low on her spine. I splay a palm over a winking dimple, simply because I can.

She stirs, mumbling, "Don't eat me."

I suppress a snort into her hair, carefully twisting to shield her against the final rays of sunset. My gaze roams her body as I relive the night that will forever be imprinted in my skull. Bruises bloom along her hips and thighs from where I gripped her too tight. A red ring circles her throat from where my belt choked her. Bite marks mar her beige skin with splotches of crimson and purple from where I sank my teeth. A bandage on the rune I carved into her chest crinkles with her every breath.

For just a moment, I'm ashamed of what I've done to her perfect body.

Then I glance at myself.

Tattoos hide most of the evidence of her vicious retaliation. Still, I can feel every ache and bruise. My arms and chest and back are clawed like a cat's scratching post. Bite marks in my shoulders and neck. A split lip from when she rode my face a little too hard. I didn't mind, but she nearly cried about it until I bit her lip and gave her a matching split.

As the moon set and the sun rose, neither of us were satiated.

We spent hours upon hours in this room, christening every surface with sacrilege. When we were both too tired to go on, I drew us a bath and washed her up while she did the same to me. I held her for a time, sprinkling bubbles over her shoulders until she fell asleep in my arms. As soon as the bath grew cold, I carried her back to bed and bandaged her chest. The moment I tucked her in and slipped in beside her, she was crawling to my side and curled herself around me like roots over rock.

I smile and kiss her head, drifting into dreams of me living an entire future with the little devil in my arms.

—◆—

When I awake, it's almost dawn and Poppy isn't here.

In an instant, I'm on my feet, tripping over myself in the dark. I throw on a set of sweats and beeline out, barely registering Jezebel's bright eyes piercing the hallway's thick shadows.

I check the manor's library. Empty.

Dining room, kitchen, the thousand other rooms in this enormous Gothic mansion.

All empty.

An intrusive thought slithers through my mind. *Did she...leave me?*

No. I know her, inside and out. She wouldn't have just disappeared after spending all that time being as close to me as humanly possible.

I dig through my pockets for my phone then hiss a curse when I realize I left it on the nightstand upstairs. I'm passing through the kitchen again when I see it: the pot of black.

Slowly, I peer out the windows overlooking the city. I spy her silhouette instantly, the reflective lettering of my work jacket glinting back at me in the fading moonlight. Filling a thermos, I tug on my boots and silently slip outside.

Poppy puffs on her vape, her windswept tresses tumbling in the wintry breeze. Seems like my jacket—drowning her like an oversized dress—is the only thing she's wearing aside from her muddy slippers.

I can taste her turmoil in the air like poison.

"You should be asleep," she rasps without looking back.

"*Bonjour,* Pot. Call me Kettle."

Her quiet laugh is a touch too weak.

I sidle up behind her, curling a knuckle beneath her chin and tugging her focus up to me. I don't know what emotion I see in those baby blues. I lean my brow onto hers and ask the question that's been eating me alive since waking in an empty bed.

"Do you regret it?"

She scoffs. "Don't insult me."

Thank the fucking angels. "Are you in pain?"

Poppy sinks all her weight into me like she was a pillar too close to crumbling out here on her own. "No, I just...I want to make the right choice. For us."

"The only right choice is what's right for *you.*"

She dips her chin then reaches up to skim her cold fingertips over the scar on my cheek. "Will you stay out here with me for a little while?"

"Only since you asked so nicely."

I kiss her chilled smile and pull her down to the ground, settling her into my lap. She takes my thermos and sips it with a grimace.

"This shit is liquid tar."

"Here's a thought: If you don't like it, don't drink it."

"Don't tell me what to do."

"Brat."

"Prick."

I chuckle as she nestles deeper into me like a cat curling into its bed. I settle my chin atop her head and stare out at the city as the sun slowly scorches the world awake. How long, I wonder, was she out here seriously considering her future with me while I was merely *dreaming* of living my future with her?

"Brontë?"

"Hm?"

Poppy twists in my arms, her eyes fusing to mine. Within them is an inferno of both heavenly and infernal flame, the brightest and the darkest parts of her looking right at mine. Her chin trembles, but she doesn't say anything.

She doesn't need to.

I know what she's feeling. I feel it, too. Like we've found the secrets of the universe in each other, sharpening that guillotine still hanging over our heads. People are cannon fodder in her world. We're now each other's atomic bomb.

"*Venez ici.*" I marry my lips to hers, kissing the tiny tremble away. "*Mon cœur bat pour toi. Sans toi, je ne suis rien. Tu es mon autre moitié dans cette vie et dans l'autre.*"

"Translation?"

"My heart beats for you. Without you, I am nothing. You are my other half in this life and the next."

She blinks tears from her lashes. "Brontë..."

"You don't have to say anything. I just want you to know how much you mean to me." I settle my palm over the bandage on her heart and the rune that I carved there. "*Je t'aime, mon amour.*"

Poppy tugs me down by my hood and kisses me. She doesn't stop until the sun is bathing us in the light of a new dawn.

WRAITH
POPPY

The person staring back at me is hauntingly beautiful. She's wearing a black lace kimono, half her sleek pink strands knotted with shuriken stars. Her arctic eyes are winged, her lips stained a midnight blue.

Too bad it's just snakeskin hiding the liar beneath.

My gaze travels up, hers along with it, to the Leviathan mask in our hands. It's a different style than the others, only half a mask. Someone had slipped it under the front door of Morgenstern Manor during the first night I shared with Brontë.

I checked the cams myself. They'd been scrubbed. I then deleted the footage of me finding the mask and tucking it into Brontë's jacket that I'd been wearing for what was meant to be me brewing coffee for him as an early morning surprise.

I've been hiding the mask since then, along with the invitation now tucked into the holster beside my mini Glock strapped to my thigh and hidden under my skirt. I've spent weeks staring at the coordinates and date beneath, waiting for this night to come. They lead to St. Aurelius's Liberal Arts. Unwilling to put Emi in any more danger than I already have, I checked the academy's website and found a masquerade event being hosted on campus tonight in honor of their founder.

The unwritten instructions were clear: come alone and wear the mask.

I haven't told anyone.

Tonight, the stars aligned. Mama and Papa are asleep. Brontë is working. Being at the manor has made it easy to keep this from everyone else.

Am I making a mistake? Probably.

But this is *my* war.

No king or queen who's unwilling to fight on the frontline deserves their crown.

Texting Brontë that I'm spending the night at Beelzebub's with Emi, I head downstairs. Jezebel meets me at the foyer, blocking my exit with a loud yowl. She sounds almost...pleading.

I crouch, scratching her cheek. "I'll be back. Keep the bed warm for me."

She huffs, pawing at my chest with a whine.

"You can't come with me."

She bats me again, and I fold her paw between my hands.

"If I don't return, protect my parents. They'll need you more than me."

She grunts, and my throat burns.

"I will *not* lose another friend, sweet girl. You will stay here, and if I don't come back, you will guard Mama and Papa for the rest of your days. Do you understand?"

Jezebel's glacial eyes search mine, an entire lifetime of unconditional and unfaltering love in their depths. What I face tonight is too dangerous for her. She may follow me into death, but it doesn't mean I'd ever allow it.

Throwing my arms around her neck, I hold her for long minutes. Her soft whimpers stab my heart and bleed me dry. I kiss her nose, giggling as she sneezes.

"Look after a certain coroner, too, would you? He's kind of grown on me a little."

Jezebel bows her neck. I tug my leather jacket on and slip out the house like a wraith, my fingertips skimming the scar over my heart carved by the man I love.

HUNT
BRONTË

"Is it cruel to be eating pizza while surrounded by corpses?" Quinn wonders aloud as she eyes the morgue coolers.

"Of course not." I scoff, happily clogging my arteries with another grease-ridden slice. "We're hungry, and they're dead. What's so cruel about that?"

She chuckles, shrugging and devouring her own slice. It's been an easy healing journey for us, repairing our broken friendship from the roots. She's slowly getting over Scull's 'disappearance,' though I'd be lying if I said I feel no shame every time she talks about him with a mournful tone. As if, subconsciously, she knows he's no longer alive.

"You look good, Brontë." A serene smile tugs her lips up. "You've been practically glowing lately."

"Sex will do that," I drawl, washing the crust down with a thermos of cold black coffee that Poppy made for me before I fucked her in my car as payment.

Quinn quirks her lips in thought. "Does Poppy have any single friends?"

"None that aren't felons."

"I assumed as much." She shrugs, sipping her can of sparkling water. "I'm starting to think that's my type."

"Fair enough. Give me your phone." She does, and I add Poppy's number to her contacts before sending Poppy a text with Quinn's number. "There. Ask her yourself."

"Right now?"

"If not now, then when?"

Quinn audibly gulps, dialing Poppy. My eyebrows scrunch when she leaves a message. Poppy should be at Beelzebub's with Emi, according to her text she sent less than an hour ago.

"Probably got caught up watching vampire anime," I say light-heartedly as I try calling.

She doesn't answer for me, either.

Heart surging into a gallop, I tap into the tracker app. Poppy has yet to discover the device I slipped from her old jacket to her new one. On the map grid, the pink dot blinks at a traffic light half a mile from Morgenstern Manor. She moves at a hurried pace, taking the highway toward the city outskirts.

A single thought emerges: *Leviathan has her.*

Panic curdles my stomach, and I lurch to my feet as everything I consumed threatens to come back up. "*Excusez-moi, ma chérie.* Grease and coffee don't mix well."

Quinn nods, grimacing as I nearly sprint out the morgue. I pause halfway up the stairs, swallowing bile as I call Emi.

"Brontë? What's—"

"Is Poppy with you?"

"No. I haven't even spoken with her today. Why?"

"I need eyes on her. *Now.*"

What I like most about Emi: she doesn't ask questions. Seconds of listening to her bash her keyboard later, she reports, "Got her. She's on her bike, heading north."

My knees weaken with relief. Leviathan doesn't have her.

But I feel my hackles rise. Why would she lie to me?

"Where is she going?"

"Let me load her maps. If we're lucky, she's using GPS…" Another grueling minute of listening to Emi's frantic typing. "Huh, that's odd."

"Quickly losing my mind over here, *mon amie.*"

"Sorry! It's just—she's headed to St. Aurelius's."

"The cemetery?"

"The academy. There's a masquerade tonight in celebration of the founder."

Clarity blooms in my cranium. "*Putain.*"

"What?"

"Leviathan. She's heard from them, and she's going in alone." I take the stairs two at a time, sending Quinn a half-assed apology text for abandoning the rest of my shift. "Watch her, Emi. Don't let her out of your sight."

"What are you going to do?"

"I'm going to finish what I started ten years ago and hunt the little devil down."

COSMETICS
POPPY

The Old Main of St. Aurelius's Liberal Arts is a sight of majestic grandeur unlike any I've ever seen.

The ancient behemoth is a harmonious blend of architectural styles: Norman, Arab, Byzantine, Gothic. Lush gardens surround the building, flourishing in the first yawns of spring. Dew coats petals like liquid diamonds. Grand statues of angels and warriors upon chariots and soaring pegasuses balance the pops of color with somber notes of gray.

It reminds me of Morgenstern Manor, and I'm even more curious about my ancestor who supposedly attended this academy.

Ahead, ushers and security guards linger around the grand arched doors open to guests pouring in from their parade of Jaguars and Teslas. Someone was pompous enough to bring a horse-drawn carriage. Buttery firelight spills from inside, Victorian music along with it. I doff my helmet and suck down a lungful of spring's balmy breath, idling at the line's rear.

This is it. No more waiting, no more planning. No more chasing dead ends.

I have one shot to right my worst wrong.

The line moves, and I don my half Leviathan mask. Ushers take the Ninja before I'm escorted inside, where mosaic floors and walls painted in breathtaking frescoes greet me. The artistry is charming yet haunting: fallen angels weeping into their hands; demons looming over mortals cowering in fear. Many pieces are incomplete. As if whoever started them died before they could finish.

I'm led through the maze of corridors with the other masked guests to a grand courtyard open to the night. A string quartet plays Bach from a shadowy corner. Tables carved into the shape of crescent moons line the walls, set for a feast that could feed an entire army. Snatching a sparkling drink from a passing tray, I pace the perimeter and scan the crowd for any familiar faces.

I lock gazes with a woman in a black, crushed velvet gown whose wild cinnamon curls and big blue eyes I instantly recognize.

What the fuck is Quinn doing here?

"Poppy?" She approaches with a bemused smile. "I didn't know you were on the guest list."

"Touché."

"Oh, Christ, this probably looks like it's something it isn't. I got an invitation when Shane was still..." She clears her throat, her lashes glistening. "I wasn't going to come, but then Brontë left work sick, and I figured instead of wasting this one chance, I'd see if maybe Shane would be here."

Too many questions war for my tongue. The first is: "Brontë is sick?"

"Anyone would be after mixing coffee with pizza."

My nose scrunches. "Gross."

"No kidding."

Not willing to lower my guard, I check my phone. "Ah, he did try calling. Along with texting me your number. You called, too...?"

"We were talking boys." She waves a dismissive hand. "Anyway, I haven't seen Shane. Have you?"

"Nope." Technically, it's not a lie.

Quinn nods, sipping her drink and casting her attention to the sea of masked guests around us. "Maybe he's running late."

"Sure, possibly."

I crane my neck to watch the people funneling in. There's hundreds in attendance. All filthy rich, judging by the couture and gold and general posturing as if someone shoved sticks up their asses.

An itch forms beneath my skin the longer I study the guests. Many know each other, exchanging hugs and familiar smiles. Which is a worrisome level of odd, considering Leviathan's members are blind to one another's identities. These people seem more like those you'd see at a church or community event.

Followers, perhaps? If so, how is that possible? Leviathan is a ghost.

I peer at a nearby trio of women huddled closely, sniggering amongst themselves, and I swear on every star in the cosmos I see fangs flashing—

A tall figure slinks through the courtyard, derailing my thoughts. Broad shoulders, generous muscles, dark hair. For a moment, I imagine Brontë beneath the mask.

But then I see his eyes, and my own widen.

They're mismatched: the right is pale ivy, the other white as death. Four brutal scars slash from his left temple to the edge of his opposite cheek. They look like they were made by an animal. Something big and pissed.

Whoever he is, he easily spies me gawking. He recognizes me instantly, jerking forward. Silver metal flickers in his hand.

I reach for my gun.

Then he sees someone behind me and freezes mid-step.

Quinn suddenly latches onto my arm, startling me. "I think I see Shane! Come on. This way."

Too shellshocked, I let her drag me through the crowd. We stumble past the strange man. A musk of citrus and cigarette smoke clings to him like a shadow. My elbow grazes his knuckles as Quinn tows me behind her.

That's when I see it: the lighter clenched in his fist.

Whoever they are, they're a smoker.

By the fucking stars. *He's* who I spoke to, the ringleader Scull took orders from. The one at the top of Leviathan's food chain.

I dig my heels in. "Quinn, wait."

"I can't do this without you." When she turns to me, tears leaking mascara down her cheeks, guilt tips a rusty blade into my ribs. "Please, Poppy. You're the only person here I know and trust. If it's not him, I'll leave. Promise."

How am I supposed to deny a heartbroken woman? "All right, Henriette. Let's find Casanova."

I throw a final glance over my shoulder, but the man is nowhere in sight. He's watching, though. I can feel those harrowing eyes on the back of my head.

Quinn rushes to the entry hall, politely shoving through oncoming traffic. When we reach the entrance with no Scull in sight, she visibly deflates and sobs into her palms like the fallen angels on the walls.

"I-I swear I thought I saw him."

"I know." I wince sympathetically and steer her toward the restroom before she has a humiliating public meltdown. "Come on, let's get you cleaned up."

Quinn rips off her mask, panting at her reflection above the sink as I wipe her bleeding cosmetics with a damp towelette. "I'm so fucking tired of always seeing him. Every day, he's just around the corner or in someone's face. I miss him, and I hate it."

My lips roll into a line. "I'm sorry, Quinn. You deserve better."

It's all I can give her without revealing the truth.

"Can I ask you something?"

"You just did."

Quinn snorts. "Brontë is rubbing off on you."

"And I'm not complaining." I smile at her small laugh. "What's your question?"

"Did you burn or bury the love of my life after Brontë skinned him alive?"

I stiffen. Stare.

Quinn's teary gaze slides to me. She's unnervingly still, the calm before the storm. Then she grins like a cat with a canary trapped under its paw.

And it all makes perfect, agonizing sense.

Quinn wasn't Scull's little, unsuspecting lamb like we'd thought. No, she's a lion—just like he'd been.

"You," I breathe.

She leans in and breathes back, "Me."

I grab my gun, but she fists my hair and shoves my head into the mirror so hard, my mask crumples. Before I can right myself, something thin and metallic and sharp pricks my neck—a needle.

I gasp, stumbling back and tripping over my own feet. I topple to the floor, my limbs too heavy. Quinn's sneer blurs as darkness envelopes my vision. She paws through my pockets, stomping on my phone and stealing my weapons. Then she lifts a small device I've never seen before.

A tracker.

"Aw, look at this. Your boyfriend has been stalking you." She crushes the tech beneath her stiletto. "We don't need him crashing our girls' night, do we?"

I try clawing her face, but my fingernails graze her skin as harmlessly as feathers.

As my eyes drift shut, Quinn croons, "Sweet dreams, princess. Your reckoning is about to begin."

RECHERCHÉ
Brontë

Dantë sifts through guns, ammo, and an assembly of military-grade equipment organized in neat rows on the kitchen island.

He keeps it all hidden behind a hollow panel in his closet. Although I never condoned his hoarding of this much weaponry, I'm grateful for it now. Even the skull masks he makes himself with human bone from the criminals I skin will prove useful for what we're about to do.

"Keep your wits, brother," I say as I check my Kimber. "Not a single Leviathan leaves that masquerade alive."

"Understood." Dantë loads a pump-action shotgun and aims out the window overlooking the deceptively calm Atlantic. "Ready to get back on this old bike?"

"*Oui.*" I clip smoke grenades onto my belt and strap a tactical vest to my torso as he slings the shotgun onto his back and slips KA-BAR knives into the sheaths on his thighs. "You?"

"As ready as I'll ever be." He slings a bandolier of grenades over his chest. "You seem pretty calm, considering. Are you feeling well enough to do this?"

It's a fair question. If I were losing my shit thinking of Poppy either afraid or dead, I'd be a liability. Nothing is more dangerous in a hostile zone than an unstable mind.

I flex my right hand, not needing to look at the runes that spell the wrath coursing through my nervous system. But instead of succumbing to the rage boiling in my blood, instead of letting it ride me, I take the reins and channel it to fuel my potential.

"*Oui,* I'm good."

"*Merveilleuse.*" Dantë and I each pick a clear Bluetooth earpiece from the countertop and lodge them in our ears. "Keep the line silent unless shit goes south."

I finish packing myself with weapons and turn to find Jezebel sitting on her haunches, tail flicking. I found her locked in the manor's library after I dropped by for Poppy's parents, who weren't there and didn't answer their phones. "You're staying here, *ma chou.*"

Eerily, the black panther inclines her head. I wouldn't be shocked if she truly is a guardian angel, sent here to monitor her charge. Her ears perk a moment before my pocket vibrates.

I check the caller ID before answering. "What do you want, Volkov?"

"Emi spread the news. I'm coming with you, Bourbon."

My hackles rise. "No, you're not."

"*Da,* I am. You're not the only person who cares about Poppy." Before I register the echo, I'm staring at Nikolai as he steps into the kitchen from the basement door. Slippery bastard snuck in here, probably through the same damn window that Poppy had all those months ago. He flicks a hand at our weapons and gear. "Got any more goodies to spare?"

I don't bother arguing any further. He's made his decision.

"Only if you can follow orders."

"No going rogue. Got it." He loads himself up with pistols and blades. "What's the plan?"

As Dantë tells him, my cell buzzes again. I answer my phone on speaker with a gruff, "Emi?"

"Poppy's phone signal just went dark. I'm trying to hack the campus cams, but they're blocked."

"Shit. Hold on, I have her bugged."

Ignoring the incredulous glares, I open the app.

There's no pink dot.

I see red, growling, "*Fuck.*"

"Has anyone tried calling Poppy's parents?" Nikolai asks.

"*Oui,* no answer. They weren't home, either. Jezebel was locked in the library."

"Let me check the manor's cameras," Emi says, typing vigorously. "Shit! They're wiped. Along with every fucking street cam in Salem."

My phone cracks in my grip. I find my brother's anguished gaze, and my chest threatens to burst.

Something strange happens when emotion triggers the most primal parts of us to wake up and open its eyes. Something inexplicable. First, the world shrinks—then silences altogether. As if the awakening of that intuition, that instinct, that beast within us all, is so recherché, even the air holds its breath.

A vibration disrupts the silence.

"I-I'm getting another call," Emi stammers, her unsteady voice grating my raw nerves. "I don't know the number."

A beat passes before Dantë barks, "Answer it, Remiel."

"Okay, okay, l-let me bridge the call." Never has a moment felt like an eternity. "H-hello?"

First, I hear the lighter. Then the modified voice growls, "St. Aurelius's tomb. Tell whoever you need. This ends tonight."

"I-I don't understand."

"You don't need to understand. You need to save the last Morgensterns while they still breathe."

Click.

My world goes mute, questions circling my skull like vultures. Dantë takes my phone before I can crush it and says more to Emi. I'm not listening. Not as I crack at the seams and breathe decimation.

Nikolai settles a hand on my shoulder. "She needs you."

I need you, Poppy once said to me.

She. Needs. *Me.*

"Emi," I say, grabbing a mask, "can you tap into our comms?"

"Already here," she reports in our ears.

"*Parfait.* I need you to call Bax. Tell him to meet us at Indigo with as much dynamite as he can get his pyromaniac hands on."

"On it."

I turn to the black panther who looks just as bloodthirsty as me.

"Oh, Jezebel." I grin wide as my sanity catapults into another dimension. The one where I'm Scythe, on a mission to flay skin from bone and make it fucking *hurt.* "How hungry are you for sinners' flesh?"

Jezebel yowls, a murderous gleam in her hellfire eyes.

CLICHÉ
POPPY

The quiet, steady crackle of burning wood slowly drags me up from an endless abyss.

Memories flash through my mind like strobe lights: frescoes; mismatched eyes; a serpent that had been lying in the shade and waiting to strike.

Quinn.

A lion wearing lamb's skin.

Fury ignites in my veins, burning me awake. I wrench myself out of the drug's grip, only to be choked by a collar clamped tight around my throat. Chains wrap my body from ankles to shoulders. My spine is straight as a sword, my boots planted on a slab of wood.

Am I chained to a fucking pyre?

Adrenaline dumps through my system as I frantically absorb my surroundings. I'm in the middle of St. Aurelius's necropolis, centered on the pentagram carved into the stone floor. The wall sconces are lit, popping merrily in the undercroft of Leviathan's founding families. Smoke and the stench of burned flesh clogs the air, thick as fog. Ash and soot stain the floor in patches, as if...

As if this is where Leviathan has been taking my family.

And *burning* them to death.

Fear washes through my rage. My head swings left, and I see Mama around the corner of the pyre. Papa is to my right. Both are chained and unconscious, their chins to their chests.

No. No, no, no—

"At last," breathes a demonic voice, "she wakes."

A pair of masked figures emerge from the farthest shadows of the crypt. I can do nothing as they approach, their robes slithering behind them like snakes. Their faces are completely concealed. As they near, their silhouettes take shape. Neither of them are built like the man with heterochromia I saw at the masquerade.

"What the fuck is this?" I snarl, struggling uselessly. "I spoke with your boss. I told him to take this up with me, not my fucking family. Where is he?"

One says, "I'm afraid whoever you spoke to, Poppy, does not speak for Leviathan."

The other says, "At least, not anymore."

"Let's not confuse her further, Acolyte."

"Why not, Magus? It's been so *entertaining* watching her spin in circles all these months."

"Mm. It has, hasn't it?"

Their sniggers sound like fiends cackling over fresh meat.

My focus darts between them, unsure who is saying what. "Is there a clause in your creepy cult handbook that says you can't show your faces to the dead-to-be? Or are you all just fucking cowards?"

They tilt their heads and share a glance. The left one moves first, doffing the mask with gloved hands to reveal cinnamon ringlets and sapphire doe eyes.

I snicker. "How underwhelming."

Quinn scoffs. "You're not even going to ask me *why?*"

"Don't insult my intelligence. You're a fucking cliché, Quinn Wildes. Raised by a cop, only to learn they're just another shade of gray disguised in blue. Drawn to the dark side, because, well, we have cookies and morally black men. Speaking of the latter, you fell in love with one. Kudos on living out the age-gap fantasy, by the way. You discovered his secret in some way or another—let's be honest, nobody cares—and became his understudy. Made up that bullshit lie about being blackmailed. Willingly helped him with the purge of my bloodline to earn yourself a place among his people. Explains why you aren't branded yet. But you will be, right? After your task is complete. Oh, and let's not forget about your fake friendship with the coroner who'd been hunting me for ten years. He gobbled up all your lies, because he sees the good in people. But you're not good, are you? You're the villain, and you always were." I smirk at her scowl. "Did I get anything wrong, *Acolyte?*"

Quinn remains damnably silent. Her superior, though, chortles as if impressed.

"You missed your calling in profiling, Poppy."

"Wasn't in the cards." I shrug. "And who are you, Magus?"

"You're not going to guess?"

"Don't want to flex too hard. Might hurt myself."

Another chortle. "Oh, how I've forgotten your fire."

My eyebrows knit as the gloves come off first, unveiling a fresh manicure and a stunning opaline ring. Then the mask slides from golden beachwaves and a misshapen ear that I distinctly remember my bullet grazing after I'd been stabbed. Thick lashes lift, and chocolate eyes solder to mine.

I shouldn't be shocked. We knew she was involved with Leviathan in some regard. Yet I feel like I'm staring at Medusa shedding her snakeskin.

"Margot." I suppose the poppet we found in the academy archives wasn't made for her, but *by* her. "Now, *this* is a surprise."

A sinister smile spiders over her Cupid's bow. "Would you like to psychoanalyze me now?"

"Not enough therapists in the world for that."

"That's what I like about you, Poppy: you've got balls. Unlike the rest of your boring family." A dismissive flick of her wrist at Mama and Papa, both still knocked out cold. "So, tell me. How is Brontë? Is he as delicious in bed as his brother?"

"Fuck you."

Margot chortles as she idly toys with the ring—the Bourbon heirloom. It reminds me of Brontë's eyes, the gemstone casting a kaleidoscope of colors over her grin. "There's a story behind this ring that isn't widely known. Apparently, it was forged by a guardian angel who fell in love with his mortal charge. He was of course banished from Heaven to live eternity in Hell. Legend says his lover ended her life early to be with him forever. That mortal was supposedly an Aurelius. When Ancient Rome fell, the ring was lost and later found on the shores of *Baie des Anges* in Nice, France by a Bourbon."

It takes me a moment to catch onto what she's really saying. "You targeted Dantë for the ring. His past didn't scare you off. You got what you wanted and left."

"*Très bien, ma chérie.* Let's try another round, shall we? While we're on the subject of ancient history, do you know what happened to our founding families?"

"They were all hung while Felix burned."

"All except...?"

"Octavia Morgenstern."

"Bravo. Why?"

"She flew from the noose on her broomstick."

Margot's dark gaze slides to Quinn. "Do you remember the story, Acolyte?"

"Of course, Magus. Upon joining our Father's inner circle, Octavia was promised a cure for her infertility. A ritual was planned to fulfill this vow, along with those promised to the other members, but the night of their sabbath was raided by witch hunters. Octavia stood at the noose alongside her peers and watched our Father burn. She prayed to Lucifer to save their lives. He saved only *her* life, and—"

My snort cuts her off. "Do you even hear yourself?"

"I assure you, Poppy," Margot says, "you'll want to listen closely."

"This is fucking psychotic, but sure. Finish your pitch. Not like I'm going anywhere."

Margot nods to Quinn, who continues, "In exchange for saving her life, Octavia agreed to bear Lucifer's child. Rumor has it they were star-crossed lovers and that he forged her a ring of black diamonds not unlike the Aurelius ring."

My attention flits briefly to Mama's ring. Swallowing suddenly becomes a Herculean effort. What are the chances this is all fucking *real?*

No. It's not real. It's just more stories told by a radical and ludicrous satanic cult.

I bark a laugh, half hoping my parents wake up. They don't. "So, you're telling me that my ancestor was in love with the Devil, and I'm from a long line of Antichrists?"

Quinn arches an eyebrow. "Who's the cliché now?"

Margot lays a silencing hand on Quinn's shoulder. "You're focusing on the wrong angle, Poppy. *Everyone* was meant to die that night. Octavia cheated death. No one does so without disastrous consequences. Look at all that's happened to your family over the years since then: your war with the Volkovs, the fall of your empire. Don't you see? A debt has yet to be paid. Death won't stop until it's collected what's owed."

I don't believe any of it, but she does. So, I play along.

The longer she talks, the more time I have to get out of this mess. Brontë will be looking for me by now, especially if he checked that tracker and found it inactive.

"Where does Sebastian fit in?"

Margot drifts to the Bonaparte casket, drawing her fingertips through the dust. "Many of us have been lying in wait for the moment we could make a move to undo Octavia's curse without breaking our most fundamental rule: We, the Church, do not engage in the Crown's affairs. There's been disagreement among our ranks regarding how to handle the death of a legacy by your hand, causing a rift in leadership and splitting all the way down to the bone. Simply put, we are at war with ourselves. Our people are now slaughtering each other. Death's curse has afflicted us as surely as you. The only way to stop it is to correct Octavia's mistake and satisfy death's craving by spilling every last drop of Morgenstern blood." Her gaze pins mine like nails in a coffin. "And begging Lucifer for forgiveness."

My upper lip curls. Here I am thinking *I'm* insane.

Margot suddenly brandishes a wicked knife from her sleeve and grabs Quinn's curls. In a blink, blood splatters the stone at their feet. Quinn gasps, hands flying to her slit throat.

And the lion becomes the lamb.

"Your sacrifice will be remembered, Acolyte," Margot murmurs, watching Quinn drop with bored apathy. "Rest now in the fires of Hell."

Rage flickers within me once more. If anyone had the right to claim that cunt's life, it should've been Brontë.

Quinn twitches in the last throes of death. Her irises dull as her blood soaks into the pentagram. Margot wastes no time, conjuring a ball of flame with a mere flick of her wrist and tossing it into the kindling circling the pyre.

"What the *fuck?*" I shout, unable to comprehend what I just witnessed. "What are you?"

"I'm a witch, Poppy." Margot kneels outside the pentagram, drawing a grimoire from her robes with a wicked grin. "Hush now. It'll all make sense soon."

Her eyes roll back as she chants Latin verses. As if she's actually planning to summon the fucking Devil.

Flames lick at the bottom of my boots. Their stifling heat scorches my lungs. Mama and Papa are still asleep, unaware they're about to be burned alive.

An impossible breeze lifts my hair, an electric current sliding over my skin. My eyes play tricks on me, elongating the shadows. I swear I see the pentagram *pulse* a vibrant, bloody red.

Not real. It's not fucking *real.*

Smoke swirls around the pyre, gripping my throat tight. My eyes slam shut against the sting. I don't know what is happening or how. Magic is fiction, not reality. Maybe I'm hallucinating. Maybe I've finally lost what little I had left of my sanity.

It doesn't matter because I'm about to die.

But it's not myself that I care about. It's my parents on either side of me, the mother and father I've been lucky enough to have my entire life. It's the people I'd be leaving behind. It's the man I fell for, the angel of a soul I trusted enough with my whole black heart.

For just a moment, I imagine what we would've looked like captured on canvas beside each other. Brontë, his arms around me like protective wings. Me, wearing a crown like a halo and clinging to him as if he's my salvation.

My king. My angel.

The love of my life.

As the heat of the flames flares hot enough to scald my skin, I don't pray to the stars.

I pray to the only angel that I believe in.

PHANTASM
BRONTË

St. Aurelius's Cemetery is crawling with Leviathan guards like maggots on a corpse.

Foot patrols monitor the graveyard, their masks like demons in the dark. Their M16s and flashlights pan over headstones. Not that they can hear or see shit in this torrential downpour drowning the forest and thick fog blinding them to a black panther and three men setting up jars of dynamite powder around the entire perimeter.

Jezebel paces between us as we work. She stares, unblinking, at the Aurelius mausoleum towering over the cemetery. Sensing something none of us can. Edging my every ragged nerve.

"We're all set, Emi," I murmur as I carefully lodge the last jar in the mud. Her drone hovers nearby, watching for hostile activity. "Tell Bax I owe him a few drinks."

"Copy. Be safe, all of you."

"We will. Over and out."

Nikolai is the first to take off without so much as a goodbye or a backward glance, KA-BARs in his fists as he vanishes into the dark. Dantë takes a step forward, but I catch his bicep, jerking him back.

"If I fall—"

"You won't."

"*If* I do, you keep moving and save her. Got it?"

His eyes lock on mine, fear thrumming under the surface of his mask. "Got it."

I nod, and he disappears into the spectral fog like a phantasm. That's it; no goodbyes.

We learned long ago to never give death an opening. It'll snatch any opportunity with greedy hands and hungry teeth.

Breathing steam through my nostrils, I pull my own blades and start moving. Jezebel prowls at my side, fangs bared.

All good plans are simple, with as little twists and turns as possible to ensure the smallest margin of error. Fanning out, we each claim overlapping sectors of the cemetery as ours to clean, working our way in toward the mausoleum from the outskirts so we don't miss a single hostile. A clear path will grant us passage into the Aurelius crypt without having to watch our own backs, and the distraction planted along the treeline will turn their heads for that split second we need to slip into the viper's den undetected.

Jezebel and I stalk as one, targeting our first victim in seamless synchronicity. They don't even hear us trailing behind them, nor do they feel death's breath on their neck until my gloved hand is over their mouth, gagging their startled shout. A swift slice through their jugular, and they drop like a weighted sack. Blood pools onto the ground beneath them like molten rubies.

For just a moment, I let myself feel the heaviness of taking a life. Regardless of who they are or the cult they serve, these people likely have families waiting for them to come home.

But I am not the one who recruited them. I am not the one who brought them here, knowing they'd be in danger of becoming sacrificial pawns in this macabre game of chess. Their blood is on Leviathan's hands, not mine.

Still, I whisper a prayer for them to find their way to where they belong.

And then I move on to the next.

Again and again, I reach for the memories I've been avoiding for so long to charge the force behind every cold-blooded murder: Mama's hazel eyes closing far too soon; my father's hot blood bathing me in death; rabid dogs chasing me and my siblings through eldritch mazes; skinning and stitching to the sound of wretched screams; seeing the woman I love lying in bed as she fought for her life.

I lose count of the bodies I leave in my wake. Behind me, I see only one color.

Red.

I never told her, but Virgil's fear for me was misplaced. She was there with me and my brother in Sleepy Hollow. She took as long to recover from the trauma as us. But she forgets what happened before that. She forgets that we were trained to be ruthless killing machines.

Murder is in our blood.

Jezebel pounces the next doomed soul as they round the corner of a gargoyle statue. This feline is a force of nature unlike any I've ever seen. Silent as tombs, deadlier than any bullet or blade. She goes for the throat, downing them without a single sound aside from a wet gargle and a heavy *thump*.

Scanning my surroundings to ensure we didn't miss anyone, I murmur, "Secure."

A moment later, Nikolai tags in. "Secure."

"Brontë," Danté growls in my ear, sounding strained. "I need h—"

He cuts off with a bark of pain, and I'm instantly running with Jezebel at my heels. We skid around a tall trio of weeping angels. Crimson blooms on Danté's right thigh as he struggles with fending off two guards at once. I target the one lifting their rifle.

The KA-BAR slingshots from my hand, clanging against the raised gun. The guard whips their head my way, and Dantë sinks his blade into their gut. I switch my focus to the other guard, lifting another knife to throw.

They fall for the bait, latching their attention onto me as Jezebel strikes from behind, ripping and shredding until they die with a whimper.

I clap my twin's shoulder, jutting my chin toward the slice in his thigh. "All right, Ghostface?"

"Never better." He grins, his pupils dilated. He's high on adrenaline.

I shake my head, muttering, "Fucking *cretin*," under my breath.

"They know you're there," Emi warns. "Light it up. *Now!*"

Dantë lurches, moving fast as if he wasn't just stabbed in the leg. He slings off his bandolier of grenades, pulls the pin from a single pineapple, and flings it back toward the treeline. The three of us immediately sprint for cover, diving around the back of a gravestone just as the thunderous *BOOM* shakes the night awake.

Faster than a lick of lightning, the dynamite catches the explosion and erupts like a slumbering volcano disturbed from its peaceful sleep and taking vengeance by ending the world. Flames spear into the sky as the forest ignites in an inferno of hot, hungry fire.

Somewhere in the chaos, I hear a madman's laughter. It takes me a moment to realize it's coming from my ear, and it sounds like Bax.

Angels above. He really is a pyromaniac.

"Volkov," I bark. "Tag in."

No response.

"Emi?"

"Looking!"

"We're wasting time," Dantë growls. "He's probably dead."

"*Putain.* Fuck it. Let's go!"

While all eyes are turned away from us and the world is deafened, we run for the mausoleum. I take the lead, popping smoke grenades as we sweep through the cemetery. Resistance meets us head-on, shouting and gunfire lost in the cacophony of the chaos. We slay every Leviathan guard trying to stand in our way. Every last one.

In minutes, we reach the Aurelius crypt, but someone beats us to the entrance—Nikolai.

"Dead." He scoffs, his mask drenched in gore. "Your lack of faith in me is truly offensive."

I'll never admit it aloud, but I'm more than relieved.

We barge into the crypt, making quick work of the guards inside. I slam the pommel of my knife into the inverted ruby cross upon the empty sarcophagus. The passageway opens, and smoke billows out in thick clouds of gray. Distant screams send shivers down my spine.

I know that voice like I know my own name.

Poppy.

Poppy is screaming.

My world falls into absolute silence.

Jezebel bolts down the stairs. We follow, graceless but swift. Emi's drone whizzes over our heads, but her voice crackles in our ears as the signal drops.

Halfway down, an impossible wind shoves the smoke past us, funneling toward the opening at our backs. It's so strong, it pushes Emi's drone up, up, up the same path we're taking down. Stumbling over each other at the bottom, we brace ourselves against the wind and absorb the scene: the last living Morgensterns chained to a burning pyre, Quinn—fucking *Quinn*—lying dead in Leviathan garb while a blond woman chants an incantation on her knees outside the pentagram.

The *glowing* pentagram.

A trick of the light. That's all it is. Because anything else isn't fucking possible.

Poppy sees us and cries, "Brontë!"

The woman whips her glare to us.

My blood freezes.

"Margot?" Dantë breathes.

Jezebel roars and launches forward at full throttle.

Then Margot pulls a pistol from her robes and shoots her down.

FIRESTORM
POPPY

Jezebel falls in a heap of black fur. She doesn't get up.

My heart stops. *Not my baby.*

My scream scrapes out my throat like the last screech of a dying beast. I snarl at Margot, whose grin grows eerily wide.

Dantë pumps his shotgun, taking aim at his runaway fiancée. But the slippery bitch is already climbing onto the pyre, banking the flames with a flick of her wrist and wedging herself behind me, where he won't be able to shoot without peppering me and my parents with buckshot.

As soon as Nikolai and Brontë train their pistols on her, Margot clicks her tongue and presses her gun to my temple.

The unnatural wind stops.

Chills spiderwalk down every vertebrae in my spine.

My eyes find Brontë's through the rippling flames. A firestorm rages in his hazel stare. *You will not die,* he seems to convey with that subtle dip of his chin. *I will not allow it.*

I nearly sob. He seems to forget that he's no death-defying god.

"Let's not play any games, boys," Margot croons, using me as her human shield. "We all know how this ends."

"*Oui,* we do," Dantë growls. "With your cold corpse rotting in the dirt."

Margot's chuckle sounds like scales slithering through thorns. "One day, Reaper. Just not today. Unless, of course, you want your mother's ring back now rather than never...?"

Dantë's finger flirts with the trigger. Nikolai orders him to stand down.

"Back off, Volkov," the former snaps, swinging his gun and training the barrel on Nik, "or you're eating lead."

"I'm not your fucking enemy," the latter snaps back at the same time Brontë barks, "Both of you—enough!"

More poison drips from Margot's lips, incantations slipping between them. She's turning them on each other, the power of suggestion magnified by whatever those words mean.

And I've had *enough* of this insanity.

I may have a gun to my head, but that doesn't mean I don't get to choose whether I fight for life or roll over and let death take me.

"Coward," I spit, my chin snapping up. My skull bashes Margot's nose with a satisfying crunch. She yelps, her head whipping back, and—

Bang!

I expect my lights to go out, but then I grasp I wasn't shot. My eyes widen on Brontë's smoking Kimber as Margot's gun falls from her hand. She clutches her bleeding shoulder, her teeth stained scarlet as blood hemorrhages from her broken nose.

Something cracks above us. It sounds like bones snapping.

Margot's gaze lifts, bloodshot whites flashing in both awe and terror. "He's here."

I see nothing but smoke.

Then every flame in the chamber snuffs out.

Time slows. Every blink is a decade; every motion, an eternity.

Impossible. This is *impossible.*

My heart rebels in my ribcage. I hear nothing but my own rapid pulse and heaving lungs. I feel a touch on my cheek so cold, it burns like winter fire. An arctic breath frosts the sweat on my temple, chilling as death.

"*Filia.*"

The voice is both young and ancient, man and beast. I shake uncontrollably as the feeling of fingertips like icy fire trail down my arms. I hear my restraints clinking, as if a claw is dragging through each link. A growl, unholy and as monstrous as a creature risen from the depths of Hell, rumbles through the dark.

That's when I see them: the eyes cracking open an inch from mine.

They're breathtaking...and they're the things nightmares are made of—draconic and glowing a radiant, vibrant violet. Swirls of flames dance within them, rippling at their edges like hellfire. I see myself within them, terror on my face, and I swear they soften in response to my undiluted fear.

My mouth opens for a scream, but then those harrowing eyes close. Upon my brow, I feel my fringe being brushed aside, replaced by freezing lips. Against my skin, the voice whispers, "*Occidere.*"

My collar shatters, and my chains snap.

Time jolts. Sconces blaze to life, scorching the dark to light. The otherworldly presence is gone—along with Quinn's body.

But I have no time to question any of it as Margot is already bolting up the stairs behind the three confused men. Dantë whips around first and takes chase. I snatch her forgotten pistol and dash from the pyre, barking, "Nik, grab my parents. Brontë, check on Jezebel."

Brontë snags my throat as I'm rushing past. He wrenches his bloodstained mask up and strikes my mouth with his. For just a heartbeat, I let myself kiss him. Earth could be falling above us, and I wouldn't even notice as he delves deep enough to taste my soul.

"Don't *ever* lie to me again, Poppy Morgenstern," he growls, voice breaking, before ripping himself away and dashing to Jezebel.

Head still spinning, I catch up to Dantë at the mausoleum entrance. He's teetering, losing his balance as blood streams down his right pant leg.

"Too far," he grinds out as he sags to his knees. "Can't get a shot."

I peer out to the cemetery as Margot reaches the edge of the burning treeline. The tall flames devour the downpour, blazing through the fog.

Steadying my breath, I line up the sight with the back of her head. It's a far distance for a handgun, but I was raised by a deadeye. I aim a few paces ahead of her, my finger finding the trigger and—

Dantë knocks into me, sending my killshot soaring straight past Margot's head. She disappears through the trees, and a furious shriek bursts out of me. Tears carve lines down to my vengeful heart. I turn the gun on Dantë, ready to maim his other leg for fucking up my shot.

But his eyes are fluttering shut.

All thoughts of revenge vanish as I drop to my knees and pull him into my lap. Checking his pulse and finding it weak, I vow to him and every star watching, "Death will not claim another life tonight."

$$\text{\textbf{\textendash}\!\textbf{\textbullet}\!\textbf{\textendash}}$$

HALLUCINATION
Brontë

ONE MONTH LATER

Poppy won't stop shivering.

We're sharing a loveseat in the library at Morgenstern Manor. She's wrapped in a blanket, a steaming mug in her grip and her head resting on my shoulder as her pet panther snores in her lap.

We're lucky Jezebel survived the shots she took. If she hadn't, I doubt Poppy would still be herself.

There's a blank space in my memory between shooting Margot while she'd been fifty feet away on a burning pyre and that pyre being empty of flames while Margot ran up the stairs *behind* me. During that same glitch in reality, Quinn's corpse disappeared.

Neither Nikolai nor Dantë remember those moments, either.

Worse yet, the bodies of every Leviathan member we'd laid waste to had vanished. Rain washed their blood away and doused the fire from the dynamite we'd detonated. As if none of it had even happened.

Poppy has yet to talk about what she saw. Virgil says she could at any point, but it's already been a month. She's been having nightmares, waking up screaming. When I'm able to calm her, she says she keeps reliving that night over and over. My lullabies help her sleep, but she's still waking with restless bruises beneath her eyes.

My gaze finds Rin's, then Alexander's. Shame weighs their shoulders down. They weren't able to protect their daughter when she needed them most. Worse, the predator preying upon their family escaped without leaving a single lead for us to follow.

Margot has vanished. Though it's unclear how many cult members are on what sides of Leviathan's internal war, we've all been watching our backs for another attack. Emi has contacted the number belonging to the man Poppy saw at Leviathan's masquerade—the same man who called to help us find her and her parents that night, leaving us constantly asking ourselves why.

No one has answered.

Leaving too many questions in the void.

"*Filia*," Poppy murmurs into her mug, baby blues swimming with the same uncertainty she's been carrying for weeks. "Does anyone know that word?"

Alexander blinks through a wine-induced haze. "It's Latin for 'daughter.'"

"And *occidere?*"

"Why are you asking, *Petit Diable?*" I interject before her father can reply.

"Just curious."

My eyes taper at the blatant lie, but I don't push her. Not while she's still recovering from that night.

"'Kill,'" Alexander says with the same narrowed gaze as me. "*Occidere* is a command to kill."

Poppy shivers again, curling into a tighter ball beneath my arm. Her parents exchange a loaded glance that sets my teeth grinding before Rin places a hand on Poppy's knee.

"What did you see, darling?"

Poppy hesitates, and then her shoulder hikes in a tentative shrug. When she looks at me with the memory of impossible wind and a glowing pentagram haunting her eyes, she answers, "It doesn't matter. It wasn't real; it was just another hallucination."

⸻⸺◆⸺⸻

A quiet week later, I'm breathing gray smoke out a window cracked to the May dawn as Poppy sits at her father's desk in his study, reading through her childhood fairytales with tears in her eyes.

"I want her back," she rasps, flipping through the leather-bound notebooks. "I want this little girl back."

I don't have any encouraging words to offer. She'll never get that piece of herself back, and she knows it. Her innocence died the day her father handed her a knife and ordered her to take a life. At her core, Poppy Morgenstern is a killer.

Leviathan spent enough time beating that fact into her bones.

"You still have a choice," I remind her. "Assume your birthright and rule. Or let the legacy of your forefathers die."

"Let's tackle that another day." Poppy sighs, closing her notebooks in a desk drawer and joining my side as she nurses her vape. "How is Danté?"

Since that bloody night last month nearly killed him, my twin has been healing at a decent rate and walking with only a slight limp. He's still beyond exhausted, using his recovery time to pour himself into gaming to distract himself from the less-than-slim chances of ever seeing Mama's ring again.

"Physically, he's fine."

"You know that's not what I'm asking."

"Not to sound like a copycat, but let's tackle that another day."

"Fair enough." She chews her bottom lip. "How has work been without..."

Without Quinn. We don't speak her name. I refuse to acknowledge she even existed. It was easy for us to plant the evidence needed for a convincing runaway story. Everyone at work had seen how devastated she'd been after Scull "left the city" and believed she'd gone to find him.

But that's not what Poppy is asking.

She's asking how *I* am without voicing the question directly. Because I never have a simple answer for how I feel about the woman I'd thought was my friend. The friend I'd given a second chance even when I shouldn't have. A second chance I'll regret for the rest of my life, as it had nearly ended in me losing the most precious person in my life.

Something wet and warm slips from my lashes.

"I'm sorry," Poppy murmurs, stepping into my side and wrapping an arm around my waist. "I shouldn't have asked."

"Don't be sorry," I say, pawing at the unbidden tear and kissing the crown of her head. "*Merci* for caring enough to ask. For being here even after my mistakes led to you and your parents in that crypt."

"That's not your burden to bear, *mon ange*." She presses a kiss to the angel guarding my heart. "You saw the good in her. Something tells me it wasn't all an act on her part, that she really did think of you as a friend, in her own twisted way. Maybe that's why Scull hadn't gone after you sooner. Maybe she was protecting you."

I don't know how much I believe that, but we'll never know now. It's the closest thing to closure I'll have, and I'm more than ready to end that chapter of my life forever.

Silence descends over us like a calm mist. It's as comforting as sitting at a campfire in the dead of winter. Poppy is my flame, and I'm hers. I toy with her hair, my knuckles brushing her spine. Goosebumps prickle her flesh as if my hands haven't been a constant presence on her skin.

I've lost count of how many times we've claimed each other. Lately, though, it's been different.

We've been different.

Everything we thought to be true was a lie. Margot wasn't murdered; she's a member of the same cult that nearly destroyed my own life twice over. Quinn wasn't my friend; she was using me to get to Poppy for her own gain.

We both saw inexplicable things that defied logic.

But we have yet to talk about any of it.

And it's driving me up a fucking wall.

"What's wrong, *mon roi?*"

"Don't ask questions you already know the answer to, *ma reine.*"

Poppy palms my cheek, thumbing the scar she gifted me. "Aren't some unknowns better left in the dark?"

"Says the woman who held a knife to my throat when demanding to know my past I also thought was better left in the dark."

"You liked it. The knife part, I mean."

"Poppy." My irritated tone causes her to flinch, and I dust apologetic kisses across her scarred fingers. "Respectfully, you're being a little prick."

"I know." She huffs a breath, ruffling her fringe. "I don't know how to describe any of it without sounding fucking insane."

"Trust me, *Petit Diable.* You can't sound any worse than I feel."

Poppy casts her gaze to the city and the rising sun beyond. "When I woke up in the crypt on the pyre with my unconscious parents, Margot and Quinn revealed themselves. And then they told me a psychotic story I have yet to wrap my head around." She briefly speaks about a supposed curse her ancestor, Octavia, triggered in cheating death thanks to the Devil himself saving her life the night she'd been destined to die. And the repercussions of that curse the longer it's left unresolved. "Margot also mentioned something about your family ring that I don't understand beyond it being a targeted object that she planned to steal from your brother all along."

"*Putain*," I breathe, raking an agitated hand through my hair. "What a fucking mess."

"There's more, Brontë. So much more."

I nod, bracing myself. "Let's hear it."

"Margot called herself a witch. I wouldn't be questioning the validity of that claim if I hadn't seen her literally conjure a ball of fire from thin air to light the pyre and subsequently cast what I can only assume was meant to be a ritual. As if that wasn't a hard enough pill to swallow, something else happened after you shot her. Something..." She shakes her head, her expression wan. "You're not going to believe me."

"Try me," I insist. Everything is making so much more sense now, even if the facts are too fantastical to contemplate being actually true.

Poppy lets her eyes drift shut, shivering even as I drape an arm over her shoulders. "Time didn't exist. Or maybe it did, and it was paused? I don't know. I felt something cold. It touched me. Not possessively, but tenderly. Adoringly. I felt its breath on my skin. First, it said, '*Filia*.' Then it opened its eyes. They were beautiful and monstrous and..." Her lips wrap the vape, and she inhales deeply, exhaling lavender smoke as her eyelids crack open. "They were that color—purple. But they were glowing, like they were made of fire. It saw my fear, and I swear on every star, it looked like it didn't want me to be afraid of it. Then it closed its eyes, kissed my forehead, and said, '*Occidere*.' That's when the restraints came loose and time resumed."

I drag on my cigar, breathing cherry smoke as I mentally digest the tale that feels more and more like fact than fiction. "Walk the path of insanity with me for a moment. Leviathan was remembered by your family as a cult, but the history of their founding father, Felix Aurelius, claims they were a coven of satanic witches. What if Margot is, indeed, a witch? That tracks with what we've learned about Leviathan thus far."

"*Hai.* But what about the creature that appeared?"

"Margot was on the side of Leviathan that believes Lucifer assisted Octavia in cheating death, which now has this insatiable hunger that must be satisfied in the form of Morgenstern blood—*Lucifer's* blood. What you just described sounds like it wasn't a creature at all. To me, it sounds like it'd been Lucifer himself, and he rose from the deepest pits of Hell to save the last of his descendants, along with commanding you to kill Margot."

Part of me wants to laugh at the outrageousness.

A larger part of me wishes my mother—an expert on all things otherworldly—was here to make sense of it all.

"If any of it was real," Poppy says slowly, puffing purple smoke, "what does it change?"

"Either nothing...or everything."

"Depending on what?"

"What you decide, I suppose." At her quizzical look, I add, "Margot may have escaped, but that doesn't mean she or anyone on her side won't be back to finish what she started. You're still a Morgenstern. You're still her target, as are your parents. You can either tuck tail and run—or stand and fight. Either way, I'm with you. Whatever you choose."

Her expression falls, and I can almost see her tucking those thoughts in a dark corner of her mind before she says, "I don't want to talk anymore."

"Poppy, you need to—"

Faster than I can register, she fists my shirt and pulls me down to her sweet lips. Her open-mouthed kiss steals whatever argument I'd been about to voice, her tongue flicking mine in silent demand. A groan climbs up my throat only to be echoed by her. Blindly tossing my cigar out the window, I palm her waist and plant her ass against the glass, shoving her red silk yukata up past her hips as the need to be inside her overrides my brain and consumes every instinct.

"Brontë," she warns, tugging the skirt back down. "Not here."

"If not here, then where?"

Poppy grabs my wrist and tows me back to the empty library. She leads me through the stacks until finding a rolling ladder. "How is this?"

"*Parfait.*"

I lift her onto a rung and unbuckle my belt, ripping her skirt up to her navel and fitting my aching cock to her weeping entrance. She whimpers, rolling her hips and impaling herself on my dick. Her inner walls constrict around me, and I nearly come undone as her greedy cunt sucks me in.

I fight against the urge to let my eyes find new homes in the back of my skull and just rut into her. I want to savor this—*her.*

Gently, I rock my hips and work myself deeper into her tight, wet heat until I'm fully seated. Arms circling my neck to hold me close, she breathes little Japanese curses against my throat like love notes.

A thousand lifetimes spent right here, in this moment, and it still wouldn't be enough. Especially not when I remember that I almost lost her again.

I don't let the intrusive thought in often, but it's a very real possibility. A hundred scenarios from that single harrowing night could've ended with the woman I love dead. With the color in my life fading back to the dullest shade of gray.

"What are you waiting for?" Poppy plunges her hands into my hair, her lips finding their home on mine. "Be a good king, and fuck your queen."

I do, tasting my name on her tongue and listening to her body sing for me. This, being inside her, reminds me that she's still here.

Alive and beautiful and certainly not a hallucination.

NORTH STAR

POPPY

"How are you feeling, *mon amour?*"

"I don't know." I fist the skirt of my black lace yukata, my palms sweaty. "It feels weird to be celebrating something as mundane as my birthday right now. Leviathan is still out there, waiting to make their next move."

Brontë bobs his head in consideration as we drift into the lot at Beelzebub's. "Haven't we earned the right to take a night off from worrying about what lurks around every dark corner?"

"I guess." We're not even inside yet, and I already want to return to the manor. This place was once my home, my haven. Now, it feels almost foreign. Like an old friend I haven't seen in so long, there's no familiarity left to find comfort in. "Let's just get this over with."

I grab the door handle, but the locks click into place.

A gun's muzzle skirts my jaw. Hot breath brushes the shell of my ear as Brontë growls, "Did I say you could leave?"

My core throbs in response, desire licking at my veins. "There is such a thing as wrong place and time, *mon ange.*"

"Relax." He ghosts the Kimber over my cheek and through my hair as I turn to face his mischievous grin. "Give me your vape."

I paw through my purse until I find the abysmally low pen. "Bax is cooking up the new batch for me, so this is it for now."

"We'll just have to share it, then."

Brontë takes the vape and hits it, draining the blue juice down to the dregs. I gape, caught between admiration and agitation.

"Greedy pr—"

He grabs my nape and latches onto my mouth with his, breathing cotton candy smoke into my lungs. I drink it down, cherishing every last vapor.

How is he this sexy without even trying?

Licking my tongue, he seals my lips with a mind-altering kiss. "Better?"

Serenity seeps into my nerves, and I lean my brow against his with a long sigh. "Better."

"*Magnifique.* Come on, let's get moving now that you've made us late."

Chuckling at my scoff, Brontë grabs my door and walks arm-in-arm with me into the café. I clutch his sleeve as we head to the corner space by the coffee bar. My friends' bright smiles greet me, and I'm passed from Brontë to Emi with a squirming Hades, then Cas and Circe and Bax, Dr. V, Danté, and finally, Nikolai.

"Happy birthday, *printsessa,*" Nik murmurs as he hugs me close. "You look radiant as ever."

I *tsk.* "Don't compliment me."

"Too weird?"

"Too dangerous." I hike a thumb over my shoulder at Brontë, whose fists are clenched in his lap as he pays half his attention to the others while watching us. "Guard dog, remember?"

Nik peels back with a smirk. "I'm not *that* threatening, am I?"

I snicker, shaking my head and sobering as his grin softens. "Thank you for being here tonight. It's a nice change of pace to see you outside a life-or-death situation."

"Didn't have a choice, really."

"Ah." My gaze briefly flits to Circe, who's also watching us. "Were you dragged here by the balls?"

He shrugs, lashes downturned. "Something like that."

"We've been through hell and back, haven't we? Could you look at me while I'm talking to you?"

His eyes anchor to mine, their gunmetal depths unreadable as I take his hand and hold it between my palms.

"A year ago, I wouldn't have ever guessed I'd be friends with you. But I also never would've guessed the thousand other things that have happened since then." I swallow thickly, suddenly battling an onslaught of emotion. "Thank you for helping them save me and my parents, Nik."

His lashes grow wet. The tears are gone in a blink, but it's enough to make my nose sting. "What are friends for?"

I squeeze his hand. "Let's catch up soon, *hai?*"

"*Da.* I'd like that."

I turn to join Brontë, but he's occupied with Jezebel.

Who should be back at the manor.

With my parents.

"*Ota ome,* darling."

Mama hugs me before I can register she's there, pecking me on each cheek. She's as lustrous as stardust in her white lace kimono. Her smile is more dazzling than I remember ever seeing.

I squint. *Why the hell is she in such a good mood?*

Better question: *Why is she here?*

I don't remember the last time I celebrated a birthday with my parents.

Papa steps out from behind her. I'm convinced my heart is going to explode the moment his wintry gaze freezes me to the spot. "Poppy."

"Papa."

"A word?" He gestures to the kitchen, where Kahula is belting out a Halsey song playing over the speakers. "In private."

I lead the way, casting a final glance over my shoulder. Mama spares me a nod as she lingers by Brontë, chatting low. The motion seems to say: *Now is your chance.*

My purse grows heavier than gravity.

I shoo Kahula from the kitchen and pivot toward Papa. "Um, what's up?"

By the fucking stars. Did my voice just *squeak?*

"Your mother suggested there was something you wished to speak about but weren't entirely comfortable sharing at home."

So much for *when you're ready...*

Dread spears my guts and sweat pebbles my brow as fear twists my insides into noxious knots.

I'm still not ready.

"Poppy." His tone is brisk. "Speak."

Trembling, I dig through my purse for the black candle that's been in my hands so much, the name carved into the wax has nearly rubbed off. I grab a match from a nearby drawer and tip the wick into the flame.

"I have no intention of continuing your legacy," I declare, my heart threatening to break my sternum. "I am starting my own chapter. Please understand that, for my health, I cannot go on living this life of—"

"Enough."

"—depravity. I am sorry for not saying any of this sooner, but you must know that I've taken the time to—"

"I don't need to hear this."

"—think about my decision, and this is it. I don't want to inherit your life, your crimes, your crown. If I do, I don't know how much longer I'll live before I die at the hands of another. Or my own."

"Poppy—"

"*Daisuki da yo.*" My voice wobbles, and my throat refuses to work. I bow my neck until my hair forms a protective veil around me. "Please don't hate me for choosing myself. I still wish to be a part of your life. I need you to know how much you mean to me, Papa. Because even after everything you put me through, you're still my North Star."

Despair rattles my breath. Tears stream down my cheeks.

There's nothing left for me to do but stand here and wait for him to disown me.

Most normal people wouldn't give a shit what he does next. My father robbed me of a childhood and stole my dreams. But he also taught me how to be a warrior and a diplomat. He taught me how to rule on my feet rather than let the world throw me onto my back and make me its slave.

Alexander Morgenstern is many things. First and foremost, he's the man who raised me.

The candle leaves my grip, and my shoulders shake.

"Poppyseed," Papa murmurs, his scent of parchment and coffee shrouding me in a nostalgic embrace. "Look at me, baby girl."

I do, lifting my damp lashes to see devastation and sorrow warring across his features. He thumbs the tears away like he used to when I was too small to hold a knife and paint the world in red.

"Your mother and I are leaving, dearest daughter."

A beat passes as my upended mind attempts to comprehend his meaning. "What?"

Papa's mouth forms a grim line as he plucks stray strands of hair sticking to my lips. "These months reminded me of how far we've strayed from our original purpose. Atop the misalignment, there is a target on our backs. Your mama and I have discussed at great length what to do and how much to involve you in our plans. We want to protect you, but we've learned our limits. If anything, you have a greater chance of survival in the company of those you've surrounded yourself with here. So, we've decided to leave the city and travel for a while. We have a local property to return to during the months we come home, but the manor is yours."

"I-I don't understand. You're...quitting?"

"Retiring," he corrects gently. "Never will you hear me say these words again, but Leviathan may have done us a favor in burning our family tree. This is your opportunity to follow whatever your dreams are now. If you wish to let this empire die, let it die. If you want to make it your own, then do so. You have no competition for the throne. You answer to no one. You have an entirely clean slate. You know what to do to get started if that's what you wish. If you need anything at any time, you have me and your mother in your pocket. Do with the keys what you will."

He pauses for me to say something, but speaking is physically impossible.

"I love you, Poppy. I never say it enough, I know that. I forgot how to be your father over the years, but I'm willing to give it another shot. No matter where you go or what you decide from here, remember that we are always under the same stars."

The love in his words...it feels like a splash of color onto life's gray palette. Sobs wrack my chest. The sound of my heart snapping free builds and builds as a roar, only to escape as a broken whimper.

In an instant, I'm clinging to him like a child and soaking the shoulder of his suit with the tears of my bleeding heart. He holds me close, rocking me gently and kissing my temple.

Like he used to when I was too young to take a life.

FAIRYTALE

BRONTË

Poppy lifts a thick stack of paper from the desk that has become ours for Bourbon Binds and plops it into my hands before drifting toward the cracked windows and puffing crimson plumes of bourbon-cherry smoke into the early June dusk.

No context, as if I'm supposed to read her mind.

This fucking woman.

"What is it?"

A tut. "Use those pretty eyes, and see for yourself."

I fan the pages and slowly realize what I'm holding. "You wrote a business plan?"

"Mhm. Mama and Papa helped. I'd like you to review it and edit as you see fit. That is, if you're still up for being my king."

Emotion ties my throat into knots. This is the most important decision of her life. She's been taking these weeks to think since we moved in together. To consider her future as a Morgenstern monarch. Not only as the last living heir shouldering the weight of centuries, but as the one person who holds all the power to reshape our city into the dream she's had since her innocence was torn from her hands and bloodied with a life of sin.

Living without fear of disappointing either of her parents—but especially her father—has unlocked the cage she was born in. I've never seen her less stressed. I've also never seen her more restless. No expectations have pressured her down one path or another. What happens from here is solely her decision. Not mine, not her father's or her mother's or anyone else's.

Hers.

"You're sure this is what you want?"

"*Hai.*" Poppy nods, red smoke filtering from her nostrils. "Leviathan has been quiet for far too long after everything that happened. Even if they are squabbling within their own ranks, one side will win, and we must be prepared for the worst. We need to arm ourselves with enough forces to protect us against them should they strike again."

"What happens after Leviathan is no longer part of the equation?"

"I'm going to make my dream come true and do what my ancestors originally set out to do: help people. I'm going to show the Hayashis that they were wrong to believe me only capable of terrible things because of my father's blood. I forge my own path, and I'll do so either alone or with the man I love by my side."

The man I love.

This is the first she's admitting it aloud.

I set the papers down and close the short distance between us. There are no words in any language that can describe the swelling of pride in my entire being.

All I have left are my actions.

My hand rings her throat just the way she likes it. I steal her next breath of smoke, cherry and bourbon flooding my senses the moment our lips touch.

"I am your king," I say, plucking the little black box from my pocket as I lower to a knee, "if you are my queen."

Poppy doesn't breathe as the small hinge creaks open. Nestled within is the Morgenstern ring of sparkling black diamonds arranged into a crown. "H-how did you...I-I mean, we haven't talked about any of this. What do you expect me to say? Is this because of my decision? Why didn't you tell me? I can't—"

"Breathe, *Petit Diable*." I stand and sweep the tears from the up-turned corners of her eyes. "What I feel for you has nothing to do with your choice. You're a friend, a fighter, a lover. Above all else, you are my home. These are what make you who you are, and that is why I love you beyond measure. You are my church, my steeple, my goddess. In this life and every life after. I'm yours, Poppy. Forever. I just wanted you to know that sooner rather than later. I think we've learned well enough by now that tomorrow is never guaranteed and, as you keep reminding me, we are only human. Not immortal vampires, sadly."

I trace the shape of her ethereal face. She still doesn't say anything.

Fuck it. She's mine, and she knows it as much as me.

My gall drives me to pluck the ring from its nest and slide it onto her finger. Her eyes light up like stars in the night sky.

"Your mother wanted you to have this." I skim my thumb over the spires of the crown. "I hope that's all right."

She rests a palm on the angel guarding my heart. "I love you, Brontë Raziel Bourbon."

"I know."

She scoffs. "Egotistical brute."

I wink. "You love it."

Poppy smiles, tipping onto her toes to whisper against my lips, "Forever?"

A calm unlike any I've felt before settles in my bones, warm as sunlight. I thread my fingers through her hair and capture her mouth with mine in a slow, tender kiss. She tastes like love. She tastes like home. She tastes like a fairytale I've only ever dreamed of living.

"Forever."

FOREVER

POPPY

"**Y**ou have lived a life anything but quiet," I say as I trail the tip of my butterfly knife over Jonas's shoulders flecked with as many scars as pinup tattoos on his thick arms.

He doesn't reply. He's still out cold.

"Did you give him too much fentanyl, *Petit Diable?*"

I lob a scowl at Brontë beneath my pink skull mask covering half my face. "Don't blame me. *You* prepped the dose."

"You didn't need to use the whole damn syringe."

"Look at him. He's enormous."

"He's smaller than me."

"Literally *everyone* is smaller than you."

He winks from beneath his own half-faced mask. "Good answer."

I whip him off. He chuckles, sinking back into the shadows of the private lounge beside a solemn Jezebel.

Voodoo & Velvet has become our favorite place to torture the rats of our city. A small chunk of my inheritance went to purchasing the nightclub and keeping this room not only permanently booked but below freezing at all times.

To keep our guests...comfortable.

Jonas Ashcroft, just like the others before him, is bound to the metal chair coated in rime. His hands are cuffed, and his personalized gag is already hanging on a thick chain around his neck: an adult-sized pacifier bejeweled with blades and barbed wire.

Fitting, for a hospital janitor who's been suffocating newborns this past year.

Fuck, it feels good to be serving poetic justice again. Leviathan is still a threat, one we've been preparing to face. This war with the cult—or coven, as Brontë keeps insisting even though I'm still trying to grapple with what we saw being real—isn't over. Upon the Morgenstern dynasty and the lives of my family lost, I will have my vengeance.

I still have nightmares about all the impossible things that happened the night my bloodline was nearly eradicated—Margot conjuring fire and performing a ritual; the ethereal being that visited and commanded me to kill her.

Tonight, though, I'm seeking solace in bloodshed with the man I chose to share my throne and spend the rest of my life with. His half-sister is a damn good therapist, but there's nothing quite as cathartic as torture.

When my victim is awake, that is.

Huffing a steaming cloud, I draw a syringe of adrenaline from my pocket. "How soon is too soon to shoot him up with this, *mon roi?*"

"Patience, *ma reine.* That's only for if we lose a pulse before we're ready to let the reaper take him."

I scoff but pocket the needle. Briefly marvel at the ring glinting on my finger. Signaling to the world that I've been claimed, and I'm all *his.*

My blade skims over Jonas's shoulders again. This time, his muscles twitch in response.

A corner of my mouth kicks up. *Finally.*

I fist his greasy bleached hair at the root, forcing his neck back and holding my knife against the edge of his...smile? Is he enjoying this?

Oh, fuck no.

My hand lifts. *Snap!*

Jezebel slinks forward.

Jonas's smile vanishes.

My hand lifts, two fingers poised. "Make it hurt, sweet girl."

Snap!

The big cat pounces, shredding skin like wet paper. Jonas screams like the infants he killed. His bones audibly crunch, his tendons snapping like wishbones. Fangs pierce an artery, and blood sprays the room.

Snap!

Jezebel reins in her bloodlust, licking her maw as I let her out the door. Jonas is a heap of tattered meat. He's still breathing, though.

But he certainly isn't smirking.

"Won't be long now, *mon amour.*"

Brontë looms at my back, his serrated KA-BAR dragging up and down my throat. His hunger for me is insatiable. As if he's lived his entire life deprived of life's darkest indulgences, and he'll never get enough.

Already, Jonas is fading. I draw the adrenaline and jam it into his heart. He gasps, his body convulsing as if possessed.

"You have sixty seconds, Scythe. Make them count."

Brontë understands his assignment. He herds me toward the mangled murderer and bends me over the chair. My palms brace the arms as my leather pants are pulled down past my ass. I gasp as he slaps a cheek with the flat of his blade.

Jonas's shit-brown eyes widen, his gurgling wails turning desperate. *Such a fucking turn on.*

Brontë grabs my hips and thrusts the entire length of his thick cock into me. I cry out as he fucks me harshly overtop the dying sinner. His strikes hit deep, so deep that I feel something in my chest loosen—a gnarled knot of anxiety that's been building within me, within *us*, for months. Chiseling away at the memories of the night we could've so easily lost each other and so much more.

I'll never forget the expression he wore when he found me in that crypt. He's worn the same expression every time we make love or fight or just lie in each other's arms. Like he doesn't believe what his own senses are telling him until all of them are filled with me.

I wonder if my own face radiates the same relief as he replaces the fear of uncertainty with the promise of inevitability. No matter where our lives go from here, we're in it together.

Pressure coils in the base of my spine, tightening into a painful twist of pleasure and agony. Brontë groans, hauling me up and glancing down as my core throbs. The muscles in his arms visibly flex around me as he pulls out a single inch from my tightening channel. The veins in his cock bulge with his own impending end.

"*Putain*, Poppy. Your tight little cunt is so perfect, I swear you were made for me."

"Or *you* were made for *me*."

"Semantics."

Brontë slams himself into me with a mighty thrust that rattles the chair. I gasp, euphoria lining my vision with constellations. I choke it back, *needing* him to plunge with me. He does it again, barking in my face, "Stop holding it, Poppy. Come for me so I can fill you. *Now*."

I couldn't even defy his command if I wanted to.

My climax barrels into me, and I cry out his name like I'm flinging my heart at him. He catches it eagerly, chasing my moans with heady kisses that threaten to throw me over the horizon again.

"One more, *mon amour*. If you want my cum inside you, I need you to fall for me one more time."

I do, and then he's growling French curses in my ear. Liquid heat bursts inside me, thick as honey straight from the comb. The mewls that escape me are pathetic, but he loves them, groaning as he laps the noises from my tongue and grinds his hips until nebulas are bursting across my vision.

"Stop," I plead through the rapture heightening to an unbearable euphoria. "*Mon ange*, please."

"Later, *ma reine*," Brontë murmurs against my lips, his kisses slowing and turning tender as he eases the pressure off my sore and hypersensitive clit, "when I'm fucking your delicious little ass and you're using that dragon cock on your pussy, the *s* word doesn't exist."

I try to scowl but end up smiling instead. "Only if you promise to let me use the dragon cock on *your* ass, *mon roi*."

"Be careful when making deals with devils, *Petit Diable*. The wrong one just might steal your soul instead."

Never. I will never get enough of this man.

A good thing never lasts just as long as forever.

EPILOGUE
REMIEL

Smoke slithers through my dreams, sticking to the back of my throat like tar. Flames lick the edges of my vision. Screams echo through decades—

A paw bats my chest.

I gasp myself awake to see Hades's emerald eyes staring back at me from above my sweaty brow. Darkness envelopes my room like it did the night of the fire that claimed my parents' lives.

That almost claimed mine.

I stumble to the bathroom and crash to my knees at the toilet with bruising force. I heave twice before my stomach empties itself entirely.

Too many emotions crowd my cranium as I brush my teeth and gurgle mouthwash. For a moment, I stare at myself in the mirror and mark each feature staring back at me: dark skin, hair like raven feathers, plump peach lips, Greek nose, aqua eyes.

And the demonic skull branding the center of my heaving sternum.

I take a deep breath and sigh it all out, donning sweats and rubbing my eyes free of sleepy dust as I scoop Hades up and meander my way downstairs.

Without Poppy here since she moved out, the café is even more quiet at midnight than it ever was before. I've stood in this place many times without any light to penetrate the shadows. It's usually a peaceful darkness, one that always swaddled me like my mother's arms when I was little.

Now, though, there's an eldritch feel to it all. I realize why when I spy a silhouette in the corner, idly swaying in a hammock.

Hades's quiet purrs suddenly cut off.

I freeze as the cherry of a cigarette glows bright in the dark. Illuminating a scarred face and mismatched eyes I haven't seen since I left Leviathan.

"E-Elder?"

"Hello, Master." He grins, silver smoke coiling above his hooded head. "I think it's time we have a little chat."

ACKNOWLEDGEMENTS

Never in my life did I think I'd be writing acknowledgements for my own book. Yet here I am, about to publish my debut that wouldn't have made it even close to this far without the most magical people in my life.

To Tyler, my real-life friends-to-lovers romance: You aren't just my compass—you're my North Star. You've been my beacon of light in this world of darkness, and thanking you will never be enough in expressing my gratitude for your endless support. You've listened to my aimless ramblings about plots and characters and themes three books down the road before this story was even drafted, and although so much has changed over time, you've been my constant. I love you, to the stars and back again.

Since diving into this journey headfirst, I've met some of the most warm and loving people. Rosaline, for your patience and wisdom in guiding me through the publishing process as much as you could—thank you a thousand times over. Kylah, for your cheerleading through the entire editing process, even as this manuscript was probably the worst formatting nightmare you'd seen like...ever—you're a true diamond, and I'm absolutely feral to work with you on the next book! Lex, Alexis, Thryn, Mel, Laura C., Laura H., Stu, and K, for your daily words of encouragement, dirty memes, and NSFW messages that have honestly helped me survive even the worst days. From the bottom of my shriveled, black heart—*merci*.

Writing is an experience unlike any I've ever known; it's a combination of dissociation, hallucination, and bouts of crippling loneliness that can't be stressed enough with words alone. I'd like to personally thank those who kept me company even when the lights were out and no one was home: Noah, Amy, Oscar, Rain, Ronnie, Oli, Poppy, Andy, Lizzy, Spencer, Taylor, and Vessel. Thank you for making my world feel less empty.

Something I've heard time and time again as a "new" author is that you shouldn't stop reading just because you're busy writing. Whether we realize it or not, we're always learning from others and growing our own skills thanks to them. So, to Jay, Brynne, Navessa, Santana, Harley, Sarah, Jennifer, Kerri, Carissa, and Rebecca: You have my humble gratitude for unknowingly mentoring me through the writing of this entire story...and I will fangirl over you all for eternity.

What's the point of books if no one reads them? To my readers, who took a chance on me as a debut author and this story as one they've never seen before: I am in constant awe that you all saw this book and said, "Give it to me." Imposter syndrome should be a diagnosis, because I still cannot believe even ONE person wanted to read it. I could say thank you as many times as there are stars in the sky, and it still wouldn't be enough. I cherish each and every one of you, and I'm beyond ready to show you what comes next!

Lastly, to my haters: Thank you for the fuel. I'll be sure to use it wisely.

ABOUT THE AUTHOR

Born and raised in a small town in central Pennsylvania, Trinity has been filling notebooks with love stories since she was a teen. She aspires to write strong yet flawed characters who guard their hearts with every last scrap of their souls until they find the ones worth letting in. She can be found under a fluffy blanket with a steaming mug and even steamier romance book.

Website: trinitylynnauthor.my.canva.site

TikTok: @trinitylynn_author

Instagram: @trinitylynn_author

Threads: @trinitylynn_author

www.ingramcontent.com/pod-product-compliance
Lightning Source LLC
Chambersburg PA
CBHW031117160726
47991CB00004B/1432